Duncan Morrison

The great hymns of the church

Their origin and authorship

Duncan Morrison

The great hymns of the church
Their origin and authorship

ISBN/EAN: 9783741188091

Manufactured in Europe, USA, Canada, Australia, Japa

Cover: Foto ©Andreas Hilbeck / pixelio.de

Manufactured and distributed by brebook publishing software
(www.brebook.com)

Duncan Morrison

The great hymns of the church

THE GREAT HYMNS

OF

THE CHURCH

Their Origin and Authorship

BY

REV. DUNCAN MORRISON, M.A.

OWEN SOUND, CANADA

TORONTO

HART & COMPANY

1890

PREFACE.

THESE notes on the Great Hymns of the Church are the result of the author's observations on the subject for years. He believes that our people in the public service would sing with the spirit and the understanding in a far higher degree, did they know more about their hymns; and that if any one would undertake simply to tell the story of each of them—giving some account of its origin and authorship, he would render them no small service, even if he should only succeed in awakening a deeper interest in the service of song, and calling forth some more competent laborer to enter the same field.

He had originally intended to confine himself in his annotations to twelve of the Great Hymns and presenting them in the shape of a series of contributions to the "Canada Presbyterian"; but ere he had finished that essay he received such encouragement from brethren whose opinions he was bound to respect, that he determined on extending his investigations and, at length, presenting the result in the form desired. For careful supervision and judicious selection of tunes his thanks are specially due to Mr. S. R. Hart, Toronto. These notes, such as they are, are now commended to Him without whose blessing nothing is good and nothing strong by the

AUTHOR.

Owen Sound, *1st Dec., 1889.*

iii

CONTENTS.

NOTES ON THE

GREAT HYMNS OF THE CHURCH.

BY THE

REV. D. MORRISON, M.A., OWEN SOUND.

Introduction.

"And they had two hundred and forty and five singing men and
singing women."—*Nehemiah* vii, 67.

THAT must have been a magnificent service in the
temple when a great army of singers, strengthened
by the noise of trumpets and psaltery, called to
one another and said:—" Lift up your heads, O ye gates,
and be ye lifted up, ye everlasting doors, and the King of
Glory shall enter in. Who is this King of Glory." We
read that there were four thousand Levites (and among
them some of the best people in the land) whose only
business was to look after the psalmody. They were
divided into courses of two hundred and forty and five
—each course having its appointed time. There was no
sermon in those days except in the synagogue. The
psalm was everything; but can we imagine anything
grander, more fitted to press home the great truths set

forth in the symbol and ceremonial of the former Dispensation, than those white robed Levites standing before the tokens of God's presence,—the smoking altars, the golden candlesticks,—under the very wings of the cherubim, chanting such psalms—as the 136th— one part exclaiming :—" Oh, give thanks to the Lord for he is good ; " then another standing in a different place responding :—" Unto Him who doeth great wonders ; " and so on till every trumpet sounding and every bosom heaving—all would lift up their voices and exclaim :— " Oh give thanks unto the Lord for he is good, for his mercy endureth forever " ?

All our churches need arousing on the subject of sacred song. All are ignorant of the power that is latent here —a power which, if fully evoked, would empty our saloons, fill our churches, and make our people strong in God and in the power of his might. It was the remark of Jonathan Edwards that, " as it is the command of God that all should sing, so all should learn to sing, as it is a thing which cannot be done decently without learning. Those, therefore, when there is no natural inability, as there seldom is, who neglect to learn to sing, live in sin, as they neglect what is necessary in order to their attending to one of the ordinances of God's worship." We read that he used to set apart whole days for singing !

With regard to these notes on the Great Hymns, the

writer has confined himself to a limited number ; and though they are not all equally great, they all bear the stamp of the royal mintage. Any hymn claiming to be *great*, must be Scriptural in its tenor and full of Him who bore our sins on his own body on the tree. The successful hymnist must take his key note, not from Parnassus but from Mount Zion. The great masters such as Spencer, Dryden, even Milton, are failures in the matter of sacred song, for they move in the cold aphelion in a path lying far remote from the central fire. However polished their lines, and classical their allusions, their treatment is cold, and cold because lacking in the Scriptural element. It is not to such hymns as theirs that the soul turns in a sad hour, but to such as, " Let not your hearts with anxious thoughts," or " Lo, he comes with clouds descending." It is to such that the soul turns. It is such that have power—that touch the imagination and fill the heart with blessed peace.

Still further a hymn should be pure in its language, faultless in its composition, its rhythm and its rhyme. Transparent simplicity is a great excellence. There is no place in the composition of a hymn for participles or complex terms. We need not go farther than the psalms for models in this respect. Whatever be the mood of the writer—jubilant, prayerful, pathetic, reverential,—the language, the style, is in every way worthy of the theme. There is a solemn beauty in those old Hebrew lyrics that wears well. We look in vain here for any word or fault or figure that would mar their majesty or offend the taste of the worshipper whether peer or peasant.

Now this is a matter that should not be lightly regarded. Many a noble hymn on account of one halting line or some crude metaphor has suffered severely. " Why did you not include in your collection Cowper's great hymn, ' There is a fountain filled with blood,' etc. ?" That is the question which the writer addressed to the convener of a committee charged with the duty of making a collection of hymns. What was the answer ? " Too much blood ; too much blood." It is a pity that a hymn of such excellence should become an offender for a word, and still more that the penalty should be exclusion from the hymnals of the church. It may be that the figure is faulty—(a fountain cannot be filled, but a cistern may)— but whether faulty or no, there can be no doubt that had every committee dealt with this hymn as that referred to, the church would have been a great loser.

Again, the reverence so conspicuous in the great hymns of the church, is a feature that should not be lost sight of by hymnists. Read the *Te Deum*, the *Dies Iræ*, the *Magnificat*, the *Glory in Excelsis*—any of the great hymns in the Scriptures, or out of the Scriptures, and note the veneration of the worshipper, the reverence of his language, the solemnity of his spirit; but we do not always find this in modern hymns. On the contrary, there is a flippancy—a familiarity running through some of them—which is inconsistent with true worship, and the relation of the creature to the Creator. In such hymns we are taught to sing of " Dear Jesus," "Sweet Jesus," etc., as if he were *altogether one of ourselves.* How different the spirit of those heavenly worshippers concerning whom we read that in approaching the eternal throne they veil their faces with their wings, crying, " Holy, Holy, Holy, Lord God Almighty ! " etc.

Again, a hymn should be full of *spiritual life.* No graces of style, depth of thought, or wealth of illustration can compensate for the want of spiritual life—the element of profound earnestness. This is another feature conspicuous in all the great hymns of the Church. They appeal to the common heart. They are for the most part, the utterance of the soul in some spiritual crisis, in the clear revealing light of heaven—when the things of time lose their importance and the great realities of the eternal would roll nearer the spirit's eye. Here, also, the great masters have, for the most part, been failures. Even Milton can hardly get a place in our hymnals. "Let us with a gladsome mind," though faultless in its composition, is but little used in our services, and but for the undertone of the 136th Psalm, of which it is a paraphrase, would be still less. His is the form to which we bow with greatest reverence in these last days, and his the shadow which is longest. The gift of poetry was vouchsafed to him as to no other in our time, but not the richer experience in divine things that filled the soul of a Wesley or a Williams with an enthusiasm which cast out all fear and made them conquerors and more than conquerors. The rod was in the prophet's hand, but the true *afflatus* was wanting to make him a sweet singer in Israel; and so when the rock was smitten no crystal tide flowed for the many thousands of Israel. Words written for mere effect are ephemeral, but words coined from the heart are pure gold. Experience, religious experience *truly* recorded in even the simplest verse, interests and never fails in inspiring interest.

Once more, a hymn designed for public worship should be addressed to God, and should be chiefly *objective* in its character. Many of the hymns of a former generation were too *subjective*—dealing with the inward state of the worshipper rather than with the glory of the Creator—dealing, indeed, with an experience all his own, or, at least, not in touch with common worshippers—plain, prosaic men and women who were not accustomed to introspection or analysing their feelings, and who had never reached the ethereal heights of spiritual joy or passed through the great storms of conviction set forth in the hymns which they were called upon to sing as praise to Almighty God. The result was that the great bulk of such hymns fell into disuse and will ere long pass into oblivion. Where now—I take round numbers—are the seven thousand hymns of the Wesleys, or the eight hundred of Isaac Watts or the four hundred of Philip Doddridge, or the sixty-six of Cowper, and the ten thousand that have flowed from inferior pens? It must be allowed that those numbers have shrunk into small space in our hymnals; and one reason of this is that so many of our earlier hymns were written in a style that could not be called popular—not fitted to voice the common wants and aspirations of men in their approach to the eternal throne; in short they were too *subjective.* But in saying that a popular hymn should be *objective* in its character rather than *subjective,* there is no intention of putting the ban on *supplicatory* hymns. The language of supplication and prayer is always appropriate and when well expressed can never fail to interest and engage the heart. Who does not know that this is the character of many of the psalms and that some of our most popular hymns that have stood the test of ages and are likely to stand the test of ages to come, *are prayers?* When will the church weary of such a hymn as

> Oh, for a closer walk with God ;
> A calm and heavenly frame ?

Again, Augustine in his day defined a hymn to be "Praise to God in a song." So far this is correct, and if so, what is to be said of such hymns, or rather poems, as "Prayer is the soul's sincere desire," "The sands of time are sinking," "Jerusalem the Golden," "The glory that excelleth?" Such must always occupy but a secondary place in the worship of God.

Again, a hymn designed for congregational use should not aim at voicing an ecstatic mood in religion. The sober, solemn beauty of Dr. Ken's three hymns are models in this respect. The preacher in dealing with the higher life of the soul often indulges in language far transcending the common experience of ordinary mortals. Instead of meeting them on the common plane of humanity, and helping them there, he rises above them, describing states and experiences too high for them to understand and the result in the mind of the hearer is a sense of unreality—a feeling of discouragement. So with hymns of this character. Fancy a strong, burly collier called upon to sing and sympathize with the angels in Pope's address to his departing soul: "Sister Spirit, come away," etc., or that, welcoming the approach of death in this swinging, rollicking measure:

> Ah, lovely appearance of death !
> What sight upon earth is so fair ?
> Not all the gay pageants that breathe
> Can with a dead body compare.

The hymnist should aim at reality and address himself to the common feelings and aspirations of the Christian.

There is one class of hymns deserving of particular notice here—hymns called *didactic* on account of the truth which they convey, and because didactic much used as

vehicles of truth. Quite a number of our Scotch paraphrases are of this character; but who ever heard the
minister giving out: "Let heaven arise, let earth appear,
said the Almighty God," etc., or, "Naked as from the
earth we came," etc., or "How still and peaceful
is the grave," etc., or "The rush may rise where waters
flow," etc.? Such hymns, that is, those purely didactic,
must always rank low as hymns for worship; but let
both adoration and instruction meet and mingle in the
hymn, as in the case of the *Te Deum*, and what will be
the effect! What a beautiful illustration have we of this
in what we call the fourth hymn, in the old arrangement
of psalms, paraphrases and hymns! "Blest morning
whose first dawning rays, beheld the Son of God," etc.!
Or in that grander pean, the 136th Psalm, "O give thanks
unto the Lord, for his mercy endureth forever," etc.

Great use was made of the didactic hymn in the earlier
days of the church, especially in the fourth century, by
sectaries in spreading their doctrines; and who does not
know that Martin Luther did more for the dissemination
of the great truths of the Reformation by his hymns than
by all his sermons and all his evangelists! The story of
the Cross, the Incarnation, the Death and Resurrection
of our Lord, and the wonders of Pentecostal days, set
forth in simple verse, were much welcomed by the people
and soon found their way into almost every home. The
result was that the crass ignorance that had so long pre-

vailed on such subjects was dispelled and the people woke up from their lethargy to enter upon a new and a larger life.

It is not for us to decry didactic hymns, for though they —that is, when purely didactic,—must occupy an inferior place in the matter of worship, yet as vehicles of truth to the mass they may be all important. "Sing on," said Melancthon, then with his banished friends in Weimar, to a little girl that he heard on the streets going over the Ein Feste Burg, a hymn in the mouth of every body— "Sing on; you don't know what sad hearts you cheer." Such hymns rendered a great service in those days, and it might be a question whether, in view of the great ignorance that prevails as to the main facts of Revelation, even in our Home Mission fields, it would not be a wise step to employ them to a larger extent than we have ever done. After all it is the penny hymn book of the child rather than the royal psalter of the sovereign that is the great power in the land.

There are, it is computed, nearly 20,000 hymns in the English language,—"the good," like Jeremiah's figs, "very good, the bad very bad, so bad that they cannot be eaten for naughtiness." Every revival produces a new crop and everywhere the new hymns are in great request, but after a season many that were received with favor lose their charm and like withered flowers are laid aside never to be taken up again. In this respect many are called—into being—but few are chosen. They are warm and fresh,—the utterances of gushing, pious souls that have felt the powers of the world to come, and that have tasted the heavenly gift, the strange sweet joy that comes from a felt interest in the great salvation; but having no root in themselves worthy of the name, they soon wither away. This has been the fate of many hymns even in our time and must be the fate of every hymn lacking in the great essentials that make for popularity.

The church needs to know more about her hymns before she can be expected to sing them as they ought to be sung. No one needs to be told that some knowledge of the hymn, its origin and authorship,—saying nothing about the music to which it is set, or the tender recollections with which it is associated,—adds greatly to the fervor of our devotions. We take more interest in the hymn "Just as I am," when we read that it was the first of a great spiritual crisis in the life of the authoress and how wisely the saintly Dr. Malan ministered to her in her darkness and difficulties; and we take more interest in the fifty-first psalm after reading of its origin and something of the part which that psalm has played in history. So with all other psalms and hymns and spiritual songs. We want to know more about them in order to sing with the spirit and the understanding. It is to meet this want that the present work has been undertaken.

GREAT HYMNS OF THE CHURCH.

HYMN I.

THE TE DEUM.

THE FIRST OF THE GREAT HYMNS AFTER THOSE OF THE
HOLY SCRIPTURE.

AS to the music we believe it has been a great favorite
with composers both ancient and modern. Handel's
"Dettengen" and "Utrecht" Te Deums, are well
known; so also the setting on a grand scale of Berlioz. In
short, nearly every writer of church music from the days of
Tallis and Byrd to our own times, has given us one or
more settings, but that called Jackson's, is the music to
which the Te Deum is generally set in these days. The hymn,
we believe, was first sung in Herne Church, Kent, England,
being carried thither by Augustine and his Evangelists.

The Latin form runs thus :

TE Deum laudamus ; te Dominum confitemur.
 Te æternum Patrem, omnes terra veneratur.
Tibi omnes angeli ; Tibi cœli, et universæ potestates.
Tibi Cherubim et Seraphim incessabili voce proclamant :
Sanctus, Sanctus, Sanctus, Dominus Deus Sabaoth.
Pleni sunt coeli, et terra majestatis gloriæ tuæ.
Te gloriosus Apostolorum chorus ;
Te Prophetarum laudabilis numerus :
Te Martyrum candidatus laudat exercitus.

B

Te per orbem terrarum, sancta confitetur Ecclesia.

Patrem immensæ majestatis.

Venerandum tuum verum, et unicum Filium.

Sanctum quoque Paraclitum Spiritum.

Tu Rex gloriæ, Christe.

Tu Patris sempiternus es Filius.

Tu ad liberandum suscepturus hominem, non horruisti Virginis uterum.

Tu devicto mortis aculeo, aperuisti credentibus regna cœlorum.

Tu ad dexteram Dei sedes, in gloria Patris.

Judex credimus esse venturus.

Te ergo quæsumus, tuis famulis subveni, quos pretioso sanguine redemisti.

Æterna fac cum sanctis tuis, in gloria numerari.*

Salvum fac populum tuum, Domine : et benedic hæreditati tuæ.

Et rege eos, et extolle illos, usque in æternum.

Per singulos dies, benedicimus te.

Et laudamus nomen tuum in sæculum, et in sæculum sæculi.

Diguare, Domine, die isto, sine peccato nos custodire.

Miserere nostri Domine, miserere nostri.

Fiat misericordia tua Domine, super nos : quemadmodum speravimus in te.

In te Domine, speravi ; non confundar in æternum.

W E praise Thee, O God. We acknowledge Thee to be the Lord. The glorious company of the Apostles, praise Thee.

All the earth doth worship Thee, the Father everlasting.

To Thee all angels cry aloud, the heavens and all the powers therein.

To Thee, Cherubim and Seraphim, continually do cry :

Holy, holy, holy, Lord God of Sabaoth.

---

* I am indebted to Mr. G. Murray, of the "Star," Montreal, for the following valuable note. He says that a book entitled the "*Te Deum*," being a vindication of that hymn from the errors and misconceptions of a thousand years, by Ebenezer Thompson has been published (1858)—that in this beautifully printed volume, we have the results of Mr. Thompson's studies for more than thirty years, and that we must confess to much gratification *at one correction of the second reading.* The verse, "Make us to be numbered with thy saints in glory everlasting," has always seemed to us wanting in point and vigor. Now the true reading, Mr. Thompson shews, is not "in gloria numerari," but "in gloria remunerari,"—not "to be *numbered* with thy saints in glory everlasting," but "to be rewarded with thy saints in glory everlasting."

Heaven and earth are full of the majesty of Thy glory.

The goodly fellowship of the Prophets, praise Thee.

The noble army of Martyrs, praise Thee.

The holy church throughout all the world, doth acknowledge Thee.

The Father of an infinite majesty.

Also, Thine honorable, true, and only Son,

Also, the Holy Ghost the Comfortor.

Thou art the King of glory, O Christ.

Thou art the everlasting Son of the Father.

When Thou tookest upon Thee to deliver man, Thou didst not abhor the Virgin's womb.

When Thou hadst overcome the sharpness of death, Thou didst open the Kingdom of Heaven to all believers.

Thou sittest at the right hand of God, in the glory of the Father.

We believe that Thou shalt come to be our Judge.

We therefore pray Thee, help Thy servants whom Thou hast redeemed with Thy precious blood.

Make them to be numbered with Thy saints in glory everlasting.

O Lord, save Thy people, and bless Thine heritage.

Govern them and lift them up forever.

Day by day we magnify Thee.

And we worship Thy name, ever, world without end.

Vouchsafe, O Lord, to keep us this day without sin.

O Lord have mercy upon us ; have mercy upon us.

O Lord let Thy mercy lighten upon us, as our trust is in Thee.

O Lord, in Thee have I trusted, let me never be confounded.

The Te Deum is to some only a name, but to the church of God it is the most precious treasure of antiquity. Its origin carries us away back, according to tradition, for nearly 1500 years—to the night of Easter 387, and to the city of Milan and its great Cathedral. On that night a distinguished man was baptized by St. Ambrose, the bishop of this diocese, whom he had recently rescued from the errors of Arianism, and who had been but a short time before rescued from the still darker errors of heathenism. This was no less a person than Augustine, who afterwards rose to great distinction, and became bishop of Hippo, (Africa). He was a burning and shining light in his day. Many rejoiced in his ministry, and to this day his "City of God" and "Confessions" are still read by thousands with no small degree of relish and profit.

On this night, according to the tradition, those two christian fathers, St. Ambrose the officiating prelate, and Augustine the recent convert, standing by the altar, the spirit of inspiration descended upon them, and they sang, as it never had been before, the Te Deum to the great congregation—sang it in alternate strophes; whereupon the pious Monica, the mother of Augustine, cried out in a rapture, "O son, I had rather have thee Augustine the Christian, than Augustine the Emperor!" This is the tradition, but it is probable that fragments of this great hymn had been in use in the church for years before—fragments, or rather detached doxologies, with which both those fathers had been familiar, and that in this grand hour, when every heart was warm with celestial fire, and the lips of both had been touched with a live coal from the altar, as well as their memories, that they merely put such detached portions together, and welded them into a homogeneous whole. For the first two centuries a formal creed had been unknown in the church, but short statements of certain truths had been promulgated, such as that bearing upon the Trinity, original sin, etc., and it was not uncommon for believers in the hour of death, especially for martyrs, to recite such statements, together with doxologies, confessions, praises, *e.g.*, Blandina, who perished at Lyons, in the year 179 A.D., saying: "I believe in the Father, the Son," etc., and the belief is that these two fathers, standing by the altar on this memorable night, in the face of the great congregation, caught up in their song those utterances in which creeds and confessions and praises were interwoven; and that then and there the Te Deum took the form and the fashion which it now wears.

This account has been called in question, and various names have been mentioned in connection with the authorship, but nothing satisfactory has been established. If the tradition referred to is to be set aside as unreliable, then it is in vain for us at this distant day to settle the question of its genesis. One thing, however, is pretty clear, that it was known in its present form in the fifth century.

It does not appear, indeed, that any hymn of human composition had a place in the *public* worship of the church till 633 A.D., the date of the council of Toledo, held by the Western church, when amongst its decretals, it issued one authorizing the use of such hymns. That they were in common use in the homes of the people, and in the little voluntary assemblies of believers meeting together, like the christians in the early morn, of whom Pliny speaks in his day (107) there can be no doubt; but up till this period (633) the only hymns used in public worship, beside those of the psalter, were the hymns of scripture, the Gloria in Excelsis, Magnificat, etc. From this time, however, they came into general use in public worship, and the *Te Deum* at once became historical. And what a history this glorious hymn has had since that early day! Who can speak of the sad homes it has cheered, the dark hearts that it has filled with holy light, the flagging congregations, even armies, that it has roused to red hot enthusiasm! Who does not know that it was this hymn that won the battle of Leignitz, and that it was this hymn the pious Fisher, one of the bishops of the church of England, chose for his farewell when led to the stake? In London, Flanders, Bavaria, where the scenes of martyrdom were so numerous, many a consecrated monk like Savonarola, and stout-hearted layman have felt its sustaining power when the rack and the thumbscrew were plied in vain. Time would fail me to speak of the victories it has won, the martyrs it has sustained in the last sad hours; and how under its inspiration they raised their voices high above the flames and found in it the appropriate vehicle of their praise. We might almost apply the language of the apostles to such martyrs—men who through faith subdued kingdoms, wrought righteousness, obtained promises, stopped the mouths of lions, quenched the violence of fire, escaped the edge of the sword, out of weakness were made strong, waxed valiant in fight, turned to flight the armies of the aliens.

Among the many instances of the power of the *Te Deum* that might be given, the conversion of Thomas Olivers, the author of the great hymn :—

" The God of Abraham praise," etc.

must not be forgotten. He was one of Wesley's itinerant preachers, and Toplady's sturdiest antagonist. In early life he was dissipated and unsettled, but one day hearing Whitfield preach at Bristol—having gone three hours before the time to secure a seat—a great change took place. The preacher discoursed on the text: " Is not this a brand plucked from the burning? " It was a word in season to Thomas Olivers. He became a new man, though for a season he had to struggle hard before he could rise into the light and liberty of God's dear children. It was a great help to him at this time,—an event that did much to lift him up from the horrible pit and miry clay,—to hear the Te Deum, in the Bristol Cathedral shortly after his hearing Whitfield. Hear what he says concerning this event: " I went to the Cathedral at six in the morning. " When the *Te Deum* was read, I felt as if I had done with " earth, and was praising God before His throne. No words " can set forth the joy, the rapture, the awe and reverence " which I felt."

But this hymn so full of precious truth and so filled in every way to stir the human soul, has suffered severely by the hand of time and the superstition of fanaticism. It soon lost its purity and its power. It soon became the vehicle of error and the minister of the rankest Romanism. Look at the following as a specimen which we copy from an English translation from the Italian lying before us.

In "The Psalter of the Blessed Virgin," the publication of which has, more than once, been authorized by the Vatican, that grand old hymn, commonly called the "Te Deum," is altered so as to make it apply to the mother of Jesus.

> We cause our praises to ascend to Thee, O Mother of God ; we extol Thee, O Mary the Virgin.
>
> All the earth worships Thee, the Spouse of the Eternal Father.
>
> To Thee, all Angels and Archangels, to Thee all Thrones and Principalities humbly bow down themselves.
>
> To Thee, all the Powers and the highest Intelligences in the heavens, and all Dominions yield obedience.
>
> To Thee, all Choirs, to Thee, Cherubim and Seraphim joyously minister.
>
> To Thee, all angelic creatures continually sing with the voice of praise.
>
> Holy, Holy, Holy Mary, Mother of God, Virgin and also Mother.
>
> *etc., etc., throughout.*

The full history of any hymn can never be written, and especially this hymn, which was first sung, according to tradition, by those two fathers, St. Ambrose and St. Augustine, on Easter eve, 387 A.D. Certainly whether the tradition is true or no, it became as early as the fifth century the greatest of the non-scriptural or non-inspired hymns of the Church, and ever since it has held the first place. Its great prominence has made it an historical document. It is to this hymn that the nation turns for giving thanks to Almighty God, when great blessings or deliverances, are vouchsafed. By order it is to be sung or said in connection with certain of the holidays and festivals in connection with the English Church, but it lies with the Ordinary to appoint it to be sung on special occasions.

The Jubilee services of the Queen in Westminster Abbey have not yet been forgotten when it was the vehicle of the nation's praise. Never since the days of the Spanish Armada was the Te Deum sung with grander effect. That, too, was an occasion of universal joy throughout the nation, for the hearts of many were failing in them for fear, when they saw the long (seven miles) procession of warships sailing down the English Channel, and felt how unprepared they were to meet such a force. But what man could never have done, God in one night did, and gave them unexpected deliverance. A storm arose, and broke the ships of Tarshish on the northern shore, seeking to make their escape in that direction. The joy of the nation was great. A commemorative medal was struck, on which were inscribed the appropriate words *Deus offlavit dissipantur*, (the Lord blew upon them and they were scattered) and thanksgiving services were held all over the land in which the singing of the *Te Deum* formed no unimportant part. On many a grand occasion this great hymn has been lifted up, and once when no lesser one would have been fitting—when Columbus discovered the first grey outline of the new world, and the crew threw themselves into one another's arms weeping for joy.

One remarkable feature of the *Te Deum* is the reverence of its language, and the reverence which it inspires. In this respect it claims kindred with all the hymns of Scripture, for all are distinguished for the solemn beauty of their language, apart altogether from the grandeur of the theme. One incident in the life of Rev. Robert Hall, which I give on the authority of Mr. Christophers, serves to shew how scriptural the style and how kindred the character of the Te Deum is to the word of God. "He had composed a sermon on a text which had touched his fine sense of grandeur and had deeply moved his heart. On completing his sermon, he turned to the concordance to find the text. It was not to be found. It was not in the Bible. It was a sentence from the Te Deum, "*All the earth doth worship Thee, the Father everlasting.*

The Scriptural character of this great hymn is certainly a noticeable feature—the solemn beauty of the language not less than the noble grandeur of the theme. It is fitted to inspire the worshipper with reverence, but this is a feature which is often lost sight of by our hymn-makers and hymn-menders. If the Te Deum, or any of the hymns of Scripture which it so much resembles, is to be taken as a model, they should beware of anything like a fondling tone, or the familiar terms of amorous address, known among intimate friends. We refer to such expressions as, "Dear Jesus ever at thy side;" "Dear Lord, accept a sinful heart;" "Dear Refuge of the weary soul;" "Dear Shepherd of thy people, hear;" "Dear dying Lamb;" "Lay down thou weary one, lay down thy head upon my breast," etc. There is no countenance in the Te Deum, or in any of the hymns of the Holy Scriptures for such familiarity, or for the use of such endearing terms common to those that stand on the same level, and come together in the daily intercourse of friendship. Many a splendid hymn in daily use the world over, is marred in this way—in daily use and maintaining their place in the favor of the people, but doing so, not because of such terms—but in spite of such terms—because, in short, of their great counter-balancing excellencies. But we look in vain for anything like this in the Word of God or the noble hymn under consideration. Such words of endearment as those referred to, are inconsistent with the majesty of the Creator on the one hand, and the sinfulness of the creature on the other; and what we say is this, that we have no precedent for addressing the Lord as if he were *altogether one of us*. Take Israel's great story of national deliverance recorded in Exodus xv. "Who is a God like unto Thee, glorious in holiness, fearful in praises," etc., or the song of Moses at the close of his weary life, Ps. xc. "O God, thou art the dwelling place of thy people in all generations," etc.; or the battle song of Deborah, Judges v. "Then sang Deborah and Barak the sons of Abinoam on that day saying," etc.: or that wonderful utterance of Balaam, son of Beor, when he took up his parable and said : "How goodly are thy tents, O Jacob, and thy tabernacles, O Israel !" Num. xxiii. So David all through the Psalter. In his highest flights of devotion,—in the moments rich in blessing, when his mountain stood strong, he is before God as sinful dust and ashes. Even those chosen ones who enjoy special familiarity with God,—who spoke to him face to face like Abraham, as one friend speaketh to another have nothing of the Salvation Army touch in their songs of praise. And the same spirit of reverence is common to all the hymns of the New Testament—the Magnificat of Mary, the Eucharistia of Zecharias—the Nunc dimittis of Simeon, the Gloria in Excelsis of the Angels—the ascriptions of praise on the part of the redeemed in heaven, as well as the angels who, in their nearest approaches to the throne of the Eternal, veil their faces with their wings and say "Holy," etc. In none of those Scripture hymns—in none of those seventy passages apart from the Psalms, which Dr. J. M. Neale has set down as poetic, have we any warrant for the use of the familiar terms of address herein condemned, and we venture to affirm that any hymn marred by such terms, is doomed to oblivion, unless sustained by a general excellency which is more than a compensation.

Another excellency in this hymn, is its strongly objective character, which we notice in contradistinction to those which are called subjective. In the one case the worshipper looks away from *himself*, forgets *himself*, and fixes his adoring eye on Almighty God and the glories of redemption ; in the other he turns his eye in upon his spiritual state—his feelings,—experience and sings like Newton :

> 'Tis a point I long to know :
>   Oft it causes anxious thought,
> Do I love the Lord or no,
>   Am I his, or am I not ?

This is a class of hymns that was entirely unknown in the earlier ages of the Church. St. Ambrose and St. Augustine. with all the hymnists of that period, dealt with the Father of mercies, and His glorious perfections. Their attitude in praising God was not one of introspection, analysing their feelings, —dealing with their experience ; but rather that of the Baptist.—*Ecce Agnus Dei qui tollet peccatum Mundi* (Behold the Lamb of God, etc). They dealt with the great externals,—letting the feelings take care of themselves, and rejoiced in their living union and communion with that great body known as the Church of God, extending through all the ages. This also is our joy and crown of rejoicing. We travel not alone. We belong to a great company, made up of the excellent of the earth, the glorious company of the apostles ; the goodly fellowship of the prophets ; the noble army of the martyrs, and the whole Church of God throughout the world. What a long procession stretching over these 6000 years ! "Some have crossed the flood, and some are crossing now." Some are safe and happy within the fold, and some are here fighting the good fight of faith ; but all alike, safe, because kept by the power of God through faith unto salvation. What a morning that will be, when the everlasting Sabbath begins to dawn, and the long week of the world is ended,—when millions shall awake from the dust, and put on their beautiful garments, and they that have turned many to righteousness, shall shine as the firmament and as the stars forever and ever ! And how feeble will all the songs of earth appear, the greatest and the best, when we hear the anthem of the redeemed in glory and lift up our voice in that new song, of which we have read in the Apocalypse when a great host which no man can number, all shining in the beauty of holiness shall ascribe glory and honor and majesty and power to him, that is the Prince of the kings of the earth, and who liveth and reigneth forever and ever !

HYMN II.

ART THOU WEARY?

THE OLD GREEK HYMN.

TUNE.—*Stephanos.*

ART thou weary, art thou languid,
    Art thou sore distrest ?
"Come to Me," saith One, "and coming,
    Be at rest."

Hath He marks to lead me to Him,
    If He be my guide ?
"In his feet and hands are wound-prints,
    And His side."

Is there diadem, as monarch,
    That His brow adorns ?
"Yea, a crown, in very surety,
    But of thorns ?

If I find Him, if I follow,
    What His guerdon here ?
"Many a sorrow, many a labour,
    Many a tear."

If I still hold closely to Him,
    What hath He at last ?
"Sorrow vanquished, labour ended,
    Jordan past."

If I ask Him to receive me,
    Will He say me nay ?
" Not till earth, and not till heaven,
    Pass away ! "

Finding, following, keeping, struggling,
    Is He sure to bless ?
" Angels, martyrs, saints and prophets
    Answer, Yes ! "

IN the absence of the original Greek on which I am not able to lay my hand I take the liberty of presenting a translation in Latin from a gifted but unknown hymnist :

AN tu fessus ? An tu lassus ?
    An tu pressus malo ?
" Ad me veni," inquit Iste,
" Requiemque dabo."

Aliquane signa monstrant,
    Quærenti ductorem ?
Pedum manuumque specta,
    Lateris cruorem.

Modo Regis frontem ornat,
    Diadema clarum ?
Diadema, immo vero,
    Attamen spinarum.

Sin repertus, sin secutus,
    Quid mihi donabit ?
Lachryma, labore, luctu,
    Multo onerabit.

Si manerem, hærens Isti,
    Quid mi prodest demum ?
Actus labor, victus dolor,
    Transitus ad cœlum.

Ut acciperet si rogam,
    Dicet, non accipiam ?
Ruat cœlum, ruat terra,
    Hoc dicet priusquam.

> Si repertus, si secutus,
>   Me beabit certe ?
> Vates, angelus et Virgo,
>   Quisque sit pro teste.

An unknown commentator furnishes us with the following
note :

"ART THOU WEARY, ART THOU LANGUID."

We wish this hymn, though, in the estimation of some,
rather long for singing at one time, were given in full in the
books.   This has led to the omission of several verses.   After
verse fourth in *our* collection comes in the original :

> ' Is this all He hath to give me
>   In my life below ?
> " Joy unspeakable and glorious
>   Thou shalt know.

> ' " All thy sins shall be forgiven—
>   All things work for good ;
> Thou shalt Bread of Life from Heaven
>   Have for food.

> ' " From the fountains of salvation
>   Thou shalt water draw :
> Sweet shall be thy mediation
>   In God's law." '

This verse comes in after the fifth in our collection :

> ' Festal Palms, and Crown of Glory,
>   Robes in Blood washed white,
> God in Christ His People's Temple—
>   There no night.

We are indebted to the scholarly pen of the Rev. J. M. Neale,
D.D., for the translation into English of this much admired
hymn.   Many of those early hymns that have been translated

again and again have suffered severely in the treatment, so that
much of the original *aroma* has evaporated, like wine often
emptied from one impure vessel to another, but this, so far as
we can judge, has lost nothing of its original sweetness and
grace. It is indeed a remarkable hymn, remarkable for its
beauty, and, considering the age in which it was produced,
remarkable for its evangelical character. Respecting the author,
Stephanos, very little is known. He is called Stephen the
Sabaite, from the circumstance that he was an inmate of the
monastery of St. Sabas which is situated between Jerusalem
and the Dead Sea. The Rev. John King in his book "Anglican
Hymnology"—published 1885—gives a very interesting account
of this religious house. In substance, he says that it was
founded early in the sixth century, and has therefore stood the
desolations of 1,400 years. Many a time it has been plundered
and the inmates, generation after generation, put to death.
Persian, Moslem and Bedouin invaders have all in turn broken
in upon its quiet and spoiled it of its treasures ; but still it
remains one of the most interesting relics of a past age and still
sheltering a busy hive of devoted ecclesiastics. On being
admitted, Mr. King found a chapel and chambers and cells
innumerable, for the most part cut out of solid rock, perched
one above another and connected by rocky steps and intricate
passages, all surrounded by a massive wall on which two strong
towers are built near the gate way, giving the building the appearance of a fortress, as if the brothers meant to defend themselves should any bold invader come near. St. Sabas, the
founder, died and was buried here in 532, so also St. John of
Damascus. He was uncle to Stephen and one of the best Greek
hymn writers of his day. This monastery is still a large institution and numbers some forty inmates, all professing to maintain the same strict discipline—the same rules of life as prevailed
in the days of Stephen and his uncle John. One of those
rules was total abstinence from animal food, and another was

to observe seven religious services *per diem*—five by day and
two by night. Mr. King and his party found those monks
very obliging, ready to show and explain everything. Among
other things they saw the gaily decorated chapel, the tombs
of St. Sabas the founder, and St. John of Damascus, and a
cave chapel, containing thousands of skulls of martyred monks.
They were also led to the belfry of the little sanctuary, and saw
the bells which send forth their sweet chimes to cheer the weary
pilgrims within sound. From a terrace they looked down, some
500 feet, into the deep gorge of the Kedron, the stream associated with all that is tender in the last days of our Lord
on earth. Down into this gorge the savage wolves and jackals
assemble at night, and in the morning are fed by the monks,
who cast down food for the hungry animals. Viewed from
this terrace the scene is one of utter and stern desolation.
What a stirring history that of Mur Sabba, and that pertaining to those early hymnists, St. John of Damascus and his
nephew Stephanos! But a more wonderful history still, if we
knew it, belongs to that sweetest lyric that has come down to
us from those early days:

> Art thou weary, art thou languid.
> Art thou sore distrest?
> "Come to me," saith one, "and coming
> Be at rest."

Into this monastery Stephen, or Stephanos, made his way
at the early age of ten, and there abode fifty-nine years—
abode, indeed, till the day of his death. He was a man of
saintly life and splendid scholarship, delighting much in the
study of theology and sacred song. Certainly if we are to judge
of his theology from this famous hymn, we should say that he
was far in advance of his compeers—that like some lofty crag on
which the sunlight first falls, gilding the summit before the sun,
coming out of his ocean bed, has yet reached the common

horizon—his soul was filled with light, when all around might
be said to be in darkness ; when the Church was taking great
strides into deadly error, when the ceremony of kissing the Pope's
toes, in token of his supremacy over all mundane things, was
introduced, when Clement, of Ireland, who preferred the deci-
sions of the Word to the decrees of the Popes, was condemned
as a heretic ; and Virgilius, a great mathematician, believing
in the rotundity of the earth and the existence of Antipodes,
brought down the frown of Pope Zachary—when in short, the
Church was rapidly taking the form and fashion which it now
wears, for it was in this century (eighth) that it developed into
the huge overshadowing apostacy that has dominated the hearts
and lives of millions, generation after generation, during these
1,200 years. Strange, that in the midst of all this degeneracy,
we should come on such a lovely hymn—a hymn without the
least flavour of the heresies of that early day—a hymn which
has still the dew of its youth upon it, presenting precious truth
to us with all the freshness of the morning, and showing how
a heart in communion with God can grow in all the graces of
the new creature in the most uncongenial circumstances.
Stranger still, when we remember that right beside the saintly
author was his uncle John of Damascus, a man that strove night
and day to introduce image worship through the whole Church.
Nor did he rest in his efforts till the innovation was finally
sanctioned at the general council, held at Nice, 784. Strange,
we say, to find such a witness to the truth in that dark day,
and to think of that solitary monk, troubled on every side,
feeding upon the sincere milk of the Word, and growing thereby, like some old tree that we have seen rooted and grounded
among rocks, where you would say there was nothing to sustain
it ; but still, striking its roots more deeply, draws its stength
from hidden springs whereby it is enabled to do battle with the
summer's heat and the winter's storms.

We have nothing in advance of this hymn in the way of

c

doctrinal statement in this our favoured day and clearer vision. Every verse in it is but the echo of the Good Shepherd. It speaks to us of rest, just as He spoke of rest, of the way to this rest as He spoke of the way; of wearing a crown as He spoke of wearing a crown; of the blessedness that lies beyond when labour is ended and Jordan past just as He spake of it; of the welcome extended to the sinner, of the everlasting safety of all who put their trust in Him just as He spake; in short, of taking up the cross, just as Christ spoke of taking up the cross.

> Finding, following, keeping, struggling,
>   Is He sure to bless?
> "Angels, martyrs, saints and prophets
>   Answer, Yes!"

We look in vain for any trace of error or superstition in this hymn. The author, in his dark day, heard much about saints and the duty of holding them in remembrance through images; but no name is mentioned here but that Name which is above every name. He heard much about masses and their virtue, and the duty of offering them for the dead; but he seems to have known of no mass but that represented by the "wound prints" of the Master. In short, the hymn is thoroughly Protestant and evangelical in its character, and in perusing it we feel that we are brought into contact with the Word of God that liveth and abideth forever; and not only with the Word, but the saintly spirit that first breathed these lines, that fed upon the same Gospel, that delighted in that same Saviour whose utterances have lost nothing of their power during the lapse of these many years, but are still spirit and life to the souls of men.

At this distant day, it is too late to raise the question as to the genesis of this hymn, the occasion in the life of its author that led to its composition; but we can easily understand how that, amid the conflicts and confusions of the time, when the vulgar glory of crowns and courts proved such a magnet for churchmen as well as laymen, that one so spiritually minded would often send forth his thoughts along the line of this hymn, and that in some glorious hour of exaltation those thoughts would shape themselves into these verses that have been so useful in the hands of the good Spirit, in the way of witnessing for God in dark days, and in bringing rest and comfort to weary and sin-laden souls.   Much of the charm of this hymn lies in its dramatic character, presenting the truths which it is intended to convey in the form of question and answer; and therefore in clearer and sharper lines than in the ordinary didactic form.   There are certain psalms, such as the twenty-fourth, one hundred and seventh, one hundred and thirty-sixth, etc., the structure of which is antiphonal,—giving us the idea that one portion of the congregation or choir took one part, and another, another; while at times all unite in a full chorus of praise.   Take one psalm the twenty-fourth, in which we have a series of antiphonies—in which two, probably, three parties share in the performance.   One part of the choir asks the question: "Who shall ascend into the hill of God, or who shall stand in His holy place?"   Another answers: "He that hath clean hands," etc.   A third party, probably the whole congregation adds: "He shall receive the blessing of the Lord, and righteousness from the God of our salvation.   This is the generation of them that seek Him, that seek thy face, O Jacob."

Stephen the Sabaite's hymn takes its form and fashion from such psalms, and much of its charm and power comes from the strophe and antistrophe.   Not unlikely the original music to which it was set in that old monastery was also in the same line, and it would be well for our Churches, especially for our young people, if more attention was given to sacred song, and the true rendering of such psalms and hymns as that under consideration.

HYMN III.

DIES IRÆ.

THE GREAT JUDGMENT HYMN.

TUNE.—*Constancy.*   From the "German Chorales," very old and much used on the Continent.

THIS great hymn, originally consisting of nineteen strophes of three lines each, is the work of Thomas of Celano (a town of Italy, of some six thousand of a population, twenty-eight miles south of Aquila).   He was born 1185 and died 1255.   He was the companion and biographer of Francis of Assisi, both very famous in their day, the one, as the father of itinerant preaching friars ; the other, as the chief poet of his country, and whose one judgment hymn roused the slumbering choirs of Europe, and is still making the hearts of every one that hears it tingle.   The earliest book in which it is found is the " Missale Romanum," printed at Pavia, 1491.   It probably first saw the light early in the thirteenth century, and through all the intervening years it has been as a light and an echo from the eternal world.

Dr. Trench's translation is as follows:—

O THAT day ! that day of ire !
  Told of prophet, when on fire,
Shall a world dissolved expire !

Oh what terror shall be then,
When the Judge shall come again
Strictly searching deeds of men !

When a trump of awful tone
Thro' the caves sepulchral blown
Summons all before the throne.

What amazement shall o'ertake
Nature when the dead shall wake
Answer to the Judge to make !

Open then the book shall lie,
All o'erwrit for every eye
With a world's iniquity.

When the Judge his place has ta'en
All things hid shall be made plain,
Nothing unrevenged remain.

What then wretched ! Shall I speak
Or what intercession seek
When the just man's cause is weak.

Jesus, Lord, remember pray,
I the cause was of the way
Do not lose me on that day.

King of awful majesty,
Who the saved dost freely free,
Fount of mercy, pity me.

Tired thou satest seeking me,
Crucified to let me free,
Let such pain not fruitless be.

Terrible avenger make,
Of thy mercy me partake,
Ere that day of vengeance wake.

As a criminal I groan,
Blushing deep the faults I own,
Grace be to a suppliant shewn.

Thou who Mary didst forgive
And who badst the robber live,
Hope to me dost also give.

Tho' my prayers unworthy be,
Yet, O let me graciously
From the fire eternal free,

Mid the sheep my place command,
From the goats far off to stand :
Set me Lord at thy right hand

And when them who scorned Thee here,
Thou hast judged to doom severe,
Bid me with the saved draw near.

Lying low before thy throne
Crushed my heart in dust I groan
Grace be to a suppliant shewn.

A still better translation is that of General Dix, an American citizen, who in the late war won distinction for himself as a soldier, but who years before had won no less distinction as a scholar in the High School, Montreal, during the family's sojourn in that city, while the father as Civil Engineer was carrying through a great undertaking. But we have only room for three verses which may serve as a specimen.

Translation by General Dix.

Day of vengeance without morrow :
Earth shall end in flame and sorrow,
As from saint and seer we borrow.

Ah what terror is impending,
When the Judge is seen decending,
And each secret vail is rending !

To the throne the trumpet sounding,
Through the sepulchres resounding,
Summons all with voice astounding.

The following is the hymn in the original :—

1. DIES iræ ! dies illa
    Solvet sæclum in favilla,
  Teste David cum Sibylla.

2. Quantus tremor est futurus,
   Quando Judex est venturus,
   Cuncta stricte discussurus !

2. Tuba mirum spargens sonum
   Per sepulchra regionum,
   Coget omnes ante thronum.

4. Mors stupebit et natura,
   Cum resurget creatura,
   Judicanti responsura.

5. Liber scriptus proferetur,
   In quo totum continetur,
   Unde mundus judicetur.

6. Judex ergo cum sedebit,
   Quidquid latet, apparebit :
   Nil inultum remanebit.

7. Quid sum miser tunc dicturus ?
   Quem patronum rogaturus ?
   Cum vix justus sit securus.

8. Rex tremendæ majestatis,
   Qui salvandos salvas gratis,
   Salve me, fons pietatis.

9. Recordare Jesu pie,
   Quid sum causa tuæ viæ,
   Ne me perdas illa die.

10. Quærens me sedisti lassus,
    Redemisti crucem passus :
    Tantus labor non sit cassus.

11. Juste Judex ultionis,
    Donum fac remissionis
    Ante diem rationis

12. Ingemisco tanquam reus,
    Culpa rubet vultus meus,
    Supplicanti parce Deus.

13. Qui Mariam absolvisti,
    Et latronem exaudisti,
    Mihi quoque spem dedisti.

14. Preces meæ non sunt dignæ,
    Sed tu bonus fac benigne,
    Ne perenni cremer igne.

15. Inter oves locum præsta,
    Et ab hœdis me sequestra.
    Statuens in parte dextra.

16. Confutatis maledictis,
    Flammis acribus addictis,
    Voca me cum benedictis.

17. Consors ut beatatis
    Vivam cum justificatis
    In ævum æternatis. *

18. Oro supplex et acclinis,
    Cor contritum quasi ciuis :
    Gere curam mei finis.

19. Lacrymosa dies illa,
    Qua resurget ex favilla
    Judicandus homo reus,
    Huic ergo parce Deus.

---

* Dr. Trench has not translated this verse,—literally "that I may forever be a companion of the blessed and live with the justified."

On a marble slab, in the church of St. Francis, Mantua, on which this hymn is engraven, there are four preliminary verses which have the tone of a private meditation :

Cogita, anima fidelis,
Ad quid respondere velis
Christo venturo cœlis.

Cum deposcet rationem
Ob boni omissionem
Ob mali commissionem.

Dies illa, Dies iræ !
Quam conemur prevenire
Obveamque Deo iræ ?

Seria contritione
Gratiæ apprehensione
Vitæ emendatione.

Then after these four verses come the first seventeen verses as given above—the received text—but instead of the eighteenth and nineteenth verses we have the following eight, strongly colored with Mariolatry towards the close, condensed into these two, eighteenth and nineteenth.

Oro supplex a ruinis,
Cor contritum quasi cinis ;
Gere curam mei finis.

Lachrymosa die illa
Cum resurget in favilla
Tanquam ignes ex scintilla.

Indicandus homo reus—
Huic ergo parce, Deus,
Esto semper (tunc) adjutor meus.

Quando cœli sunt movendi ;
Dies adsunt tunc tremendi ;
Nullum tempus pœnitendi.

Sed salvatis læta dies ;
Et damnatis nulla quies,
Sed dæmonum effigies.

O tu Deus majestatis,
Alme candor Trinitatis,
Nunc conjunge beatis.

Vitam meam fac felicem
Propter tuam genetricem,
Jesse florem et radicem.

Præsta nobis tunc levamen,
Dulce nostrum fac certamen,
Ut clamemus omnes.   Amen.

That is literally :—

I, a crushed heart, as if in ashes,
Supplicate Thee from my ruins,
Oh have a care of my final state.

On that mournful day—
When man shall rise from ashes,
As fire from a spark !

And man answerable to Thee is to be judged,
Spare him, O God,—
And be Thou always my helper.

When the heavens are to be shaken,
And the awful days come,
It is no time for repenting.

But joyful will the day be to the saved,
And no quiet to the damned,
But the pictured state of devils.

Oh Thou God of majesty,
Benign splendor of the Trinity,
Now join me with the blessed.

Make my life a happy one,
For the sake of Thy mother,
The offspring and root of David.

Guard us then and be a relief,
Make the ordeal sweet,
That we may all celebrate Thy name, Amen !

It seems probable that the received text as translated by Dr
Trench, etc., is the truncated form—or remnant of the original
hymn as found on the marble slab at Mantua. The first four
verses are cut off as having the tone of a private meditation,
and then the last eight are condensed into two, eighteenth and
nineteenth, which make up the nineteen verses as in the received
text,—the more forcible because of their brevity, and the more
welcome because of their omission of anything like Mariolatry.

Dies Iræ is a hymn, wonderful for its simple majesty,
almost artless in its structure, the solemn grandeur of the
theme, the felicity of its diction, the strength of its imagery,
and the spirit of awe with which it inspires us ; for it touches
the imagination as well as the heart, and gives us a sense of
the solemnities of the judgment to an extent far beyond anything we know of either in ancient or modern hymnology.

The testimony of those who have the best right to speak on
the subject has given to it the highest place in the whole range
of the ancient hymns. Daniel, in his *Thesaurus Hymnologicus*,

says : " By universal consent it is regarded as the highest orna-
ment of sacred poetry, and the most sacred treasure of the Latin
Church." Similar is the testimony of Trench, Mrs. Charles,
etc.   Then among its admirers may be set down a long list of
famous names, consisting of soldiers, statesmen, churchmen,
poets, historians, musicians—musicians that have rendered no
small service in wedding to it immortal song.   Among those
admirers are included the names of Mozart, Haydn, Goethe,
Johnson, Dryden, Scott, Milman.   There is probably no human ✓
composition that has won such favour and made such an impression on the heart of Christendom.   And instead of being
on the wane, like many once popular hymns, it is becoming
more highly esteemed with passing years, making for itself a
way into all the churches, having already secured for itself a
place in more than twenty of their hymnals !

    How does it come that a hymn so broadly Papistic in its
origin should be received with such favour by evangelical
Protestants as well as unflinching Roman Catholics — that
churches that once would not allow their ministers to put on
a black gown have nearly all given it a place in their service
of song ?   One reason is that while it is Roman Catholic in its
origin, it is not Roman Catholic in its teaching as revised
and as it has been used for generations.   It has no smell
of the cloister about it.   It never betrays its origin or casts
a shadow over that new and living way which has been opened
to the holiest of all.   It is not so with the *Stabat Mater
cruce* (a mother was standing by the cross), the hymn that
ranks next to this in the polish of its verse and the solemn
beauty of its theme.   With all the exquisite tenderness and perfect finish of the *Stabat Mater* it is sadly marred with Roman
Catholic error, and this must always stand in the way of its
popularity and general acceptance in the Protestant Church.
It is in the last two verses where those errors chiefly appear,
and consist in an invocation to the Virgin :

Never shall the mingled tide,
Flowing still from Jesus' side.
May my lips inebriate turn,
And when in the day of doom,
Lightning-like He rends the tomb ;
Shield (Mary), oh shield me, lest I burn.

So the shadow of the tree
Where Thy Jesus died for me
Still shall be my fortalice ;
So when flesh and spirit sever,
Shall I live, *Thy boon* forever,
In the joys of Paradise.

(Translated by Lord Lindsay.)

From all such invocations and errors the "Dies Iræ" is
entirely free. Moreover the fact that the translations of this
great hymn, "Dies Iræ," are almost innumerable, shows what
a hold it has taken of the Church. Dr. Lisco, of Berlin (1843),
has collected eighty-seven, nearly all German, and who can tell
the number that are to be found in the French and English
tongues? Who can count the dust of Jacob? We have ourselves seen over a dozen of those translations, including Alford's
"Day of Anger, That Dread Day," Irons' "Day of Wrath, Oh
Day of Mourning," etc., but by far the best is evidently that of
Major-General John A. Dix, U.S.A., the gentleman already
referred to.

It is astonishing what labour has been expended on those
numerous translations—how many gifted pens have been employed on them, seeking to render the original Latin into the
vernacular of their respective countries. Astonishing not only
for the number but for the long patience with which they pur-
sued their work in some cases, extending over half a lifetime—
all trying to give a finer touch to some line or bring out in
happier form the thought of the author. Franklin Johnson,

e.g., of Cambridge Mass., Nov., 1883, says he spent fifteen years in his version, pruning and polishing all the time, and yet at the close of his performance was far below his ideal ! He speaks of the difficulty of rendering in English that which has such power and sweetness in Latin, and adds :

> The marble shows the form and face,
> But who will give it vital grace ?

Time would fail me were I to attempt a narrative of the deeds of even a tithe of the writers that have given themselves to this. Mr. Murray, of the *Star*, to whom I am indebted for information that leaves little doubt as to the authorship, has investigated the long obscure history of this hymn, chiefly on our account, and I am free to say that his word may be regarded as the last that can be said on the subject.

Reference has already been made to the scriptural character of this hymn, to the fact that it rises above the creed of its author or the author's church, and deals with the destinies of men and the mercy of God in Christ Jesus, in language pure and undefiled. Is not this a matter for thankfulness ? Is it nothing to say that this great judgment hymn has been in use for seven hundred years witnessing for God and truth amid all the corruptions of the Papacy—lifting up its strong, clear voice, like the trumpet of the archangel summoning the dead to the bar of God ? The song, as well as the sermon, is a vehicle of instruction, and in many cases better than the sermon. That is the case now in these days of greater light and privilege, but how much more must the people have been indebted to these hymns in past ages ? Whatever may be said about the mummeries of Romanism and the scandals of the clergy, that church has always had a splendid service of song, often a choral service ; and if the people failed to learn anything valuable from the pulpit, they could hardly fail to learn something

valuable from the choir. They were ever hearing of heaven
and hell, human guilt and the tender mercy of God in Christ,
the work of the Holy Spirit and the Jerusalem which is above.
Such hymns as the Te Deum, Jerusalem the Golden, Veni
Creator Spiritus, Dies Iræ, and such processional hymns as the
Vexilla Regis (the royal banner forward goes), left no excuse to
the people for being entirely ignorant of the great truths which,
through faith, are able to make us wise unto salvation. That
church has ever been rich in hymns—hymns that were witnesses for God and truth, amid all the mummeries of the ritual
and the effete performances of an often perfunctory priesthood.
But this hymn—the Dies Iræ—which rose like a flaming star
in the dark night of superstition, when the bullfight was the
chief amusement of the people, and the lust of temporal power
the chief passion of the priesthood, must ever be regarded as
the greatest and the one most frequently in use of all the ancient hymns ; for, apart from the fact it must be statedly sung
in the Sistine Chapel, Rome, it forms the Sequence for the dead
in the Roman Catholic burial service, and, of course, is in daily
requisition the world over. It is not a hymn expressive of the
higher life of faith in Christ Jesus—the glorious liberty of the
children of God—but rather one of bondage, deprecating God's
wrath and pleading for God's mercy in the last sad hour. It
takes its colour and character from the century which gave it
birth, when the vision of God had grown dim and the spiritual
life of the Church was running low ; but still it is a hymn
which has touched many a heart with the powers of the
world to come, and helped to prepare them for the great
assize, and among those may be named our own Sir Walter
Scott. He had in the days of his rising fame—before his eye
had grown dim, or his right hand had lost its cunning, —
penned the much admired Lay of the Last Minstrel, and he
closes the beautiful performance with the words :

The mass was sung, the prayers read,
The solemn requiem for the dead,
And bells tolled out the mighty peal
For the departed spirit's weal ;
And ever in the office close
The hymn of intercession rose ;
And far the echoing did prolong
The solemn burden of the song,
    Dies ira, dies illa,
    Solvet sæclum in favilla,
While the pealing organ rang
With it,—meet with sacred strain—
To close my lay so light and vain,
Thus the holy father sang :

That day of wrath, that dreadful day,
    When heaven and earth shall pass away ;
What power shall be the sinner's stay,
    How shall he meet that dreadful day ?

When shrivelling like a parched scroll,
    The flaming heavens together roll ;
When louder yet, and yet more dread
    Swells the high trump that wakes the dead,—

Oh, on that day, that wrathful day,
    When man to judgment wakes from clay ;
Be Thou the trembling sinner's stay,
    Though heaven and earth shall pass away.

It was to these verses he himself turned in his last hour, to this hymn ; and not to it alone, but the blessed Word from which it is drawn. A few days before his death, we are informed by his biographer, Mr. Lockhart, there was a lucid interval of that distressing malady for the removal of which he had travelled to London, Italy, Malta, etc. He was again in his own home ; and in one of those calm moments when he was comparatively free from pain, he desired to be drawn into his library and placed beside the window that looks down upon the Tweed. "Read to me now." "From what shall I read," said Mr. Lockhart. "Can you ask? There is but one" (book). I chose, says his biographer, the fourteenth of John, and at the close of my reading he said: "Well this is a great comfort, I have followed you distinctly all through, and I feel as if I were yet to be myself again." Can we conceive of a grander testimony in favour of the Bible? "There is but one" (book), said this great man, when standing face to face with God, that can meet the case. Not his own beautiful poems; not his own enchanting works of fiction. Miserable comforters were they all. He had come to a point where one blessed word of the Lord Jesus was regarded as better than all the wisdom of this world, when one ray of the excellent glory would bring more cheer to his soul than all the splendour of Abbotsford, where the romance of life must give place to sober truth, where the highest works of genius must pass away like the aurora borealis of northern skies, and give place to the solemn realities of the eternal world.* Soon after this touching scene, the deepening shadows fell on the bright spirit that had revelled in its own creations for a quarter of a century, that had touched the lyre with such a master hand, that we still hear the reverberations from afar, and the strong man staggered, and his feet stumbled on the dark mountains; but even then, the ruling spirit, strong in death, was running in its old channels, and those that were nearest heard amongst his fading utterances the cadence of this great hymn :

> Dies iræ, dies illa,
> Solvet sæclum in favilla,
> Teste David cum Sibylla.

We often, says Lockhart, (Vol. II., pp. 734, Life of Sir W.

---

* Albert Barnes on the subject.

D

Scott) heard distinctly the whisperings of the Dies Iræ, together with fragments of the psalms in his last days. In like manner this great hymn haunted the Earl of Roscommon, who had written an English version of it, as we learn from "Johnson's lives of the poets." His last utterance was two lines of that version :—

> My God, my Father, and my Friend,
> Do not forsake me in the end.

We gratefully accept of this, the greatest of all our ancient hymns and the most precious treasure of the Latin Church. What was its origin,—what the circumstances that led to its genesis we cannot tell ; but plainly the Divine Spirit has made large use of it in stirring dead souls with the "powers of the world to come," and lifting them up to a higher life. For many generations it has been a witness for God, breaking in upon the slumbering choirs of Europe like a spirit from the Eternal World. Like the "Imitation of Christ" by Thomas a Kempis, it remains as a monument of the truth that in ages of general declension, God has His hidden ones that He nourishes in secret ; and that beneath the drifting and accumulating mass of heresies and superstitions, there is now, and ever has been, an under current of simple faith in Christ that kept alive and verdant some less noticed portions of the blighted vineyard of the Lord.

HYMN IV.

COME, HOLY SPIRIT, OUR SOULS INSPIRE,

OR VENI CREATOR SPIRITUS.

TUNE.—*Veni Creator*, BY DR. DYKES, MUS. DOC.,

COME, Holy Ghost, our souls inspire,
    And lighten with celestial fire ;
Thou the anointing Spirit art,
Who dost Thy sevenfold gifts impart.

Thy blessed unction from above
Is comfort, life, and fire of love ;
Enable with perpetual light
The dulness of our blinded sight :

Anoint and cheer our soiled face
With the abundance of Thy grace :
Keep far our foes, give peace at home ;
Where Thou art guide no ill can come.

Teach us to know the Father, Son,
And Thee, of Both, to be but One ;
That, through the ages all along,
This may be our endless song :
    Praise to Thy eternal merit,
    Father, Son, and Holy Spirit.

IN my notes on the great hymns of the Church it seemed to me that some one bearing on the Holy Spirit should be selected ; and in looking over this class of hymns I have no hesitation in giving the first place to the one named.   At a very early period we find hymns set to the praise of the Father and the Father alone, to the Son and the Son alone, and it is not wonderful that ere long we should also find hymns to the Holy Spirit and the Holy Spirit alone. For the most part the recognition of the Holy Ghost in their ascriptions of praise on the part of the early Christians is to be found in the doxologies; and it was from the lips of confessors and martyrs who witnessed for God in a dark age, and who drank of the wine of the great mystery—it was from such lips that those strains rose in their most triumphant notes. It was poor Blandina * who perished in 177 A.D., at Lyons, that cried out in her last moments: "I believe in the Father, the Son and the Holy Ghost, one God, blessed forever!" Poor girl, she was roasted in a red-hot chair. Her tormentors put her in a net and exposed her to the fury of wild bulls. They whirled her about on instruments of torture till her senses were lost; but in her lucid moments she gave this as her dying testimony: "I believe in the Father, etc."

But the name of the Holy Spirit in the doxology was not enough to satisfy the heart of the Church as it advanced in years, especially amid the fuller lights and richer unfoldings of the Word, and we do not wonder at finding all along the line hymns springing up bearing on the one theme—the praise of the Holy Spirit; but the grandest of them all, as it seems to me, is that which I have selected for our meditation this day:

"COME, HOLY SPIRIT,"

or *Veni Creator*, as it is called. And here, at the outset, let me acknowledge my indebtedness to Mr. Carter, a distinguished hymnologist, for much of my information. Now, who was the author of this hymn? What was *its* genesis? Under what circumstances did *it* spring into being? These are questions we cannot answer—questions no one can answer. One thing is

---

* Referred to in th notes on the Te Deum.

clear, the hymn belongs to a far-off age, probably to the times of Charlemagne, and there are some that believe that this great monarch was himself the author. He was a very religious though not a spiritually minded man. He was the greatest soldier as well as the most distinguished literateur of his day, Eighth Century. To his pen we owe more than one great work which has survived the wreck of centuries, and to his beneficence we are indebted for the University of Paris. It was around his court that the learning and splendor of Europe lingered, and it was here where the leading spirits of the day caught their inspiration. What more likely than Charlemagne was the author of " Veni Creator." But all is conjecture: there is nothing certain. Like the Nile, which had for ages conceal-ed its source in spite of all the efforts made to solve the mystery—like this has been the history of this wonderful hymn, and like this, too, it has continued to minister to the wants and refresh the hearts of thousands who never raised such questions as those which I have propounded. Not a few of our great hymns have had a very obscure origin and a very feeble history for years—a mere thread like a silver line of water from the hills. In his last days Perronet was ministering to a mere handful of worshippers, so few indeed that he could easily have accommodated them all in his own house; but it was in these circumstances he introduced that imperial song that sounds like a bugle blast :

All hail the power of Jesus' name !

So with this great hymn under consideration. A hymn which kings have sung upon their thrones, which countless clergy have used under cathedral arches, which many a lonely pilgrim has fed sweetly upon in his wanderings, and which many a quiet heart, living a divine life amid coarse cares and hard duties, has found to be a leaf from the tree of life which is for the healing of the nations.

Do you ask wherein lies its excellency? I answer, look at its contents. Mark what it says of the Spirit. It owns Him Creator and Paraclote ; that is, man's maker and man's daily comforter. It calls Him a living fountain and a fire, and it dwells upon His love and heavenly unction. He is addressed in stately verse as able to give light and courage—as able to drive away every foe, to give us a saving knowledge of the Father and the Son, and that blessed peace that passes all understanding. It is a rich hymn, and its wealth, like ointment poured forth, is fragrant, and must have been all the more fragrant in those early days when such terms were comparatively new and congregations for the first time lifted up their voices in the praise of that good Spirit that leadeth into all truth.

From the *Psaltereum Romanum* I copy the original :

VENI Creator Spiritus
        Mentes tuorum visita,
Imple supernâ gratiâ
Quae Tu creasti pectora.

Qui Paraclētus diceris
Altissimi donum Dei
Fons vivus, ignis, caritas,
Et Spiritalis unctio

Tu Septiformis munere,
Dextrae Dei Tu digitus,
Tu rite promissum Patris
Sermone ditans guttera

Accende lumen seusibus,
Infunde amorem cordibus,
Infirma nostri corporis
Virtute firmans perpeti.

Hostem repellas longius,
Pacemque dones protinus
Ductore sic Te previo
Vitemus omne noxium.

Da gaudiorum premea,
Da gratiarum munera,
Dissolve litis vincula,
Astringe pacis foedera.

Per Te sciàmus da Patrem,
Noscamus atque Filium,
Te utriusque Spiritum
Credamus omni tempore.

Sit laus Patri cum Filio,
Sancto simul Paraclēto,
Nobisque mittat Filius
Charisma Sancti Spiritus.

Gloria Patri Domino
Natoque qui a mortuis
Surrexit ac Paraclēto
In seculorum seculum.   Amen !

For nearly twelve centuries, this hymn has been used on great
State and Church occasions, such as the consecration of sover-
eigns, popes, cardinals, bishops and archbishops.   In the Coronation Services of our illustrious Queen we have an illustration of the manner.   Conducted to the altar in Westminster
Abbey she kneeled down there, and placing her hand on the
great Bible she took the oath which the Sovereign of these
realms has to take ; she then kissed the book and this hymn was
sung by the great congregation, the Queen kneeling meanwhile.
Then her Majesty seated in St. Edward's chair—a gorgeous
cloth of gold being held over her head,—the Archbishop of
Canterbury anointed her with holy oil in the form of a cross as
the Sovereign of the British Empire.

The first instance of the use of this hymn on record was at

the translation of some Benedictine relics in 898, but it is doubtless older than this. The translation beginning :—

> Come Holy Ghost, our souls inspire,

Appeared first in the Ordinal of the English Prayer Book in 1662, and is attributed to Bishop Cosin, but previous to this, 1552, there appeared the version that originated with some of the early reformers beginning :—

> Come Holy Ghost, eternal God,—

There is also to be added Dryden's somewhat effeminate translation beginning :—

> Creator Spirit, by whose aid,

What a history this hymn has had ! Who would undertake to write it? It has been sung at the election of many an unworthy Pope, for it became part of the order of the day on such occasions ; it has been used by many an humble monk in his cloister, who had learned in spite of surrounding darkness to feed upon its truths, and many a family around the domestic hearth, Roman Catholic in name but Protestant in heart. It has been a light shining in a dark place, ministering to the faith of the Church and witnessing to the personality and continuous presence of the Holy Spirit, when the priest was unfaithful, when the doctrine of the Atonement was obscured and many an obstacle stood in the way to the holiest of all.

One very important aspect of this hymn is that it has become the father of many more, or rather the model after which hundreds of a kindred sort have been fashioned, such as the *Veni Sancte Spiritus* of Robert II. of France, translated by Dr. McGill, one verse of which I must give :

> Holy Spirit, God of light,
> Come and on our inner sight
> Pour Thy bright and heavenly ray.

This was written by a king—a king who flourished in the eleventh century, and evidently Robert II. had this hymn in his eye when he penned his version. Already the Church had wandered far away from the divine simplicity, had taken up with the doctrine of the real presence in the Eucharist, had introduced symbolic candles into the chancel and covered the altars with crucifixes—in short, had gone a long way in materializing the great doctrine of the Atonement; but the doctrine of the Trinity still remained as well as the proper divinity of our Lord, together with the doctrine of the Holy Spirit working on the hearts of men; and such hymns as that under consideration did much to preserve these articles of the faith once delivered to the saints.

In the next century we come upon the celebrated hymn of the German Abbess of Hildegarde, in which however, we have little more than an echo of *Veni Creator*. It is a sort of prose poem, beginning with *O Ignes Spiritus Paracleti*, of which we must also give a specimen :

O sweetest taste within the breast ! O grace upon us poured,
That saintly hearts may give again their perfume to the Lord ;
O purest Fountain we can see, clear mirrored in Thy streams,
That God brings home the wanderers, that God the lost redeems.

Once more this same hymn re-appears in reformation times in the hands of Luther. His thoughts, as we know, were mainly concerned about salvation through Christ and not the Church ; but a movement which was to re-establish an unfettered relationship between the soul and God, to keep an open way to the throne of the Eternal for the humblest believer without the leave of prince or prelate, was not likely to escape his notice. Hence his *Chorales*, the very first of which is a fair rendering of the *Veni Creator*. And so on, coming nearer to our own day, we have Bishop Cosin's translation of this same hymn, than which nothing could be finer, and which we have adopted into our hymnal and honoured with the first place there, as it behooved us to do. It is really an admirable translation, and the compilers of the Book of Common Prayer have shown their sense of its value by inserting it in the orders for ordination and consecration. Dryden's translation, has never reached the popularity of Cosin's and never will, and the same may be said of even Charles Wesley's

> Come, Holy Spirit, our hearts inspire.

This, too, is certainly a great hymn, and differing in details from the great unknown, though evidently it had been present to Wesley's mind at the time when he sat down to write his version. But apart altogether from the question of intrinsic merit, this hymn of Charles Wesley has caught the heart of Methodism and set it on fire, and, as Carter says, the Methodist that does not know it would be as little worthy of his spiritual heritage as a Scotchman who does not know " The Lord's my Shepherd." The same writer adds that " it has been sung before the sermons in the Methodist societies the world over for the last century; that it has helped to maintain among them their great faith in the Spirit's power, and we doubt not it has been answered in showers of blessing again and again."

Now go back to the days of Charlemagne and trace the history of this great hymn through the intervening centuries, forming a sort of staple for scores of other hymns on the Holy Spirit—giving its character and colour to them all—and say whether we have been indulging in exaggeration when we claim that it should be set down as one of the great hymns of the Church? God gave a great blessing to the world on that day when it saw the light, not only for what it is in itself and for what it has done in itself, but in leading so many gifted men to try the same theme and strike the same golden chord. In this respect—I may say in both, but chiefly in the latter—it has done much to sustain the faith of the Church in days of darkness, when the priest was chiefly exercised about ceremony, and candles, and crucifixes, penance and indulgence, and discussing such questions as the tenuity of devils and how many of them could dance on the point of a needle; but this hymn, together with the troops that followed it and sprang from it, was a constant ministration, and doubtless it has proved spirit and life to thousands. In this respect it has been a still small voice often heard above the clang of the war trumpet, the shout of the crusaders, the roar of lions, the crackle of the burning fagots ready to consume the martyr—and always a voice of power even when rising on the clear melody of infant lips or in the faltering accents of old age. In this respect it has been a fire continually burning, now breaking out in one form and now in another, now in that of "Robert the sage," now in that of the ancient Abbess of Hildegarde, now in the Antiphones of the Venerable Bede, and now in the *Chorales* of Luther, but chiefly in the heart of Charles Wesley, to whom the world owes so much, and still more in the heart of the Anglican Bishop to whom we are indebted for the noble translation which forms the first of the list of hymns to the Holy Ghost in our Presbyterian Hymnal.

HYMN V.

JERUSALEM THE GOLDEN.

TUNE.—*Ewing.*

JERUSALEM the golden,
  With milk and honey blest,
Beneath thy contemplation
  Sink heart and voice opprest.
I know not, O, I know not,
  What joys await us there ;
What radiancy of glory,
  What light beyond compare !

They stand, those halls of Zion,
  All jubilant with song,
And bright with many an angel,
  And all the martyr throng :
The Prince is ever in them ;
  The daylight is serene ;
The pastures of the blessed
  Are decked in glorious sheen.

There is the throne of David ;
  And there, from care released,
The shout of them that triumph,
  The song of them that feast ;
And they who, with their Leader,
  Have conquered in the fight,
For ever and for ever
  Are clad in robes of white.

O sweet and blessed country,
  The home of God's elect !
O sweet and blessed country,
  That eager hearts expect !
Jesus, in mercy bring us
  To that dear land of rest ;
Who art, with God the Father,
  And Spirit, ever blest.

THE original poem of which this is part, consisted of three thousand lines, but in the hands of the Rev. John M. Neale, D.D., who translated it into English, it became one of four hundred and forty-two lines. Dr. Neale, however, begins with the line *urbs Syon aurea*. Immediately on its publication—1859—it became immensely popular. Mr. Duffield says that in 1885 it was the seventh in rank among all the favourite English hymns. As a whole it is too long for devotional purposes, but it has been broken up into several pieces and re-arranged, so that out of the original four hundred and forty-two lines of Dr. Neale, we have several hymns of moderate length— all of great beauty and power. "Brief life is here, our portion" (*hic breve vivitur*) is one piece. "For thee, O dear, dear country," (*O bona patria*) is another ; Jerusalem the glorious (*urbs Syon inclyta*) is another. Dr. Neale was a clergyman of the church of England, an advanced ritualist, and to such an extent did he carry his ritualism that he was "inhibited" for fourteen years. For the sake of supporting himself, he took to writing stories for children—stories which have had an immense sale and in many respects furnish a model in the way of story telling, especially as regards dealing with historical facts. Dr. Neale graduated in 1840 (Cambridge), having won for himself great distinction as a classic, taking the Seatonian prize, no less than eleven times—a position to which no other had ever attained or came near attaining. He was, indeed, a marvellous scholar, qualified in every way, scholarship, sympathy, taste, admiration for the ascetic life, to translate the Latin hymns of

the mediæval age.   He was besides a splendid story teller and
withal a devoted christian, · one whose works of philanthropy,
prove how the ideal and the real may flow on together, the one
acting and reacting upon the other.   It is to him we owe the
sisterhood of St. Margaret, which is simply a training school
for the best class of nurses—an institution which was established in 1859, and which in many respects is a model institution
of its kind.   But there is nothing which Dr. Neale has done,
—not even his long work of faith and labor of love necessary
for the founding of this institution that will do more for the
glory of God and the good of souls,—nothing that will be more
lasting in its results and prove richer in its fruits than the
translating of this old Latin hymn, the first notes of which were
heard in the cloisters of Cluny nearly eight centuries ago.
He has thereby unsealed a fountain from which many a one
that never heard his name will drink,— a fountain that will
continue to flow for ages, and minister to the faith of the
church when scores of hymns now popular, will be swept away
like fuel for the burning.

We can only afford room for a specimen of this long poem
in the Latin :—

> Urbs aurea, patrea lactea, cive decora,
> Omne cor obruis, omnibus obstruis et cor et ora.
> Nescio, nescio, quæ jubilatio lux tibi qualis ;
> Quam socialia gaudia, gloria quam specialis.
> Laude studens ea tollere ; mens mea victa fatiscit ;
> Sunt Syon atria conjubilantia martyre plena.
> Cive micantia, Principe stantia, luce serena ;
> Est ibi pascua, mitibus afflua, præstita sanctis.
> Reges ibi thronus, agminis et sonus est epulantis.

The scholar will notice that these lines are all hexameter,
made up of five dactyles and one spondee,—that each line is
divided into three parts, —the second part rhyming with the first,
and the third part, rhyming with the third of the preceding line
thus :—

Regis ibi thronus—agminis et sonus—est epulantis.

Then as a rule the author makes no use of the *Cæsura*. Think
of the labor, the patience of going through three thousand lines
—and such polished lines—in this fashion! He used to maintain that he could never have done so but for the fact that he
had been upheld by divine inspiration!

The subject of the hymn is the advent of Christ to judgment,
the joys of the saints, the pains of the reprobate. Dr. Neale
calls the hymn a "bitter satire on the fearful corruptions of the
age in which the poet, Bernard lived. As a contrast to the
miseries of earth the poem opens with a description of the peace
and glory of heaven, of such rare beauty as not easily to be
matched by any mediæval composition on the same subject." With respect to its power in giving a fresh and cheering
view of the glory to be revealed, there can be no manner of
doubt. How many a pale face, through this hymn, has become
radiant with its holy light! How many a sufferer has been
helped in his last hours and patiently endured, seeing Him that
is invisible! No better illustration can be found than that
which Dr. Neale himself furnishes—the case of a little boy to
whom the Doctor ministered in his last hours. The sufferings of
the child were very great, but on hearing this hymn repeated,
even the whole four hundred and forty-two lines he would lie
still, and feel so lifted up that he was scarcely conscious of the
agony that was preying upon his vitals. The light affliction
which was but for a moment, was nothing to him in view of
the revelations of this hymn. And when we think of the
warm, sympathetic nature of the Doctor, so spiritually minded,
and so tender, we need not wonder that such a case should
have afforded him the sweetest satisfaction · more so probably
than all the eulogies with which he was favored for his literary
deeds. He died in 1886, at the time of which he held the
wardenship of Sackville College, East Grinstead, England.

Fourteen years of "inhibition"—ecclesiastical censure—enforced silence as regards the pulpits of the establishment! Still they were not years of idleness or fruitlessness. On the contrary, they are now turning out to be the richest and the best in his life. The perversity that led a Pusey and a Newman into dangerous error—that has destroyed many a gifted mind —that at one time threatened to destroy our Protestant England, was rebuked and put down. Out of the eater God brought forth meat and out of the strong he brought forth sweetness for it was during this enforced silence that the most of Dr. Neale's mighty works were done, not the least of which was the translating of this old hymn of three thousand lines. We owe under God some of the richest portions of the Scriptures to the enforced silence of St. Paul in Cesarea, Rome, etc. We owe to the enforced silence of Rutherford, those heavenly letters which he wrote in a cell in Aberdeen jail—letters which have lost nothing of their power during the lapse of these two hundred years.—We owe to the enforced silence of John Bunyan the story of the Pilgrim's Progress, which has lighted up the path of many a pilgrim since his day; —and we owe to those fourteen years of "inhibition" during which Dr. Neale was silenced, the translation of "Jerusalem the Golden," for which the entire church of God is thankful to-day.

Still Dr. Neale was only the translator, not the author, —the angel with the golden key that opened the prison door for the apostle. The author is Bernard of Morlaix—not St. Bernard his contemporary. It is not often we have two men of the same name, same generation, same country—almost the same neighborhood, devoted to the same pursuits and winning for themselves almost equal honors. The Bernard of whom we now write never found a place in the saints' calendar, but he has won for himself a place in the saints hearts —a place to which many of the saints in the calendar never made their way. He was born at Morlaix (Bretayne) of English parents, and became an inmate of the very illus-

trious Abbe of Cluny, whose church was then the most
magnificent in France. The situation of the Abbey is on the
little river Grône in the department of the Saône et Loire, in a
lovely valley between two mountains,—say two hundred miles
southeast of Paris. Into this celebrated Abbey, Bernard made
his way; but in spite of the heavenly surroundings and engagements, prayer, penance, reading, meditation, musical services,
and the grandest ritual of his day, Bernard was far from being
at rest. He was conscious in his own soul of a terrible warfare,
the hot contendings of rival powers, and this he knew was only an
index—weather glass-like—of what was going on in the coarse,
common world around him. In the penitential sigh, in the
groaning of the midnight hour, he heard the echoes of a doomed
world, and caught the sound of the swelling waves of destruction,
even as a child in his fancy, hears the ocean sound, ever as he
applies the kindred shell to his ear which was picked up on the
shore long years ago. To him the world was a doomed world.
The Judge was at the door. The great seething mass of
humanity, rotten to the core, unless rescued by the church, was
ripe for destruction; but he would hold himself in readiness,
keep *his* loins girt and *his* lamp burning, and so he sings :—

> The world is old and sinful,
> Its passing hour is near ;
> Keep watch, be hushed and sober,
> The Judge's knock to hear.
>
> Rise Christian, rise to meet him.
> Let wrong give way to right,
> Let tears of godly sorrow,
> Melt into songs of light.
>
> The light that has no setting,
> Too new for moon or sun,
> So crystal-like and golden,
> So like its Maker, One.

The transition from these lines to Jerusalem the Golden the
hymn under consideration was easy, and in its three thousand

E

lines he gives full scope to his meditations—bringing out in rich
contrast the heavenly state of the righteous. To these meditations, doubtless, is to be traced the genesis of this great hymn.
How different is the Abbey of Cluny now with all its surroundings from the time that Bernard farmed and wrote iambics
—the people, the country, the dominant ideas of society? Many
a storm has raged during these centuries around this venerable
Abbey, but this glorious hymn remains the same as when it
received the finishing touches of its author—shining like a
silver star, cheering many a weary pilgrim in the dark night,—
a witness for God now, and a witness in mediæval days when
the priest was unfaithful, and the gospel was obscured and
truth was poisoned at its sources. Amid all changes it has
been lifting up its voice for God, a still small voice indeed,
but still never altogether suppressed. It has held its own
against all comers—the shout of the gladiator, the roar of
battle, the crackling fires of martyrdom, the groaning of the
prisoner appointed to die, the hot contendings about popes and
emperors and doctrines and decrees, and the wassail and the wine-
drinking of many generations. We speak of old hymns, but
truth never becomes old; beauty never, holiness never, love
never; so with truth and the natural imagery in which it is
presented. The leaves fall but the tree remains. The gospel
is presented in one form, in one age; in another form, in another
age because better suited to that age; but still the same, the
everlasting gospel which the apocalyptic angel has to preach
unto all them that dwell upon the earth; and every hymn in
full accord with this gospel of the kingdom must be a power in
the world. "The old story has had its day, and will no longer
satisfy men. Give us something new—something better suited
to the age and our higher attainments." In such terms do some
in their ignorance and arrogance speak who likely know little
of the gospel, but not those who have felt the plague of their
own hearts, seen their own weakness in an hour of temptation,
realized in some measure their dependence on an Almighty Arm,

their need of cleansing and the blood of sprinkling—realized, in short, the powers of the world to come and the glory of a kingdom, whose limits transcend the stars and of whose duration there is no end. To all such the gospel is ever fresh and fragrant as the morn—a thing of beauty and a joy forever; and any hymn like that which issued from the cloisters of Cluny in a far past age, will be welcomed as a ray from the excellent glory.

Nor can I suffer this hymn to pass away from my hands without noting the lofty form of piety which we find in its author, Roman Catholic, though he was. It is, in many passages, a painful, even a revolting task to read the history of that church, and the excesses into which many of its dignitaries fell, but beneath all that dark exterior there were many precious souls that kept themselves unspotted from the world, that in spite of all the errors and excesses of the time, could say in their solitude—Truly, our fellowship is with the Father and his Son Jesus Christ. Where can we find a loftier form of piety, self-denial, pure consecration, than in the two Bernards of Cluny, whose hymns are now so much in favor; or in Fenelon arch-bishop of Paris, a Roman Catholic, in name, but a Protestant in heart; or Thomas a'Becket, whose blood was shed by the hands of an assassin on the altar steps of England's oldest cathedral; or Thomas a'Kempis whose wonderful book, "Imitation of Christ" after the lapse of three centuries has still such a hold on Christendom; or Cardinal Newman whose hymn "Lead kindly light" so often guides our devotions? Protestantism is not a narrow ecclesiasticism that can see nothing good beyond its pale, but a form of that broad charity that can recognize grace wherever it is found; a brother beneath the monk's cowl, or the soldier's uniform or the quaker's quaint dress; in short, anyone that has learned to do the will of the Father. During the revolution in Italy in 1848, there were some sad overturnings and desolations; and among these a famous monastery on the inside walls of which were found some expressive pencillings. One read:—*O Salvator beate, me absciderunt ecclesea tua, sed non potuerunt me abscidere seipso.* The inference is that some one not sufficiently docile, excommunicated, had been immured in this cell, enclosed by the wall on which these words were written—but who realizing the communion of saints and their fellowship with the Father and the Son, gave utterance to these words:—*O blessed Saviour, they have cut me off from thy church, but they cannot cut me off from thyself*; and he might have added, and I am persuaded that neither death, nor life, nor things, etc. How many like this unknown brother in the Roman Church, but better than their Church, living a divine life in obscurity, bearing the ban of ecclesiastical ostracism, but realizing their communion with the Father and the Son and with all the saints, could use the same language? We refuse to unite with the Roman Catholic church in their prayers and invocations, but not in their praises. We do not care about their forms, but we welcome their hymns and sing as heartily as they, "Lead kindly light"; "Jerusalem the golden"; "Come Holy Spirit"; "The world is very evil, etc.": and what is no less interesting, our Protestant hymns are making their way *to them* and finding a place in *their* collections. Strange that in the ritualistic section of the English church Watts, and Charles Wesley and Doddridge should find a place in their hymnals beside St. Bernard, Venantius Fortunatus, Thomas Aquinas, and Keble—that such hymns as "Jesus shall reign where'er the sun," and "Hark the herald angels" should find a place among the invocations to the saints and the virgin —the adoration of the real presence and the processional peans on high days! Jerusalem the Golden is no longer a Roman Catholic hymn. Rock of Ages is no longer a Protestant hymn, an English church hymn, a Presbyterian hymn, but the *Church's* hymn—God's great sacramental host ever growing in numbers and in power, and will continue to do so till she goes forth fair as the moon, clear as the sun, and terrible as an army with banners.

HYMN VI.

EIN FESTE BURG*

THE GREAT REFORMATION HYMN, BY MARTIN LUTHER.

TUNE.— *Worms.*

(Supposed to have been written in 1498 by Luther.   It is well harmonised and full of the pathos of the original.)

THIS hymn has been called the Marseillaise of the Reformation—the battle song of the Church militant in its terrific conflict with the Roman hierarchy.   It is a translation or rather a paraphrase of the forty-sixth psalm, and a noble paraphrase it is; for although some of the lines may be rugged, the strength and majesty of the original are well preserved, and apart altogether from its historic associations, is fitted in a high degree to stir the heart and minister to the faith and the courage of the believer.

> A SAFE stronghold our God is still,
>   A trusty shield and weapon;
> By His right arm He surely will
> Free from all ills that happen.
>   For still our ancient foe
>   Doth seek to work us woe:
>   Strong mail of craft and power
>   He weareth in this hour;
>   On earth is not his fellow.

ᴴ Cut on Luther's grave stone.

Stood we alone in our own might,
Our striving would be losing ;
For us the one true Man doth fight,
The Man of God's own choosing.
Who is this chosen One ?
'Tis Jesus Christ, the Son,
The Lord of hosts, 'tis He
Who wins the victory
In every field of battle.

And were the world with devils filled,
And watching to devour us,
Our souls to fear we need not yield,
They cannot overpower us ;
Their dreaded Prince no more
Can harm us as of yore ;
His rage we can endure ;
For lo ! his doom is sure,
A word shall overthrow him.

Still must they leave God's word its might,
For which no thanks they merit ;
Still is He with us in the fight,
With His good gifts and Spirit.
Even should they, in the strife,
Take kindred, goods, and life,
We freely let them go,
They profit not the foe ;
With us remains the kingdom.

A RX Deus est firmissima,
Præsidiumque verum ;
Per omnia pericula,
Per omnes vices rerum,
Nam inimicus stet,
Maligna agitat,
Vi et astutiâ

Armis invidiâ,
(Non similis,) utetur.

Si nobis fideamus nos,
Sit hostis triumphator ;
Sed fecit hos tutissimos,
Quibus est Salvator.
    Quis sit? inquirisne?
    Jesus, certissime,
    Sabaoth Dominus,
    Deus ipsissimus,
In pugnis semper victor.

Sit mundus plenus dæmonum,
Hiantium nos vorare ;
Non timeamus impetum,
Vult Deus nos servare ;
    Heus ! tenebrarum dux.
    Maligne, furens, trux !
    Ludibrium tu sis,
    Damnatus, debilis,
Te fugat parvum dictum.

Salvator regnat ubique,
Pro nobis et debellat,
Dat Is opes libere,
Et inimicos pellit.
    Perimant omnia
    Bona terrestria ;
    Perimant corpora,
    Stant tamen optima ;
In secula seculorum.   S. T. RAND, D.D.

As to the genesis we must look to the life of the author, especially the Diet of Worms, for it was then (1521), as is generally believed, it was composed. He was born at Eisleben, Thuringia, Nov. 10, 1483 ; and "born again" about twenty years after, when a flash of lightning killed a young companion

by his side, and when he resolved to enter a monastery and take
the cowl and the vows of a monk.   This, he thought, was the
first sure and certain step toward the higher life of the soul.
He was admitted to the monastery of Erfurth in 1505, a
monastery of the Augustinian order; and there he soon discovered that though a man may flee from the world he cannot
flee from himself—from his sins and the retribution that cleaves
to them.   He had been deeply impressed by the sudden death
of his friend in the thunder-storm referred to, and had taken
some steps in the divine life, but he had not entered into liberty.
We still find him dimly groping his way after the light, spending much time over an old Latin Bible, and humbly, thankfully
receiving instruction from Staupitz, the Vicar-General of the
establishment—a man who had passed through a similar experience to himself and had made his way to the light within
the walls of the monastery.   But Luther was far from being
happy.   His heart condemned him, for, do what he might in
the way of penance and duty; it still pointed, even on his best
day's performances, to a long arrearage of duty at night.   Very
great were the penances he imposed on himself, severe the
austerities that he practised with the view of satisfying his
conscience and securing that blessed peace for which he longed
and longed more than they that seek for hid treasures; but
in vain.   He was miserable.   His strong iron frame gave way;
his falcon eyes sank deeper in his forehead and the once round
and rosy youth looked like a spectre as he walked up and down
the corridors.   Still he prosecuted his studies with amazing
industry and attained to such mastery and familiarity in dealing with the Scriptures that everyone that heard him, even at
an early stage, was impressed.   Then his prosperity was equal
to his industry.   In two years from the time he entered the
monastery he was ordained to the priesthood, and in the year
after he was raised to the professoriate in the new university of
Wittenburg (1508).   He was made a D.D. of Erfurth in 1512

and in April, 1516, was made vicar of his monastic order, in which capacity he visited extensively the various cloisters of the province of Saxony, to which he belonged.

It was in 1510, when he visited Rome, the occasion on which that great spiritual change took place, which was followed with such mighty results to the world. It was then, and not till then, that he was enabled to shake off the *incubus* that was crushing his spirit and darkening to his view all the promises of the Gospel. Doing penance on the stairs of Pilate—creeping up and down like other pilgrims, he presented a sad spectacle; but suddenly there flashed into his soul a passage which he must have often met before—*the just shall live by faith.* Then it is not by laborious acts of penance? So Luther reasoned, and the result of his reasoning was liberty—even the glorious liberty of the children of God. He rose from his knees strong in God and in the power of his might, like a giant refreshed with new wine. He went to Rome as a mediæval ecclesiastic, full of admiration and reverence for his Church, but he returned disgusted with its abominations, with what he had seen with his own eyes and heard with his own ears in that city of churches and priests and friars and nuns and ecclesiastics of many names. Still, at this stage, he had no idea of raising his voice against the Church. His idea was simply reformation, and to this he bent all the tremendous energy of his nature. He would now in his lectures and sermons make it clear as day that the facts of man's spiritual experience were of more value than their expression in stereotyped church forms—the church forms that were prescribed—the only forms she would recognize.

His first encounter (1517) was with Tetzel on the subject of Indulgences—that is the liberty, on the authority of the Church, for a given price, to take a plunge into sin! A few days after the encounter he posted up on the church door of

Wittenburg ninety-five theses against the sale of such indulgences. This was a blow that struck right home, and so
the Reformation began. The Pope in his wrath (Leo X.) issued
a bull upholding the indulgences, and placing Luther under the
ban (boycot), declaring him a heretic. How did Luther treat
the Pope's bull? Cringe, fall down upon his knees and sue for
mercy? No! but in effect hurled the bull back in his face.
Nay, more than that. He had a fire kindled at the eastern
gate of the city (Wittenburg) and at the head of a procession
of professors and hundreds of students of the university of
the city, walked forth with the offensive bull in his hands till
they reached the gate, whereupon Luther flung the sacred
missive into the flames, and another professor did the same with
a copy of the Canon Law of the Church of Rome, saying:
"Because thou, O godless book, hast long afflicted the saints,
be thou also afflicted and consumed in everlasting fire!"

The result of all this was the Diet of Worms (1521) to
which Luther was summoned to meet the Papal Nuncio, Cajetan
by name, to answer for his sins before the princes and high
estates of Germany. The Nuncio contended that Luther should
not be heard on the ground that he by the bull of the Pope
had already been condemned, but the Emperor Charles V., who
presided on the occasion, thought that he should be allowed a
hearing, and he was heard accordingly. The legate loses his
temper. He will "not dispute any longer with such a beast,
he has such wicked eyes in his face and such horrid thoughts
in his head," and so the meeting was broken off, but great was
the sensation and tremendous the enthusiasm with which the
doctrines of the Reformation were received. But the meeting—
this historical occasion was one to which the Reformer looked
forward to with much anxiety. He spent the preceding night
in prayer, and many of his supplications that night consisted of
two words, "More light! More light!" It was in view of

this meeting, this Diet of Worms, that Luther wrote his translation of the hymn under consideration.

A sure stronghold our God is still, etc.

And here many illustrations might be given of the power of this regal hymn—power to cheer, comfort, to inspire with manly courage. In this respect this hymn has had a wonderful history. Luther himself was accustomed to sing it in times of despondency or in seasons of danger when the sky was dark, and a storm from enemies was impending. "Come Phillip, he would say to Melancthon, "let us sing the forty-sixth Psalm," and then would raise his splendid tenor voice on *Ein feste burg*, "A sure stronghold," etc. "Sing on my little maid, you don't know what famous people you comfort." That was what Melancthon himself said on one sad occasion on hearing a little girl singing this same hymn on the streets of Weimar. And so he might speak thus for many a desponding spirit has gathered a strange strength from its inspiration, and among these, it is said, Queen Elizabeth on one sad occasion. But the most interesting case that has come under public notice, probably, is that of Gustavus Adolphus, King of Sweden, the great christian hero that came to the rescue of the German Protestants 24th June, 1630, one hundred years after the famous protest was entered at the Diet of Spires by Martin Luther and his friends—the occasion from which the term Protestant took its rise. He landed on the coast of Pomerania with 30,000 troops, all in sympathy with their leader and the brave Germans that had been scattered and peeled by many years of harassing warfare. They united into a strong phalanx and marched together to successive victories, and ultimately in the case of the chivalric Gustavus Adolphus to death. Here is what Duffield says of him: At the battle of Leipzig the king bade his army sing Luther's hymn, *Ein feste burg*, "A sure stronghold our God is still." So he did again in his last struggle at Lutzen with Wallenstein, on that occasion with the accompaniment of the drums and trumpets of the army. Then he knelt beside his horse and offered this prayer, "Oh, Lord Jesus Christ, bless our arms and this day's battle for the glory of Thy holy name." Then he arose and went along the lines encouraging his troops, and gave the men their old slogan, "*Got mit uns*—God with us," as their battle cry. "Now let us begin!" The fog which had hung over the plain was thinning away, and the king had only a buff coat on. "God is my armour," he said to his servant who wanted him to put on his coat-of-mail. Later on he exclaimed, "Jesu, Jesu! help us to fight this day for the honour of Thy name." About eleven o'clock the fatal bullet struck him from his horse, but by this time he had won the battle. As he fell he cried out, "I seal with my blood the liberty and religion of the German nation." Then he said, "My God, my God!" and finally, "Alas! my poor Queen!" It is not strange that the name of Gustavus Adolphus should be dear to Protestant Germany, and that an association bearing his name should seek to perpetuate the principles for which he lived and died, and that ever as the association meet from time to time, they should sing, "A sure stronghold our God is still."

Luther wrote only about seventeen hymns altogether, and probably translated from the Fathers about as many more, but each and all were a power in the land. One great purpose which they served was the spread of the truth. They flew, we are told, as if on the wings of the wind from one end of Germany to another. Sometimes one song would win a whole town as by one blow. A poor weaver walks through the streets of Madgeburg, singing one of the hymns of Luther, and makes a sensation. The mayor lays hold of him and throws him into prison; but the hymn has done its work and two hundred sturdy citizens march up to the mayor and demand his release, and he is released accordingly.

To mention one case more. Luther hearing a poor lad from Prussia singing one of his hymns before his door—a lad that knew nothing about the authorship—took him in and asked him where he had learned it; and finding that he had learned it in Prussia, that his hymns were being sung in the churches in that land, that the truth had already spread so far, his eyes filled with tears of holy joy. And what shall we say of such hymnists as Decius, the monk so long bound in affliction and iron, that heard the sound of the Reformation in his cell and entered into liberty—the minstrel whose one song, "Glory in excelsis," was so greatly blessed? And Schneesing, whose joyful pæans celebrate the day of illumination when the darkness rolls away from the weary spirit of the penitent, and the Sun of Righteousness arises with healing on his wings? In person he was weak and withered, but his soul strong in God and in the power of his might was living in the light of God and daily drinking of the wine which he had mingled. And what shall we say of Neumark whose song of comfort and trust in Providence, "Leave God to order all thy ways," has been such a blessing to the Church and met with such a welcome in his day that when the people of New Brandenburg heard a baker's boy sing it in the streets, it was at once caught up by them and carried from town to town till it became a household word throughout the land! And Gerhardt whose contribution to the hymnology of the German Church, is in some respects the richest and best of all, whose one hundred and twenty hymns are still in great favour, and for the most part, are likely to be for generations to come? They may not have the strength and majesty of some of those of the great Reformer but in literary finish, in sweetness and poetic grace, they excel his, and they are no less fragrant with the one grand Name and the promises, which are great and precious to those that believe.

Time would fail us even to enumerate the great masters of sacred song in this favoured land. Germany is pre-eminently the land of hymns. No country has been more blessed in this respect. What a power they have exercised! They have been the means of quickening, illuminating and comforting the hearts of the people for ten generations. Our covenanting forefathers had no such advantage—no such spiritual songs to cheer them in their long and arduous struggles—no Luther to sing to their children as he sang to his little Hans "concerning the Child Jesus," the song that is now the chief Christmas song in Germany. They had to content themselves with the Psalms of David and celebrate the praises of Christ and redemption in verse, in which His name often does not appear! How the Germans would have acted in such circumstances it is not for us to say; but one thing is clear that God did a great thing for them when He raised up such minstrels as we have named—men whose hearts were open to the sweet loving light of heaven, and whose lips had been touched with a live coal from the altar. False teachers have again and again arisen to teach another Gospel and bring them into bondage; broad school men like Strauss have sneered at the evangel of Luther and sought to eliminate the miraculous and the spiritual from the sacred page; infidels, sitting in the seat of learning, where the best youth of the country were to be taught, have done their work; but so long as these songs of Zion are in favour with the people the great Reformation truths are safe, and they will still continue to be safe and to warm the hearts of the people and help to bind them as with a golden chain to the throne of the Eternal.

HYMN VII.

JERUSALEM, MY HAPPY HOME.

Tune.—*Southwell.* Admirably adapted to the words.

JERUSALEM, my happy home,
 Name ever dear to me ;
When shall my labours have an end
 In joy, and peace, and Thee ?

When shall these eyes Thy heaven-built walls
 And pearly gates behold ?
Thy bulwarks with salvation strong,
 And streets of shining gold ?

Oh when, thou city of my God,
 Shall I thy courts ascend,
Where congregations ne'er break up,
 And Sabbaths have no end ?

There happier bowers than Eden's bloom,
 Nor sin nor sorrow know ;
Blest seats ! through rude and stormy scenes
 I onward press to you.

Why should I shrink from pain and woe,
 Or feel at death dismay ?
I've Canaan's goodly land in view,
 And realms of endless day.

Apostles, martyrs, prophets, there
 Around my Saviour stand ;

And soon my friends in Christ below
  Will join the glorious band.

Jerusalem, my happy home !
  My soul still pants for thee ;
Then shall my labours have an end,
  When I thy joys shall see.

JERUSALEM, urbs aurea
  Urbs cara semper mi
O quando acta opera,
Pleroma gaudii ?

Quandoque cernam mænia,
Et portas gemmeas,
Et aureas vias cæli,
Quas, Deus, teneas ?

Cœlestum formas lucidas,
Vitreum juxta fretum,
Eternum quoque Sabbatum,
Et sepiternum cœtum ?

O otium Eden suavius—
Quô neque sons nec mæror !
O sedes vos faustissimæ
Protendo vobis fruar !

Cur mala illa formidem
Se mortem etiam ?
Amœna ultra Jordanis
Nam modo videam.

Apostoli, vates, martyres
Stant circum thronum Diē ;

Et cito sim fidelibus,
Collatus quoque ibi.

Syon ! mi domus aurea
Te specto propius ;
Sed quum est pura anima
Te fruar amplius.

THE original of this very popular hymn is obscure. It appears that one signing himself " F. B. P."—*alias* Francis Baker, priest, had for some offence been imprisoned in the Tower nearly three hundred years ago, and that he, whiling away the weary hours in his cell, prepared a MS. containing twenty-six verses—one hundred and four lines —beginning thus :

Hierusalem, my happy home !
   When shall I come to thee ?
When shall my sorrowes have an end,
   Thy joyes when shall I see ?

O happie harbour of the saints !
   O sweete and pleasant soyle,
In thee noe sorrows may be found,
   Noe griefs, noe care, noe toyle.

It is prefaced in these terms : A song by "F. B. P." to the tune of Diana. This MS. some years ago found its way to the British Museum, and Dr. Horatius Bonar, finding it there, and attracted by the splendour of its imagery and real excellence, copied it *verbatim et literatim*, and published it in 1852. In a monogram on the hymn he states that he found it in a MS. volume of religious songs without date, but apparently written in the early part of the seventeenth century, and that in this MS. volume of religious songs he found this, which is now

F

known to be a copy of a portion of a longer hymn on the same subject by another hand.

Dr. Hatfield has shown on very fair grounds that this paper signed " F. B. P." is not an original—that the original is a long hymn of thirty-one double stanzas, consisting of two hundred and forty-eight lines; whereas that of "F. B. P." contains only twenty-six verses, consisting of one hundred and four lines,—that there are many variations and transpositions,— that upon the whole there is reason to believe that "F. B. P." simply reproduced from memory such portions of the original as had cleaved to it, and had committed them to writing, and that this writing ultimately found its way to the MS. department of the British Museum, whence after the lapse of a couple of centuries, Dr Horatius Bonar excavated it and published it just as he had found it with the monogram referred to in 1851.

How, then, about the original? Who was the author? Can any satisfactory account be given of him and his claims? The answer is that Wodrow, the distinguished historian of the Church of Scotland, makes the author to be the Rev. David Dickson, D.D.,—a divine that filled a large space in the public eye from 1583—1662. He was the only child of John Dickson, a pious and wealthy merchant of Glasgow. He received a thorough education in the university of his native city, and soon rose to distinction. At the early age of twenty-seven he was appointed Regent or Professor of Philosophy in the same university, devoting himself, with his associates, Boyd and Blair, to the revival of godliness among the undergraduates. After some years we find him occupying the still higher office of Professor of Divinity in the same university, and in 1638 he was chosen to fill the highest seat in the gift of the Church— that of Moderator of the General Assembly. He took an active part in public affairs during the Commonwealth, and at the Restoration lost his professorship by refusing to take the oath of supremacy. It appears from Wodrow, the historian, that he ranked very high—ranked, indeed, among the ablest and most influential ministers of his day, and yet so modest that he never made use of his title D.D. He was, moreover, very conscientious, so much so that he suffered himself to be deposed from the ministry—parish of Irvine—the birthplace of James Montgomery, one hundred and fifty years afterwards—rather than comply with the obnoxious "Articles of Perth." He was, however, soon restored to his parish, where he laboured with great success till 1641, when he was appointed Professor of Divinity in the University of Glasgow.

But may not this Rev. David Dickson, Professor of Divinity in the University of Glasgow, be the copyist and plagiarist? "F. B. P." and he were evidently cotemporaries. "F. B. P." was a prisoner in the Tower, probably died in the Tower, and what more easy than to perpetrate the literary theft? Is it not possible that he took this MS., which found its way into the British Museum and is still lying in the British Museum, and made use of it, extending and amplifying the one hundred and four lines into two hundred and forty-eight? Who was there to stand up in defence of the obscure—the unknown "F.B.P.," lying in prison or in his grave? That is the position which Dr. J. M. Neale and others have taken, but it is not a position which is at all tenable. The MS. which "F. B. P." left behind him shows, from internal evidence, that it was written about 1616 or 1617, and it is clear from Wodrow, the historian of the Church of Scotland, whose accuracy in matters of detail has never been questioned, that David Dickson by this time had risen to great eminence as a scholar, as a Christian labouring for the conversion of souls, and as an author both in poetry and prose. He was then,—the date or supposed date of the MS., 1617 (according to King, "Anglican Hymns"),—about thirty-four years of age, and had been for seven years Professor of Philosophy in the University of Glasgow, winning for himself the fairest name. And if he was guilty of this literary

theft, "impudently appropriating to himself what belonged to
another," he must have done it after this time—after the MS.
of "F. B. P." made its way to the British Museum, or at least
after "F.B.P." had any power over it, *i.e.*, that David Dickson,
so modest as to refuse to use his title of D.D.—so conscientious
that he suffered himself to be deposed from the ministry rather
than act contrary to his convictions, was guilty of doing the
meanest and dirtiest deed of his time. Is such a supposition
possible? Does it consist with the dignity, the conscientiousness,
the high character of one of the best men of his day? The
testimony of Wodrow is this (having enumerated some of
Dickson's works): "Besides these he wrote . . . some
short poems on pious and serious subjects which, I am told,
have been very useful when printed and spread among country
people and servants, such as, 'O Mother, Dear Jerusalem!' and
one somewhat larger, 8vo., 1649, entitled 'Christian Love,' to
be sung with the common tune of the Psalms." "F.B.P.'s"
performance was plainly a reproduction from memory of such
verses or lines of the original as he could think of.

Still there is considerable obscurity about the authorship of
this poem of thirty-one double stanzas consisting of two hundred
and forty-eight lines. Dickson, if he did write it, did not put
his name to it, but this is not unlike the man. One thing is
clear, the poem belongs to his day and it would appear, took
kindly to the version of "F. B. P." when it was published, all
the more probably, from the fact that the original was too
long—that a shorter hymn presenting the same truths was
better adapted to the purpose he had in view. The latest information, Duffield tells us, on the subject comes from the Rev.
James King's "Anglican Hymnology." He makes out that
Dickson expurgated this hymn of "F. B. P." and offered his
own in "O mother, dear Jerusalem." Thirty years later the
Rev. William Burkitt, vicar of Dedham, reprinted "F.B.P.'s"

pieces with changes of his own; and finally it has come down to us in the form here presented.

Still, though the present form of the hymn may be the more acceptable, it was under the old form, "O mother, dear Jerusalem!" that it made its way to the popular heart and became such a favourite with both young and old. Many a lonely cell, many a dark home, many a pale face has been lighted up by its revelations. Snatches of it used to be heard among the hills and glens of Scotland—in the fishing boats along the coast—among the harvesters in the barn after the labours of the day—from the children on the Sabbath evenings after their questionings were over, for with the children this hymn has always been a favourite, and in many a child's heart the hymn lived long after he had left the parental roof and blossomed in other scenes and in other circumstances, where it might be thought everything was given to salt—given up to the curse of perpetual barrenness. A young Scotch lad who was on his deathbed at New Orleans, says Dr. Belcher, was visited by a Presbyterian minster, but the dying man wanted no minister to speak to him. He shut himself up against all the efforts of the good man to reach his heart. Somewhat discouraged the minister turned away, and scarcely knowing why,—without anything like design or aim, but guided by that good Spirit that leads into all truth,—he began to sing:

> Jerusalem, my happy home,
> Name ever dear to me.

That was enough! a tender chord had been touched—a flood of early recollections burst in upon the soul of this youth—days of innocency when he, a free and happy child, went out and in, with no stain upon his name and no cloud upon his heart. With bursting tears he said to the minister: "My dear mother used to sing to me that hymn." He was now open to the truth, open to the consolation of the Gospel. God gave the penitent peace, the blessed peace that passeth all understanding, and now both mother and son are rejoicing in the eternal light, delighting themselves in the glories of the New Jerusalem concerning which we read : " And I John saw the holy city, New Jerusalem, coming down from God out of heaven, prepared as a bride adorned for her husband," etc.

We must not close our comments on this hymn without noting some features of its great excellence i.e., its Scriptural character, its simplicity and freshness, its easy graceful rhythm. The fact that it and its predecessors have for over two hundred years stood the test of every form of criticism and held their high place in spite of their quaintness and great length and almost juvenile simplicity, together with the fact that so many gifted pens have been employed in condensing, changing, and embellishing the original thirty-one double stanzas, until the two hundred and forty-eight lines have been reduced to twenty-eight—is an evidence of essential nobility and a promise that it will continue to hold its present high place in the hymnals of the Church for generations to come. Yet, it is to be borne in mind that a hymn is, or should be, direct praise to God— "praise in a song." This was Augustine's definition of a hymn fifteen hundred years ago, and there are few that will dispute that definition—provided always that hymns of an experimental (subjective) character, as well as those that are the burden of a prayer, like " O for a Closer Walk with God," are included in the definition. But it is strange how many that may be called good hymns offend in this respect. The one under consideration does ! It is rather a poem than a hymn. It is not directly praise to God. It is a eulogy of the material glories of heaven rather than an expression of gratitude to God for such a home. Much the same may be said of such hymns as : " The sands of time are sinking," "The glory that excelleth," "The spacious Firmament on high," etc., etc. Such hymns or poems please ;

they touch the imagination; they live in the memory and
minister to a sort of sentimental piety which is not altogether
a stranger to a heart still bent upon its sins, unblessed, un-
changed and unforgiven.   Did not Irish Moore write, yes—even
write very pretty poems about heaven, how that there was
nothing true but heaven, when he was yet a stranger to God,
and that holiness, without which no man shall see the Lord !
Such hymns are not *red* enough to disturb the carnal mind, or
if disturbed to meet its great wants, its sense of justice, its
longings for light, its feelings of gratitude when light and life
are vouchsafed.   Hence such hymns as that under consideration
must always occupy a secondary place in the service of the
Church.   They serve an end in its ministration, but not the
highest end.   They have little or no power over the unrenewed
heart; but when the heart *is* renewed, when the fountains of
the great deep *are* broken up, they minister to its faith, they
touch its hidden springs and brighten its ethereal eye, especially
in the hour of sorrow when the glory of the world fades upon
the view and lover and friend are removed into darkness.   It
was in such an hour that Watts wrote " There is a land of pure
delight," and it was in such an hour that the beloved disciple
who was banished to the Isle of Patmos for the Word of God
and the testimony of Jesus, was uplifted by such contemplations,
" I, John, heard a great voice out of heaven, saying ' Behold
the tabernacle of God is with men and He will dwell with them
and they shall be his people, and God Himself shall be with
them   .   .   .   and wipe away all tears from their eyes; and
there shall be no more death, neither sorrow nor crying ; neither
shall there be any more pain for the former things are passed
away.' "

HYMN VIII.

THE GREAT EVENING HYMN.

BY BISHOP KEN.

TUNE—*Canon.* BY THOMAS TALLIS.

ALL praise to Thee, my God, this night,
For all the blessings of the light;
Keep me, O keep me, King of kings,
Beneath Thine own almighty wings!

Forgive me, Lord, for thy dear Son,
The ill that I this day have done;
That, with the world, myself and Thee,
I, ere I sleep, at peace may be.

Teach me to live, that I may dread
The grave as little as my bed;
To die, that this vile body may
Rise glorious at the awful day.

O may my soul on Thee repose,
And may sweet sleep mine eyelids close!
Sleep that may me more vigorous make,
To serve my God when I awake.

When in the night I sleepless lie,
My soul with heavenly thoughts supply;
Let no ill dreams disturb my rest,
No powers of darkness me molest.

Praise God, from whom all blessings flow ;
Praise Him, all creatures here below ;
Praise Him above, ye heavenly host ;
Praise Father, Son, and Holy Ghost.

LIFE so beautiful as that of Dr. Ken could not but be followed with a peaceful death. The great doctrine of the cross was dear to him and that section of the English Church which gave it prominence. "I die," he said, "in the communion of the Church of England as it stands distinguished from all Papal and Puritan innovations, and as it adheres to the doctrine of the Cross." At his desire he was buried at Frome, under the east window of the chancel in the early morn, just at sun rising. There, in the midst of that solemn scene and as the daylight was breaking, his own anthem of praise was sung, "Awake my soul and with the sun, etc."

Latin Translation of The Evening Hymn.

LAUS nocte tibi, mi Deus,
   Ob dona tua in dies ;
Custodias me, Rex regum,
Sub alis tuis securum.
Ignoscas mala quæ feci
Ob Christum Filium tui,
Ut ante palpebræ clausæ
Sim pace, secum, mundo, Te !

Doceto agere vitam,
Ut non sepulcrum metuam ;
Vel mori ; ita oriens
Permagno die sim lucens.
Quiescat Te mi anima !
Et somnus cludat lumina,
Refectus ita serviam
Te melius, quum revigilam !

Et si insomnis, ministres
De Se suaves memorias ;
Et mala somnia absint,
Quietum meum non turbent,
Laudate Deum quo dotes ;
Laudate Eum humiles ;
Laudate Eum seraphim ;
Tres, Patrem, Natum, Spiritum.

If I were asked to name the hymn that probably has been most frequently sung during these last two hundred years, it would be the one under consideration. Is there any verse in Scripture so often repeated as the doxology which closes this hymn, " *Praise God from whom, etc ?* "

The mention of a midnight hymn may sound strange in modern ears, but Ken's model was Latin and not English ; for as yet English hymnody was scarcely born. His ideal was not gathered from Spencer or Addison, or Watts, or John Milton. True, they had commenced to write in Ken's day (1637—1711) but as yet had awakened no very favorable response on the part of the people. His ideal was found in the hymns of the early christians who had hymns for all seasons, morning, noon, evening, midnight, and early cock-crowing. Those hymns were simple, but popular. The fisherman in his boat used them, the vine dressers on the hill, the soldier in his rounds, the shepherd on the plain, and the mother in her household duties, all delighted in them and gathered instruction from them. But the Church was slow to receive them, even the best, into her services ; but events at length occurred which led the Church to give them welcome. During the militant period of the Milan Church, when Arianism united with Imperial patronage, threatened to lay waste this famous See and silence its faithful ministers—when St. Ambrose saw his magnificent cathedral invested with troops ; those hymns so rich in thought, so fragrant with the name of Jesus, were transferred from field and forest to the Basilica, and did much to sustain the enthusiasm of the people during their defence, and the weary days and nights appointed to them. Little wonder that the soldiers of Justina, the Queen mother, an Arian, failed to produce anything like an apostacy from the faith, when in Europe's grandest cathedral were heard sounding forth such hymns as: *Christe qui es et Deus!* Among the hymns transferred from the house to the church at this time—fourth century—was St. Hilary's morning hymn, *lucis largitor*; St. Ambrose's hymn for cock-crowing, associated with the repentance of Peter,—*Eterne rerum conditor;* the midnight hymn, containing allusions to the slaying of the firstborn and the sudden coming of the bridegroom, of which we must give one verse in English in the way of a specimen :

> It is the midnight hour ;
> Prophetic voices warn ;
> To Father and to Son once more
> Now be our praise upborne ;
> And to the Paraclete,
> The perfect Trinity.
> God in one substance Infinite,
> Let there be ceaseless praise !

Ken had his eye on those old Latin hymns, for his biographer tells us that at that famous school to which he was sent—Wykeman's near Winchester,—the pupils were accustomed to sing as a morning hymn : *Jam lucis orto sidere.* Should we ever have had his own grand morning hymns but for that early Winchester exercise? The probability is that in after life when he used to chant his hymns to the melody of the lute, he only gave forth the echoes of that noble old hymn that had touched his heart while yet in his teens.

What was the genesis of this hymn? The answer is : Bishop Ken, deprived of his See for conscience sake, had (1703) gone on a visit to his nephew, Rev. J. Walton, then

Prebendary of Salisbury. During his sojourn there, a great storm arose one evening and swept over the entire island. It blew down a stack of chimneys, which falling, cut through the bedroom in which Ken was lodged without injuring a hair of his head; but the same storm, rushing upon Wells, the seat of the cathedral he had filled so worthily, hurled down another stack through the chamber of another bishop, not sparing *him*, but killing him on the spot, and *that* the bishop that had supplanted Ken! When we think of the strange discrimination of the storm, one bishop taken and another left—Ken's great piety, his poetic nature, we can easily understand that he would be greatly moved at what had taken place. We require to know these things before we can enter into the spirit of such lines as :—

> Teach me to live that I my dread
> The grave as little as my bed.
> Teach me to die that so I may
> Rise glorious at the judgment day.

Ken, no doubt, had a desire to do for the youth of Winchester in English what the old masters had done for them in Latin. But the immediate circumstances which gave rise to the evening and the midnight hymns, were, it would seem to us, the great storm referred to, that burst over the island in 1703.

Dr. Ken was the son of a barber-surgeon, born at Little Birmingham, Hertfordshire, England, July, 1637. At the age of thirteen he was sent to the famous school at Winchester, for which in later years he prepared his manual of prayers, and to which he added his three famous hymns. His were troublesome times. In the year in which he was born, Charles I. was forcing Episcopacy upon Scotland—an act which drove the nation into rebellion and led the people to band themselves into a solemn league and covenant to maintain their beloved Presbyterianism—some of them adding to their signatures "till death," and others it is said, opening a vein that they might write their names in blood. In the year that Oliver Cromwell assumed the reins of government, (1650) young Ken entered this famous school, then under the management of Rev. John Harris, D.D., a Presbyterian, a covenanter, and a member of the Westminster Assembly of Divines, that had just closed its sittings. Here he rapidly grew in favor with God and man. From this he passed with ease and honor into Hart Hall, Oxford, gaining a fellowship and taking his M.A. Degree in 1664. He was ordained shortly afterwards and successively held the positions of tutor in Oxford, chaplain to the Princess Mary,—daughter of James I. and wife of William Prince of Orange,—chaplain to the fleet under Lord Dartmouth at Tangier, chaplain to Charles II. His chaplaincy to the Princess Mary involved his removal to the Hague, the city in Holland where the king of that country then resided. One incident occurred during his sojourn here which should not be withheld because of its bearing on the life of the poet. Charles II., his patron and his prince, made a visit to the Hague to his neice, the Princess Mary. He came in great state with a courtly retinue; but there was one member of that court against whom Ken had special objections, and yet for this member he was desired to provide apartments under his roof. Ken refused and expected a storm. Still the king showed no resentment, suffered no word of censure to fall from his lips. Not only so, but shortly after this when he wanted a chaplain for himself, Ken was the man that was chosen. When the lords of the household and the dignitaries of the church were arguing, one for this and another for that favourite, the king said: "Where is that good little man that refused lodgings to poor Nell at the Hague?" The end of the controversy was that Ken was appointed Royal Chaplain to Charles II. The office, however, was one of short duration, for not long after this the king died, and one of Ken's duties was to attend the death-bed of his sovereign. It must have

been a grief to him to give place at last to a Roman Catholic
priest who administered to Charles the "sacraments" of that
church, of which he was secretly a member; and it must have
been a still greater grief to see fluttering around his master in
his last hours, courtiers and courtesans that had lived on his
bounty, and to hear that almost his last words in this world
were addressed to his brother James in behalf of the Duchess
of Portsmouth, adding, "And don't let poor Nellie starve."—
(Eleanor Gwinn.)

Shortly after this, Thomas Ken was raised to the See of Bath
and Wells, but in 1688, when James II., at heart a Roman
Catholic, reissued his Declaration of Indulgence, ostensibly
granting liberty of conscience to all in matters of worship, but
in reality taking Romanism under his wing, and requiring all
bishops to see that the same was published in all their churches
on the two Sabbaths, 20th and 27th May, 1688, Ken with six
other bishops refused, not that he was intolerant or in any way
sympathized in the efforts that had been put forth to produce
uniformity; but in reading the document he felt that he would
be compromising the liberty of the church and recognizing the
right of the sovereign to interfere in matters that lay beyond
his sphere.   He felt also that such an action would prove fatal
to the Protestantism of England,   He refused, and amid the
ten thousand parishes in the country, not one hundred complied.

The seven recusant bishops of whom Ken was one, prepared
a humble petition to his majesty James II., praying to be released from the obligation of causing the Declaration in question
to be read in their respective Sees—a petition that his majesty
was pleased to pronounce treasonable !   The bishops were thrown
into the Tower to await their trial, not because they had refused
to read the Declaration, but because they had presented a
petition praying to be released from that duty.   But the trial
became a triumph in behalf of liberty of conscience—one of
the grandest known in the history of England.

On the accession of William and Mary (7th Feb. 1689) Ken refused to take the oath of allegiance, because of his dislike of the type of Presbyterianism presented by them; and so with certain others was deprived of his bishopric as a nonjuror. But on the death of his successor, Dr. R. Kidder, Queen Anne offered to restore it to him, and on his declining gave him a pension of £200 a year. Beneath the roof of his devoted friend, Lord Weymouth, Wiltshire, he spent his remaining days, for he never married. For nearly twenty years his pen was busy making large contributions to theology both in prose and poetry; but his fame rests chiefly on his three great hymns, and, as Montgomery says, had he endowed three hospitals he could not have done more for humanity. We cannot dispose of this hymn without noting its great power in the church still, and this is true of his other two hymns as well. They have lost nothing of their quickening and refreshing powers during the centuries that have passed since they first saw the light. It is only the other day that a scene took place in a railroad car which furnishes an illustration of this. At a city station a gang of hilarious revellers entered the car,—the hour a little after midnight. Many of the travellers were half asleep; others were settling themselves comfortably in their wraps and rugs, preparing for their long night journey. Suddenly one of the gang began to roar out a profane song. The passengers were shocked. They would gladly have silenced the vile singer, but how was it to be done? Strangely enough another voice, sweet, clear, childlike,—the voice of a little girl, waked up from sleep is heard singing:

> Glory to thee my God, this night,
> For all the blessings of the light;
> Keep me, O keep me, King of kings,
> Beneath thine own Almighty wings.

Only a few notes were sung when the hint was taken, and

another voice joined, and another and another. Manly basses
and tenors threw in their deep tones with all their strength,
and soon a full and powerful volume of song to the glory of
God poured forth, and the voice of the profane singer was heard
no more. What a blessing this and those other two hymns of
Ken have been during these 200 years! Think of the homes
they have blessed—the weary spirits tossed on sleepless beds
they have comforted! From childhood's lips, from the faltering
accents of old age, how often have those beautiful lines fallen!
In the home of the peer as well as the peasant they have held
a place, second in rank only to the sacred Scriptures, and it
may almost be said of them,—there is no speech nor language
where their voice is not heard. Their line is gone out throughout
all the earth and their words to the world's end. Ken was the
first that struck out an English hymn that met with universal
favor as a hymn for devotional purposes, whether public or
private. Great has been the favor with which his three hymns
have been received—popular as ever at this distant day—due
very much to their strong simplicity, their warm but not overstrained devotion, and their delicious rhythm. These hymns
still hold their place in the front rank, and as long as pure
English, crystalline perspecuity, and unaffected fervor are
sought after, these three hymns of Bishop Ken will command
admiration.

HYMN IX.

ROCK OF AGES CLEFT FOR ME.

THE GREATEST HYMN IN THE LANGUAGE.

TUNE.—*Petra*, by Richard Redhead.

MORE than a hundred years have passed since a young lad in England, who belonged to a pious family, but was himself far from God, was to find God by strange means. Many a prayer his widowed mother had offered up in his behalf, and many a loving counsel she had spent on him in vain. To all entreaties whether on the part of his mother or others, he answered by inwardly resolving *not* to become a Christian.

In the providence of God, however, it happened that he and his mother had to visit some friends in Ireland, and that on a certain Sunday they went to a place, Dodyman, in a barn where a good man, though unlettered, was to preach. His text was, " But now in Christ Jesus, ye who sometimes were far off, are brought nigh by the blood of Christ," Eph. ii. 13. James Morris, though not very eloquent, was very earnest. He put the question to those unsaved, whether they would give themselves that day to Christ or remain rebels. Every time the preacher repeated the question, this young man said *No ;* and at the close of the sermon his heart was harder than ever. But when the sermon was finished, the minister gave out the hymn, beginning :—

> Come, ye sinners, poor and wretched,
> Weak and wounded, sick and sore, etc.

G

The congregation, stirred by the earnest address of the preacher, sang the hymn with their whole heart; and what the sermon could not do for the young man, the singing of the hymn did. The truth made its way into his soul and overcame all opposition. It was the voice of God, and the result was that his pride, his impenitence, everything that stood in the way, was removed. This was Augustus Toplady, son of Major Toplady of the British army, the author of the greatest hymn in the English language.

In reference to this remarkable incident he said in after years, — "Strange that I who had been so long under the means of grace in England, should be brought nigh to God in an obscure spot in Ireland, amidst a handful of people, met together in a barn, and under the ministry of one who could scarcely spell his own name! The excellency of the power must be of God." He assures us that this was the beginning of days with him—that this local preacher, James Morris, was a minister of God to his soul—that under the *afflatus* of the Divine Spirit he rose to a higher life, and that soon after he resolved to dedicate himself to the ministry. Follow that youth of sixteen summers a few years more, and you will find him taking honors in Trinity, Dublin; then taking orders in the Church of England, and by and bye (1762) settling down in the vicarage of Broad Hembury—a delicious retreat on the banks of the Otter, nestling amid the peaceful hills which are overlooked by the western slopes of the Black Down Range. Here, amid the humble lace-workers of the district, he labored for several years. Here, too, he wrote some of his soul-stirring hymns, and some of his controversial works on Calvinism *versus* Arminianism which, by the time he reached his death (1778) extended to six large volumes. He is described by a contemporary as a man of "ethereal" countenance and a light immortal form. His voice was music. His vivacity easily caught the listener's eye, and his looks and movements would have interpreted his language, even had there been no such solemnity in his tones . . . From easy explanations he advanced to rapid and conclusive argument, and warmed into importunate exhortations, till conscience began to burn and feelings to take fire from his own kindled spirit, while he and his hearers were together drowned into sympathetic tears."

His hymn, "Rock of Ages," is now pretty generally accorded the foremost place in our English hymnody. It stands *first* by a vote of the readers of "Sunday at Home," who were asked by the editor of that journal to send lists of what they considered the best hundred hymns in the language. The vote for this stood 3,215; the next highest was: "Abide with me," vote 3,204.

If we had room for giving illustrations of the power of this hymn—in quickening and refreshing weary souls that never felt any trouble about the metaphors employed in the first verse or raised any questions, as to their propriety—what a record we should have! Canon Baynes, in a lecture some years ago, said that Dr. Whewell on his death-bed, found his greatest comfort in this hymn; and who does not know that it was the favorite of Prince Albert who once sat so near the throne, and that more than once he called for it in his last days, and even in his dying hour? Roundell Palmer, the first authority on a matter of this kind, gives the highest place to the "Rock of Ages." The original hymn we copy from his book of praises, with the exception of the second line of the last verse :—

" That Rock was Christ."

ROCK of Ages, cleft for me,
    Let me hide myself in Thee ;
Let the water and the blood,
From Thy riven side which flowed,
Be of sin the double cure,
Cleanse me from its guilt and power,

Not the labours of my hands
Can fulfil Thy law's demands ;
Could my zeal no respite know,
Could my tears for ever flow,
All for sin could not atone ;
Thou must save, and Thou alone.

Nothing in my hand I bring ;
Simply to Thy cross I cling ;
Naked, come to Thee for dress ;
Helpless, look to Thee for grace ;
Foul, I to the fountain fly :
Wash me, Saviour, or I die.

While I draw this fleeting breath,
When my eyelids close in death,
When I soar through tracts unknown,
See Thee on Thy judgment-throne ;
Rock of Ages, cleft for me,
Let me hide myself in Thee.

Latin translation by the Right Hon. W. E. Gladstone.

JESUS pro me perforatus,
    Condar intra Tuum latus.
Tu per lympham profluentem,
Tu per sanguinem tepentem,
In peccata mi redunda,
Tolle culpam, sordes munda.

Coram Te, nec justus forem
Quamvis tota vi laborem,
Nec si fide nunquam cesso,
Fletu stillans indefesso ;
Tibi soli tantum munus ;
Serva me, Salvator, unus !

Nil in manu mecum fero,
Sed me versus crucem gero ;
Vestimenta nudus oro.
Opem debilis imploro ;
Fontem Christi quæro immundus,
Nisi laves, moribundus.

Dum hos artus vita regit ;
Quando nox sepulchro tegit ;
Mortuos quum stare jubes,
Sedens Judex inter nubes ;
Jesus pro me perforatus.
Condar intra Tuum latus.

Yet this hymn with all its popularity cannot be looked on
as a model in the matter of composition.   Keble whose hymns
are so finished—so remarkable in this respect, would never
have thrown such incongruous metaphors together as those
in the first verse.   The pierced side becomes the riven rock—
its cleft is the hiding place, and at the same time, a fountain
of cleansing; but in spite of the confusion of thought—the
incongruity of the conceptions, the great, warm beating heart
of humanity, catches the sense and even obtains a stronger
view of the great underlying truth of the atonement without
which no hymn can be great or long retain its place among our
"psalms and hymns and spiritual songs."

The genesis of this hymn is wonderful, shewing among other
things how feeble are the instruments that God sometimes uses
for the accomplishment of his ends.   Little knew the unlettered
man, James Morris, what he was doing that day in speaking
to the people in the barn from that glorious text, "But ye who
sometimes were far off," etc.   Little did he know that, amid
that handful of hearers that waited upon him, was a young
man, who, though struggling against the truth, was to be such a
minister of the truth, which, like lightning that leaps in the dark

clouds on Alpine heights, often makes its way into dark minds, and kindles a fire that will grow in brightness and beauty while ages roll on. And little did Catharine Bate, his godly mother, know what a great work she was doing for God in rearing that child—quietly bearing with him from day to day, giving him line upon line, here a little and there a little of the Word of God.

The genesis of this great hymn is indeed wonderful, but its history is still more wonderful. Think of the power that it has exercised on the Church! To give only one illustration we mention the case of a native of Madagascar who had come under its spell. In the jubilee year of our beloved Sovereign embassies from the chief courts of the world came to do her honour. Among these was an embassy from the monarch of Madagascar. One of those in the embassy was a Hova, a man of years, dark skinned and intelligent, and desiring for his people's sake to make a good impression, he, in offering his congratulations recalled many incidents of his long journey around the Cape in a sailing vessel; and when he had told all he could recollect, he asked if it would be agreeable that he should sing—that he had one song in his heart that had whiled away many a weary hour in his pilgrimage through life. The expectation was that the venerable Hova would sing something heathenish and national—something social or convivial—but to the astonishment of all, he began in a thin sweet tenor:

> Rock of Ages, cleft for me,
> Let me hide myself in Thee!

He sang it through all its stanzas, each verse growing more subdued and tender. At the close there was profound, awkward silence, which it was difficult to break, for some were affected to tears in seeing the coming back of seed sown on the waters in missionary faith and zeal,—all were taken by surprise, little expecting to hear from the lips of the Hova on this grand occasion the sweetest of the songs of Zion. His name, says the reporter of the day, was as startling in length as his performance was surprising :—Right Hon. Lord Rainiferongalarovo.

The quickening and refreshing power of this hymn is due, under God, to the fact that it appeals to the native sense of guilt in every heart; and not only guilt but guiltiness, that is, the disposition to repeat again and again, in yet darker forms the sins of the past. This was the burden of the confessions of David, Paul, Augustine, Luther, Knox—in short, of humanity, saint and savage, in our best hours. What was the origin of the Church in Travancore, India? There is nothing more romantic in all history. A man holding a high position in the south of that country about the beginning of the present century, deeply impressed with a sense of guilt, set out on a pilgrimage seeking peace. Much he longed for this blessing; and many a pilgrimage he had undertaken before with the same end in view, but all in vain. No washing in the Ganges; no priestly incantations; no mystic spell or charm lingering around costly temples had any power over him. At length he turned his face towards home, and on his way had to pass a bazaar where a large concourse of people had gathered. He saw through the open door of the large building, some one—Koloff, the celebrated pupil of Schwartz—standing before the people and preaching to them. Koloff had been making special references to sin, and the provision made for sin in the gospel.

The word came to this poor devotee with power. He drank it in. He remained to the close and told the missionary how he had found peace. "This," said he, " is the thing I have been looking for so long. Here is the light, which nothing in all my wanderings to those great shrines, Tangore, Seringham, and others where I have been, has been able to offer to my weary soul.

This scene took place at the beginning of the present century when the churches were taking their first step in the direction of the heathen world ; and this pilgrim being a man of distinction, with abundant resources at his command, sought and obtained a missionary to go south with him to his country, and in a few years he had 90,000 Shinars gathered into congregations and many thousands of little children in the mission schools— all educated and trained in the doctrines of the cross, qualified to sing in their own tongue this great gospel hymn !

Rock of Ages, etc.

Augustus Toplady, the author, was one of the best men of his day ; but with all his unction and heavenly fire he was a bitter controversialist. He was a Calvinist of the sternest type not— slow to charge even John Wesley with giving " a known, wilful, palpable lie to the public. His forehead was petrified and impervious to a blush." . . . "He was hatching blasphemy." On the other hand, John Wesley speaks of Toplady in terms of equal asperity. "I don't fight with chimney sweepers. He is too dirty for me to meddle with. I should only foul my fingers." Happily, this style of controversy is obsolete among christian brethren, and the principal of toleration is better understood. Who would suppose that brethren who had drunk so deeply of the Master's spirit—that were all on fire for the salvation of souls, could make use of such language ? How changed is all that now with those two ethereal forms that stand so near the eternal throne ! Where are all those controversies—those ponderous volumes which were filled with such angry disputation, each combatant contending, as he supposed, earnestly for the faith once delivered to the saints ? Laid upon the shelves and hardly ever opened save by the curious, while the songs which they sang are in greater request than ever, ministering to the Church in all its sections and bringing them into yet closer relations, and

will continue to do so till we all come in the unity of the faith
and of the knowledge of the Son of God, into a perfect man—
unto the measure of the stature of the fulness of Christ, that
we henceforth be no more children tossed to and fro . . .
but, speaking the truth in love, grow up unto Him in all
things which is the Head, even Christ.

HYMN X.

OH FOR A THOUSAND TONGUES TO SING.

BY CHARLES WESLEY.

TUNE.—*Southwark*, by Christopher Tye.

O FOR a thousand tongues to sing
  My great Redeemer's praise,
The glories of my God and King,
  The triumphs of His grace !

My gracious Master and my God,
  Assist me to proclaim,
To spread, through all the earth abroad,
  The honours of Thy name.

Jesus, the name that charms our fears,
  That bids our sorrows cease ;
'Tis music in the sinner's ears,
  'Tis life and health and peace.

He breaks the power of cancelled sin,
  He sets the prisoners free ;
His blood can make the foulest clean ;
  His blood avails for me.

He speaks, and, listening to His voice,
  New life the dead receive ;
The mournful, broken hearts rejoice,
  The humble poor believe.

Hear Him, ye deaf; His praise, ye dumb,
    Your loosened tongues employ ;
Ye blind, behold your Saviour come,
    And leap, ye lame, for joy !

Latin translation—Same measure.

O MILLE mihi linguæ sint
    Ut decus celebrem
Regis—tropœas gratiæ
    Terrarum per orbem !

Rex, Deus, meus magister,
    Tam plenus luminis,
Adjuves me ut edicam
    Honores nominis.

Jesu, O nomen prepotens
    Timores hominum ;
Est dulce ægris animis—
    Pax, vita, gaudium.

Is frangit mali catenas.
    Solvitque miserum ;
Valebit ejus sanguis mi
    Expurgans sordidum.

Is dicit, vocem audiens
    Percepit mortuus
Vitam ; quin triste cor gaudet,
    Creditque frigidus.

Audite surdi, muti vos,
    Solutis tuis linguis,
Videte Regem, cæci vos ;
    Laudate Eum hymnis.

HIS is the first great hymn that fell from the pen of Charles Wesley. He had indeed tried his hand once or twice before this (1737), but those attempts were comparatively failures. He and his brother John had about this time received a great blessing—such light and cheer in the Gospel as they never had enjoyed before. They had been visiting the Moravian settlements in Germany, and had conversed much with Peter Böhler, the distinguished missionary there, and learned from him the doctrine of a present repentance and a present salvation, and the duty of proclaiming this to the world. Before this Charles had enjoyed the Gospel ; but the date of his full passage from darkness to light he makes May 21, 1737, and exactly a year after this he penned the hymn under consideration—superscribed: " For the anniversary of one's conversion."

It may be called his first and grandest hymn, and very appropriately it is placed first in that collection used by the Methodists the world over. This was the rise of a great volume of song—a volume which continued to flow for fifty years—till it reached the number of seven thousand, of which four thousand were printed in his day, though little more than six hundred are now accessible, except to the curious. From the day he wrote this hymn till the day when his bright eye grew dim, and his feet, like the patriarch's, were gathered up in his bed, he was engaged more or less in adding to his collection, and it mattered little to him where he was,—jogging along on his quiet horse to keep an appointment, staying over night in the house of some friend by the way, or rambling by the sea shore,—he was ready to jot down on saddle bag or table cover the delightful thoughts that were uppermost in his soul— thoughts that easily fell into graceful numbers and, having once fallen, remained so, for it was seldom that he retouched his lines, or recast his thoughts.

It is impossible to write intelligently of Charles Wesley without at the same time writing of John, the two great apostles of a revived Christianity—the one great as an organizer, the other as a minstrel, and both as evangelists; the one like a battering ram, breaking up the formalism of the day, and the crumbling walls of a system from which the glory had departed, and the other, like a fire, melting hard hearts, and fusing heterogeneous masses, hitherto strangers to God and to one another, into a common brotherhood, prepared to witness for Christ, and count all things but loss for His sake.

Methodism has had a wonderful history, and the fact that millions to-day sing the hymns, and follow the rules of the Wesleys—that all their societies, large or small, throughout the world, bear their *imprimatur*—is evidence of its supernatural character, and furnishes an event than which there is nothing more remarkable in the history of the Church. Those brothers certainly did a great work in their day, and richly the Divine Spirit had prepared them for that work. They were polished shafts in the hands of the Master—scholars who had won for themselves a splendid name, and carried with them the air and the *cultus* of England's most famous university; and, more than all, they carried with them the baptism of the Holy Spirit in no common degree. Walking in His light, they saw all things clearly; for theirs was an intensely realistic faith, dealing with the unseen, and lifting them far above the level of the common coarse world, its temptations and its storms. Their eye was upon a far-off home, upon the great realities of the eternal world, and their heart was in communion with God. This made them strong—strong to suffer or to serve, to live or to die, and to finish their course with joy.

We desire to tell the story of this hymn and particularly to give an account of its genesis. It came into the world in a storm. The courage, the enthusiasm necessary for leading a forlorn hope—*e.g.*, storming the Redan when the hearts of many were failing for fear—was nothing compared to the courage which animated the Wesleys when, all alone, they took to the meadows and the market-places, the highways and the hedges—when they mounted tables and scaffolds to preach the Gospel of the kingdom, and break up the stately formalism of the age. We wonder at it, and yet we need not, for the joy of the Lord was their strength. How with the light which they had—the glory which was revealed to them—could they do otherwise? It was not that they had taken hold of the Gospel, but that the Gospel had taken such hold of them that they could not be held back. They were urged on by a power not of themselves, but above themselves and independent of themselves together. This is that devine enthusiasm of which Professor Seely speaks. We see it in the Wesleys. We see it every day. There is a young girl connected with the Salvation Army of this town that furnishes the author with an illustration. She had attended his ministry for years but, it seems, without receiving any benefit, finally she became irregular in her attendance, worldly in her spirit, and disappeared from his view; but, at length, coming under the spell of a strange voice, and meeting with truth presented in a new form, her eyes were opened to the glory of the Master, the riches of His grace, the duty of a present and entire consecration. She took her ground; she entered into covenant with God, but in doing so she secretly resolved not to take a conspicuous part in the Army—not to walk the streets at the sound of the drum, and sing hymns to the amusement of spectators. But as the light became brighter in her soul, and the grace, that bringeth salvation, became richer in her experience, all this reserve passed away; and it was nothing that she should have to face ridicule and scorn and contumely. She was prepared for it all. She gladly took her place in the ranks, and braved the storm. Such was her feeling that she could not be held back, but rather desired to share with the Master the scorn of the world. He would not make this reference but for the fact that he had had sufficient opportunity under his own roof to verify the reality of the great change that has taken place—to witness a conscientiousness which is beautiful, a patience where formerly there was none, a brightness, a radiancy which sometimes mounts to a joy unspeakable and full of glory. If the Salvation Army were made up of such converts, what a power it should be in the world! He confesses that this one case has done much to reconcile him to the eccentricities of the order, and that he never looks upon the little handful of recruits on the streets walking under the beat of the drum, without respect, and thinking that there may be among them bright spirits in daily communion with the Eternal.

Now the same feeling that led this young girl to witness for Christ in her way was the feeling that led the Wesleys to witness for Christ in those dark days in the manner indicated; and the full *genesis* of this noble hymn cannot be given without stating the circumstances. What was the condition of the country when they took their ground, and opened their mouths in those songs so fragrant with the One Grand Name? Religious stagnation everywhere. England had cast off Romanism, but she had not yet taken heartily to Protestantism; and the Nonconformists—those early witnesses for a purer faith, were, to a great extent, silent, and Nonconformity itself, as if exhausted with its efforts, had lapsed into stolidity, and in some cases a frigid Arianism. In the Church of England, according to Burnet and others, the character of the inferior clergy had reached its lowest point. Many were grossly scandalous in their lives, others were caught in the meshes of the Arian heresy; while the greater part who came to be ordained were as ignorant as the people whom they were to teach. Professing christians were paralyzed by the influences of error, and the existing ministry in all the churches was powerless to attack the vices of society. The vitality of truth, the power of rebuke, the presence of the Divine Spirit, were lost, and the light in which so many had rejoiced for a season was gone. It was in these circumstances that the Wesleys lifted up their clarion voices, and broke in upon the death and dormancy that everywhere prevailed. From the day that they took their stand as the heralds of a richer Gospel than had generally been proclaimed in the stately churches of the realm, they felt that they had crossed the Rubicon, and that they had cut themselves off from the Church of England and every church. This took place April 2, 1739, a few months after the birth of this hymn. On this occasion John met on Somerset Hill, near Bristol, with three thousand people. On many of these the Spirit of God fell; to many something of the Pentecostal fire was vouchsafed, so that on retiring to their homes they could say: "We have heard strange things to-day!" The dignitaries of the Church looked on with amazement, and wondered at their boldness; but the common people, to a great extent, heard them gladly for they delivered their message with all plainness of speech, free from the shackles and subtleties and jargons of theological lore—and that with all the spiritual fervour of a new found joy—with lips that had been touched with a live coal from the altar, and the grandeur of an intensely realistic faith that often moved to tears those long unused to weep. They took the truths—the very truths which were so offensive in St. Paul's day—the very truths which were lifeless, and dry as summer's dust, in other mens' hands, and gave them forth to the crowds on the mountain side that were famishing for the bread of life. They broke in upon the slumber of ages. They shot their fiery darts all around without respect of persons, and strong men, convinced of sin, fell down in mortal agony, and from the multitude the Lord rescued His own, and made them witnesses of His power. What was the result? A storm of persecution that we cannot understand in these days. To name the Wesleys in polite society was an offence. To speak of their hymns and their singing was an impropriety. To waylay them and beat them—to make bonfires of their meeting houses—was thought proper. They were stoned, scorned, insulted, and in

many places their very appearance was the signal for disorder
and violence. A singular entry still remains in the parish
book of Illogan, Cornwall, in confirmation of these views :
"Expenses at Ann Gartrell's (tavern) for driving off the
Methodists, 9s." This is the record of the fact that the church-
warden, placing himself at the head of an angry mob, drove
the Wesleys and their followers beyond the parish boundary,
and afterward regaled his accomplices at this ale house. Long
and fierce was the persecution that those servants of the Most
High had to bear, but they never quailed, never lost hope,
never cast away their confidence, which has had great recompense
of reward. Though beset with hired ruffians by the way,
wronged in the courts of justice, insulted in every form, they
never forgot their high calling, or the dignity becoming christian
gentlemen. John, the chief power in this great movement, is
especially named for his high and heavenly demeanour during
the long-continued storm. In his piercing eye and tender tones
of persuasion, sometimes melting into tears, there was the very
gentleness of Christ ; and on his calm, intellectual features, at
once delicate and classical, we look in vain for any shadow of
resentment—anything, indeed but genuine benevolence.

Now these were the circumstances in which the hymn was
born, and when we think of the storms which the Wesleys had
to bear in opening their mouths as the heralds of a brighter
day, we will be the better able to understand the force of these
lines :

> My gracious Master and my God,
> Assist me to proclaim, etc.

One hundred years have passed away since Charles Wesley
closed his earthly labours. The sermons he preached have long
ago been forgotten, and the generation to whom he ministered
have been gathered to their fathers ; but the hymns he jotted

H

down by the way side, on scraps of paper and shelving rocks by the sea shore are yet a power in the land, giving form to the creed, and colour to the sentiment, of the Methodist societies throughout the world.   And what a power those hymns are ! It was thought by some that, on the emancipation of the slaves in the Southern States, Methodism, strong in that quarter, would be powerless in restraining them from deeds of violence, and that a carnival of blood would be the consequence; but the penetrating power of his hymns, fragrant with prayers for patience, forgiveness, christlikeness, had so melted into the soul of the negro as to make Christ's law of love supreme over all the excitements and temptations of the hour.   John Wesley acted wisely in giving great prominence to his brother's hymns. Without them he could never have accomplished the work he did.   Without them he might have transplanted something like Moravian rigidity into British soil, but not the warm spirit of devotion, the glowing piety, the enthusiasm of the many thousands of his descendants.   Without them Methodism could never have been the force which it is in the world, or its societies been indoctrinated as they have been indoctrinated in those truths which through faith make wise unto salvation.

HYMN XI.

JESUS, LOVER OF MY SOUL.

CHARLES WESLEY'S GREAT HYMN.

TUNE.—*Hollingside.* BY REV. J. B. DYKES, MUS. DOC.

JESUS, lover of my soul,
    Let me to Thy bosom fly,
While the nearer waters roll,
    While the tempest still is high.

Hide me, O my Saviour, hide,
    Till the storm of life is past ;
Safe into the haven guide ;
    O receive my soul at last !

Other refuge have I none !
    Hangs my helpless soul on Thee ;
Leave ah ! leave me not alone ;
    Still support and comfort me.

All my trust on Thee is stayed,
    All my help from Thee I bring ;
Cover my defenceless head
    With the shadow of Thy wing.

Thou, O Christ, art all I want ;
    More than all in Thee I find ;
Raise the fallen, cheer the faint,
    Heal the sick, and lead the blind.

Just and holy is Thy name ;
  I am all unrighteousness :
False and full of sin I am ;
  Thou art full of truth and grace.

Plenteous grace with Thee is found,
  Grace to cover all my sin :
Let the healing streams abound ;
  Make and keep me pure within.

Thou of life the fountain art,
  Freely let me take of Thee ;
Spring Thou up within my heart,
  Rise to all eternity.

Latin translation—Same measure.

JESU, amans animæ,
    Serva tuâ sub pennâ,
Mare volvit altius,
Et quum hiems propius.
Conde, conde me Jesu,
Duc me integrum portu ;
Tandem me recipias
Quando acta tempestas

Aliud non auxilium,
O relinque ne solum ;
Verto Te miserrimus,
Attamen carissimus ;
Nudum caput protege,
Sanctis tuis college ;
Esto Tu præsidium,
Proxime refugium.

O. Christe, es Fons omnium,
Spes, pax, solatium ;
Data donis inopem ;
Cæcum duc at debilem.
Sum vilus et infensus
Semper labi et propensus,
Inops caecus, inquinatus.

Tu graciosus et clemens ;
Lapsos erues volens ;
Tu ignosces, recipies,
Sordidum et ablues.
Salutaris Fons vivens
Beate semper et beans ;
Sali recens in corde
Seculorum secula !

CHARLES WESLEY, the author of this celebrated hymn,
may be set down in some respects as a phenomenon. He
was number eighteen of the nineteen children born to his
father and mother. In stature he was very small, as were also
his father and his more famous brother, John. In disposition
he was warm and impetuous, but very frank and amiable. In
the matter of sacred song he stands alone as an author. To him
it was a passion—a refuge to which he was ever ready to turn.
On and on through life his thoughts fell easily into poetic
numbers, and at the great age of 80 years, when the shadows
were falling, he called his wife to his dying bed, and, at his
last, dictated the hymn "In age and feebleness extreme," etc.

Charles Wesley has written hymns which, in point of excellence, cannot be surpassed, and in point of number outdoing
any other genius, man or woman, that ever lived, having, with
his brother John, composed nearly as many as all other modern
authors put together! Solomon in his day wrote one thousand
and five songs—a specimen of which we have in the Book of
Canticles; but Charles Wesley's are computed at about seven

thousand, and among these one hundred and sixty-six, on the
Lord's Supper and over two hundred on the Trinity! In 1746
he published under the title Gloria Patri twenty-four; and in
1767 one hundred and eighty-two, called "Hymns on the
Trinity." It cannot be expected, of course, that all these are
perfect. How could they? How can any one mind, no matter
how fertile, confining itself to one theme and touching only one
string of the golden lyre, strike out something entirely new
every time,—something fresh and fragrant as the morn,—so
commanding as to meet with universal favor as a real contribution
to the service of song? In point of fact, very few of those
two hundred hymns to the Trinity are ever used, though some
of them have great poetic merit; still, not one of them is to be
named with Heber's "Holy, Holy, Holy," etc. And out of all
his seven thousand, including his brother's, only twenty-seven
have found their way into the recent Presbyterian collection,
and not one of these addressed to the Trinity! We are not
surprised that Montgomery, than whom no one was better
qualified to speak on the subject, should have put it on record:
"Charles Wesley was probably the author of a greater number
of compositions of this kind—with less variety of matter or
manner—than any other who can be named."

Yet while this charge may be broadly applicable as a whole,
we can never forget such imperial hymns as "Oh! for a
thousand tongues to sing," "Oh! for a heart to praise my
God," "Hark, the herald angels sing," and this, "Jesus,
lover of my soul." Had he never written any but these, his
would have been no small contribution to the Church—a legacy,
indeed, of unspeakable value, for they bear upon them many a
seal of the Divine approval; and though more than a century
has passed since they first saw the light, they have still upon
them the dew of their youth; and it does one good to think
of the thousands of voices in every land that are lifted up
every Sabbath in those hallowed strains which give utterance

to the feelings of penitence, joy, love, hope and the aspirations of a purer, nobler life.

But certainly, if we should be asked to name the greatest and the best of the hymns of Charles Wesley, we should have no hesitation in saying: "Jesus, lover of my soul." What was its genesis? What were the circumstances in which it was written? It is plain from the recorded life of the Wesleys that many of their hymns owed their origin to some incident in the history of those great men. It was while spending a day at the Land's End, England, that Charles first thought of the hymn beginning:

> Low, on a narrow neck of land,
> 'Twixt two unbounding seas I stand.

The point of rock on which the adventurer stands is about three feet broad at its termination and about two hundred feet perpendicular over the sea, at the foot of which the waves break with great violence. On his right hand is the Bristol Channel, and on the left the English Channel, and right before him the Great Atlantic. Here, indeed, is a situation fitted to teach, to inspire such a man as our poet, and the hymn referred to is the fruit of that memorable day.

Again, the hymn beginning "See how great a flame aspires," was written after spending a season among the Newcastle colliers. Stevenson, of missionary fame, tells us that the imagery of the first verse was suggested by the furnace blasts and burning pit-heaps which to this day illuminate the whole neighborhood in which they are found. Once more, the earthquake, March 8, 1750, gave rise to nineteen new hymns, among which is that very grand one, "Lo, He comes, with clouds descending," etc.

But what was the *genesis* of "Jesus, lover of my soul?"

The story is that the poet, in his early evangelistic tours, was overtaken by a dreadful storm, when the courage of the seamen was tested to the last degree of endurance, and that, in the violence of the tempest, a bird seeking shelter made its way to the vessel laboring in the gale, and alighted upon the breast of the poet, utterly unable to hold out any longer. To a nature so sympathetic, so full of pity and poetry, such an incident must at once have been both impressive and suggestive. The sight of such helplessness on the one hand, and such a storm on the other, could hardly help to bring before him the helplessness of the sinner amid the storms of broken laws and crushing penalties, and, at the same time, the tenderness of Him who rides upon the storm, and whose love many waters cannot quench nor the floods drown.

One thing clear from the life of Charles Wesley is that this hymn was penned near to the time of his conversion—in some respects a remarkable conversion—resulting from some intercourse with Peter Böhler, the Moravian missionary, with whom the two Wesleys were going to Georgia with the view of evangelizing the Indians. They returned to London, however, where Charles was prostrated by sickness, and then it was that the words of Peter Böhler proved spirit and life to his soul. He had formerly rested on what is called a legal righteousness, well pleased with himself, like the young man in the Gospel, but under the instructions of this godly man—instructions rendered all the more impressive by this stroke of sickness, which at one time seemed likely to be fatal—his self-righteousness failed him, and the arrows of conviction left him a poor and helpless suppliant at the foot of the Cross like the bird battered and broken down by the storm of which we have been speaking. But renouncing his self-righteousness and opening his eyes to the glory of a kingdom that cannot be moved, and a righteousness whiter than snow, he entered into liberty. He had now, when this hymn was penned, had several months' experience of the new life. He had tasted its strange, sweet joy. He had risen to a higher level in the divine life and had come under a mightier influence than he had ever known in the days of his carnality.

This is the story of the *genesis* of the hymn—various versions of which we have seen, none of them probably accurate—all more or less apocryphal, and yet all founded, we believe, on something, like that given, and we can easily understand that, viewed in the light of his spiritual experience, the incident referred to must have made a deep impression on him. The memory of that sick bed in 1738, the experience of that season of grace that followed him through life, like the memory of Bethel in the case of the patriarch, followed him down to his dying hour, ever stimulating and ever sanctifying. That one day (May 27, 1838) threw its glory over all his life—over all that went before and all that came after. It is clear that during those fifty years that followed this great event, a brighter light every day shone on his path and a richer experience grew in his soul, and a mightier power every day flowed from his life, even the power of an endless life till he stood perfect in all the will of God. Now think of the incident of the bird taking refuge in the storm in his breast and see how he must have felt!

Among the many illustrations of the power of this hymn, I quote the following from Duffield: Several years ago a ship was burned near the English Channel. Among the passengers were a father, mother and their little child, a daughter not many months old. When the discovery was made that the ship was on fire there was great confusion and the family became separated. The father was rescued and taken to Liverpool, but the mother and infant were carried overboard by the crowd. and, unnoticed by those who were doing all in their power to save the sufferers, they drifted out of the channel with the tide, the mother clinging to a fragment of the wreck with the infant at her breast. Late in the afternoon of that day they were spied by a vessel passing. The officers watched for a time, and as no vessel was near from which any one could have fallen, they concluded that the object they beheld could not be a human body. Still, the captain sent out a boat with a couple of men to ascertain the facts, and, as they approached, the sound of a gentle voice broke upon the ear: Jesus, Lover of my soul," etc.

It is, indeed, a wonderful hymn and has already a wonderful history. It is a hymn for all classes, all ages, the old and the young, the learned and the unlearned. Henry Ward Beecher, speaking of it, says: " I would rather have written that hymn of Charles Wesley than have the fame of all the kings that ever sat on the earth. It is more glorious. It has more power in it. I would rather be the author of that hymn than hold the wealth of the richest man in New York. He will die. He is dead already and he does not know it. He will pass after a little while out of men's thoughts. What will there be to speak of him? What will he have done to stop trouble or encourage hope? His money will go to his heirs and they will divide it. Then they will die and it will go to their heirs, growing smaller by each division. In three or four generations everything comes again to the ground for redistribution. But that hymn will go on singing until the last trump brings forth the angel band, and then I think it will mount up on some lip to the very presence of God."

HYMN XII.

GUIDE ME, O THOU GREAT JEHOVAH!

THE GREAT WELSH HYMN BY WILLIAM WILLIAMS.

TUNE.—*Pilgrimage.*

"Thou leddest them in the day by a cloudy pillar: and in the night by a pillar of fire."

GUIDE ME, O Thou great Jehovah!
  Pilgrim through this barren land;
I am weak, but Thou art mighty;
  Hold me with Thy powerful hand,
    Bread of heaven! bread of heaven!
Feed me now and evermore!

Open now the crystal fountain,
  Whence the healing streams do flow;
Let the fiery cloudy pillar
  Lead me all my journey through.
    Strong Deliverer! strong Deliverer!
Be Thou still my strength and shield!

When I tread the verge of Jordan,
  Bid my anxious fears subside;
Death of death, and hell's destruction,
  Land me safe on Canaan's side.
    Songs of praises, songs of praises.
I will ever give to Thee!

Now look at this through a Latin version same measure:

DUC me, magne O Jehovah,
  Peregrinum terris his:
Debilis sum, tu benignus,
Manu tua teneas!
  Panis cœli,
Nunc et semper pasce me!

Pande jam crystallum fontem,
Aquæ vitæ hinc ab Te;
Ignis, nubis et columna
Tota via ducat me!
  Liberator!
Aegis, robur, semper sis!

Ripam Jordan veniente
Metus meos spargito;
Tibi Hades, Mors sint nihil;
Salvum ultra facito
  Et psaliam
Seculorum secula.

WILLIAM WILLIAMS, the author, was born near Landovery, Wales, 1717. He was one of that godly company that centred around Lady Huntingdon's parlor —the founder of sixty-two churches, the benefactress of hundreds of poor students—a lady whose name is an honor to womanhood, and one whose life to this day is a constant benediction. What Gerhardt did for Germany in the matter of sacred song —what Charles Wesley did for England, Williams did for Wales. Great ignorance with its attendant evils prevailed throughout the Principality at this time and had been prevailing for generations. The schoolmaster was a sort of phenomenon —now here, now there—giving a few months' instructions in one neighborhood and then passing on to another like the cir-

culating libraries of former days; and it would seem that up to
this time Wales was all but destitute of psalm and hymn; but
the great awakening which resulted in the translation of the
whole Bible into the Welsh tongue turned attention to this
want, and under the wave of blessing that set in from England
many a cold heart was stirred to its depths and many a tongue
long silent was unloosed to sing the glories of redemption and
proclaim the riches of divine grace. Foremost among those
great revivalists were the Wesleys in England. It was from
this country the Welsh revival came; here also great lethargy
had prevailed. Many a bold reformer had lifted up his voice
before this, both in the English and in the Nonconformist ranks,
but they scarcely raised a ripple upon the stagnant waters.
The Elizabethan age has been called the golden age of English
literature, but it was not the golden age of the Church of
England. The rigid oath of the Queen, together with the
uniformity everywhere insisted on, was not favorable to piety,
to the reformation of manners or the missionary enterprise—
certainly not to the composition of hymns designed for the
worship of God. Both Bishop Burnet and Bishop Butler speak
of their Church as in a lamentable state in their day. The rise
of Nonconformity, indeed, had been attended with considerable religious activity, but it, too, as if exhausted with its own
witnessing, sank down into icy formalism, sometimes Arianism.
It was in these circumstances the Wesleys and others arose and
broke in upon the lethargy of ages and the godlessness of the
nation and stirred it to its depths. Then the awakening which
followed soon made its way into Wales. Here one of the
earliest fruits of the "great awakening" was the conversion of
William Williams, the author of this noble hymn, "Guide me
O Thou Great Jehovah." He had given himself to the study
of medicine; but one Sabbath morning, while scarcely out of
his teens, he steps into the churchyard of Talgarth where he
heard a sermon from Howell Harris that made all things new.

The result was that he gave himself to the ministry, on which he entered with all the enthusiam of his nature. Taking the whole Principality as his field of labor he went about preaching the Word, but not before taking Mary Francis as his partner and life companion, (1735). It is said that during a ministry of forty-five years he seldom travelled less than forty miles a week, equal to two thousand a year!

It was soon found out that he could do more than preach—that his was the gift of song as well as eloquence. This discovery was made at one of the meetings of the association with which he was connected—an association of Wesleyans — for, though ordained a deacon of the English Church, he was denied ordination for the priesthood because of his consorting with the Methodists. Moreover, he was rebuked again and again by his diocesan till at length, wearied out by reproofs and restraints, he withdrew from the English Church and cast in his lot with H. Harris, Rowland, Whitfield and the Wesleys. At this meeting a trial was made of the poetic gifts of the preachers present, and such was the superiority of Williams, that he was advised to cultivate the gift that God had given him and prepare a hymnal for the connection— "The Welsh Calvinistic Connection." The result was the publication of "Alleluia" in 1745, followed by three other publications of the same kind—all of which, bound in one volume, were speedily adopted by the "Connection," and to this day they constitute their Psalmody. The hymn under consideration was written about 1760 in Welsh, the native language of Britons, that is, when he was forty-three years of age, and probably not very long after he had left the English Church and entered upon the great work of his life. In 1772 it was translated into English, probably by the author, and inserted in his "Gloria in Excelsis"—a collection, says Mr. Lowry, of Plainfield, (a very accurate hymnologist,) that was prepared by request of Lady Huntingdon for Whitfield's Orphan

Home in America—and in the following year printed as a leaflet with the heading, "A favorite hymn, sung by Lady Huntingdon's young collegians by the desire of many christian friends," followed by the prayer, which the Free Church has adopted for its hymnal. "Lord give it Thy blessing!" It is a glorious hymn both as regards poetry and finish, but it owes not a little to the polishing hand of Keble.

It was in these circumstances that William Williams and the godly band with whom he was associated entered upon their work, and with their clarion voice made the whole country ring. They took the old truths which had been stowed away in musty folios—the great doctrines of the cross—the doctrines of the Reformation with which Martin Luther had startled the world and the Church in the neighboring country, and presented them to the people with all the terrible earnestness of men that had been raised up for a great mission, and everywhere those truths were spirit and life to the souls of men. There was much hankering, and hesitation, both in the English Church and that of the Nonconformists as to those truths, as if their ministers had made a covenant with death, but there was no hesitation with the Wesleys or their followers. They would make no compromise with the world. They would utter no uncertain sound as to their mission. In full view of the great realites of the eternal world, they went forth strong in God conquering and to conquer, breaking up the frigidity of the Church on the one hand and rebuking the rottenness of society on the other. Standing up between the living and the dead, with the tables of Sinai in the one hand and the benedictions of the gospel in the other, they proclaimed the solemn truth of God to the thousands that gathered around them from day to day, and wherever they went God gave testimony to the word of His grace and granted signs and wonders to be done by their hand, reminding us of apostolic days. This was the character of William Williams' ministry. He was a great power in his day, and many rejoiced in his light—in the truths which he taught and the "glorious liberty" which he proclaimed.

People waited upon him in thousands, followed him from place to place, learned his songs and recited them to those that tarried at home, and with them divided the spoil. The Lord gave the word and great was the company that published it. The miner in his subterranean retreat sang a new song, as also the vine-dresser on the hills, the fisherman on the lake, the sentinel pacing his rounds, the milkmaid at her work and the weary traveller on his way. His songs, even more than his sermons, were greatly blessed, and their effect on the people to this day is astonishing; indeed the veneration in which they are held is little short of devotion. This hymn in particular has been greatly blessed. Christophers in his book gives a beautiful illus-tration—too long to be introduced here—of its power in sus-taining an aged saint amid weary days and nights that had been appointed to her. In this case it was, indeed, a leaf from the tree of life. On this she fed and found strength in her last hours. Singing it in an undertone, she was asked, "What are you singing?" She replied:—

> When I tread the verge of Jordan;

and it was with these lines on his lips also that Robert Flock-hart, the great field preacher of last century, passed away into the eternal world. Time would fail were we to speak of the history of this hymn in respect to its power—the sad hearts it has cheered—the dark hours that it has filled with holy light—the dying beds to which it has ministered—the music that it has made in the mines in Cornwall and around the shores of Anglesea and Cardigan Bay. God gave a great gift to the Church when he raised up this sweet singer in Israel.

So much as to the *genesis* of this great hymn. But it is doubtful whether anything can be known of the immediate cir-cumstances in which it took its rise. It must have been an outflow of christian experience such as would come to a Calvinist like William Williams, all aglow with the work that was before him. Such hymns as this are born, not made, and are the natural offspring of faith and hope in a glorious hour of exaltation. Consider the circumstances. There was darkness over all the land. In the parish church the feeble light was fading; in the Wesleyan camp the laborers were few, and in the Congregational chapels, to be found here and there, at long intervals, there was often nothing on which a hungry soul could feed. Disquisitions, sometimes very learned, sometimes very foolish, were heard in those chapels, such as the origin of sin and how long Adam and Eve remained in a state of innocence, but the great Name which is above every name, and which should be like ointment poured forth in every service, was kept in the background, and the hungry people, weary with the world's cares, longing for rest and the refreshment which they sought in the sanctuary, had reason to say, "They have taken away my Lord and I know not where they have laid Him." What more natural than the utterance of this hymn on the part of William Williams? He felt his need of divine strength and guidance, and under the pressure of heavy care cried out "Guide me O Thou great Jehovah." It was in these circumstances that the hymn was written, or, as has been said, born, for such hymns are not written—are not the elaborate manufacture of an artist sitting down in cold blood to perform his task, but the outflow of blissful experience, the vision of the soul in a glorious hour when she sees the King in his beauty and the land that is afar off. The same thing may be said of "Shall we gather at the river?" "Take my Life and let it be," "I heard the voice of Jesus say" (likely, though its author cannot say) "Safe in the Arms of Jesus"—the utterance of a blind woman, F. J. Van-Alstyne, said to have written five thousand pieces, and this, "Safe in Arms," etc., in twenty minutes. These were all born in this way, and not unlikely this was the case with this great hymn of William Williams.

I

HYMN XIII.

JESUS SHALL REIGN WHERE'ER THE SUN.

WATT'S GREAT MISSIONARY HYMN.

TUNE.—*Warrington.* Composed by Rev. R. Harrison St. Alban's England,—a grand old tune worthy of the high place assigned it.

JESUS shall reign where'er the sun
   Does his successive journeys run ;
His kingdom stretch from shore to shore,
Till moons shall wax and wane no more.

For him shall endless prayer be made,
And praises throng to crown His head ;
His Name like sweet perfume shall rise
With every morning sacrifice.

People and realms of every tongue
Dwell on His love with sweetest song ;
And infant voices shall proclaim
Their early blessings on His Name.

Blessings abound where'er He reigns ;
The prisoner leaps to lose his chains ;
The weary find eternal rest,
And all the sons of want are blest.

Let every creature rise and bring
Peculiar honours to our king ;
Angels descend with songs again,
And earth repeat the loud Amen.

THE original consisted of eight verses—rather many for an ordinary service, and so the compilers of our hymnal have only made use of five in their selection, a translation of which in Latin we furnish.

JESUS regnabit sol ubi
    In tota orbe it mundi ;
Ejusque regna extendent
Mutantes lunæ dum manent
        Et nihil magis temporis.

Sabâque Shebâ venient
Reges, coramque Hoc cadent ;
Et nomen—sicut tus fragrans—
Altare omni oriens
        Præclarum erit per orbem.

Gens omnis Illo serviet,
Amorem ejus et canet ;
Carebunt neque tenerûm
Canores voces infantûm,
        Per gloriosos annos hos

Felices regnante Hoc cuncti ;
Captivi erint liberi ;
Defessis suave otium ;
Pauperi opes Gentium,—
        Argentum, aurum et gemmæ.

Calore cuncti sub solis
Ferantque aptos honores ;
Cœlestes novum et carmen ;
Terrestres spondeant : Amen !
        Per seculorum secula.

The metrical version of the psalms in common use in the days of Isaac Watts (1674-1748) was that of Francis Rouse,

Provost of Eton. This was the first hymn book of English Protestants, for in turning from the Church of Rome they also turned away from all mediæval hymns, good and bad, orthodox or heterodox. Other versions had been tried, such as that of Patrick Sternhold and Hopkins, Tate and Brady—an English Church affair, sanctioned in 1693, but now little used —but Rouse's version, with all its roughness and Judaism and metrical infelicities, was the favourite, and has held its place for over two hundred years, and seen every rival go to the wall. With many to this day it is the only hymn book that is used in the worship of God. And when we think of its history, its traditions, associations and, above all, its fidelity to the Word, we will cease to wonder that many are slow to admit any other hymn book to the level of the psalms. These are the true Hebrew melodies, and no hymn book has ever been tested as to its value as these Songs of Zion. They were the only vehicles of praise known to our covenanting fore-fathers. They have been heard from the "utmost corners of the land," in the "moorland of mist," in the hiding places of the mountains, in the cell of the prisoner, and on the scaffold of the martyr. But in the days of Isaac Watts this version of the psalms was new, and had no such recommendations. Stennet's "Hymns for the Lord's Supper" did not appear till 1683, and Mason's "Songs of Praise" till 1697. These last found some favour in the English Church on account of the author belonging to that Church, but the great bulk of the Protestant population had no hymn book but Rouse's metrical version of the psalms. And to an ear so musical and a taste so refined as that of Dr. Isaac Watts, those psalms, in many respects, were anything but agreeable, and accordingly he resolved to supplement them with a hymn book, and in 1707 he published his first work containing two hundred and twenty-two psalms and hymns and spiritual songs. Some excellent pieces like those of Bishop Ken's the Morning and the Evening Hymn, had found their way into the

homes of the people, but as yet the modern hymn book was
unknown in the Church of God. This great want being met
by Dr. Watts, he must be regarded as the father of English
hymnody; and, as Miss I. Bird says, this place is now to him
freely accorded.

In this day when every man has a psalm, it is hard for us
to realize the greatness of the work of Isaac Watt, in making
the reformation he did make in the matter of praise. He had
not only a hymn book to prepare for the Church, but had to
face a wall of prejudice so inveterate and invincible that to
this day, in the case of many, it has not been overcome. I
mean the prejudice against the use of hymns of mere human
composition in the worship of God. Watts had to face the
storm, the first drops of which he felt when he stood before the
long-faced deacons of his little Dissenting Church in South-
hampton upon the occasion of introducing his first hymn—65th
Paraphrase. They remonstrated but he insisted. They were
old, he was young, but he had the courage to stand on his feet,
and repeat hymn after hymn till he put a book into their
hands containing two hundred and twenty-two psalms and
hymns and spiritual songs—a book which gave a great lift to
the spiritual life of the Church—a book in which christians
were no longer compelled to wrap up the shining glories of the
Redeemer in the shadowy language of types and figures, but a
book that enabled them to come to God in the matter of praise
as well as in the matter of prayer by a new and living way with
the name of Christ on their lips.

Here, however, we speak of him not as a hymn writer, but
a psalm translator. The rough verse and Judaic colouring in
which Francis Rouse had presented the great truth with which
the Hebrew text was charged, did not meet his view, and so he
undertook the task of preparing a new version of the psalms.
His design was not only to make better verses, but to divest
the psalms of their Judaic character—in short, to present them

in the sunlight of the Christian dispensation. With this end in view, he says : " I have entirely omitted some whole psalms, and large pieces of many others ; and have chosen out of them such parts only as might easily and naturally be accommodated to the various occasions of the christian life, or at least might afford us some beautiful allusions to christian affairs. These I have copied and explained in the general style of the Gospel. I have chosen rather to imitate than to translate ; and thus to compose a psalm book for christians after the manner of the Jewish Psalter. . . . I have expressed, as I may suppose David would have done had he lived in the days of Christianity." The work was at length prepared for publication, and it issued from the press in 1719. The hymn, "Jesus shall reign where'er the sun, etc.," was written it is believed for some missionary occassion—a thing almost unknown since the days of the apostles. It is his translation of the 72nd Psalm ; and though scarcely equal to Montgomery's translation of the same, " Hail to the Lord's Anointed" in point of literary finish, is even a greater favourite, and must ever be looked upon as one of the great hymns of the Church. This is all I believe, that can be said in regard to the genesis of this noble hymn.

It is still to such a hymn as this we turn in our missionary gatherings when we would seek to rouse the sleeping energies of the Church, and quicken her faith as to the future of our world, still in a sense waiting for redemption—even the glorious liberty of the children of God ; and it is in view of the sublime prospects unfolded in the sacred page that our faith seeks for such a vehicle of song—such an expression of our hope. In 1862 this triumphant hymn was sung at a great missionary meeting in Fiji, when five thousand exchanged heathenism for Christianity, and during the quarter of a century that has transpired since, how often has it been sung on similar occasions? There is no peradventure in its prophecy—no falter in its tone. In *our* little forecastings we can only say *perhaps*, and in our

little efforts we often fail; but the Master faileth never. He
will not fail nor be discouraged, till the isles wait for His law.
Why should there be any faltering in its tone? The work of
redemption was no peradventure in the hands of Christ;
and the carrying it forward no forlorn hope for the work of
illumination will prove equally certain in the hands of the
Spirit. We see not yet all things put under Him, but
we see that in every passing age a decided advance on the
kingdom of darkness. Never was any cause at such a low ebb
as that of Christ's when He was taken down from the cross
and commited to Joseph's new tomb. His enemies were everywhere triumphant; the devils in hell were jubilant, and the
friends of Christ, the apostle band that followed Him and the
holy women that ministered to Him, were all scattered—each
one to his own home. But Christ beneath the grave was
mightier than Christ above the grave; and an energy new and
strong took possession of His disciples such as the world had
never before witnessed, in virtue of which they became witnesses
for Him both in Samaria and to the ends of the earth; and
though commanded again and again to be silent in regard to
that great name they loved so well on pain of prison and death,
they would not; but, with their latest breath, maintained that
Christ *was* risen from the dead and had become the first fruits
of them that slept.

That was a remarkable utterance of Napoleon to his attendant
on him during his exile in St. Helena, which, upon the authority
of Canon Liddon, of St. Paul's, London, who has recently
investigated the facts, we are disposed to regard as reliable.
What did Napoleon—now drawing near to the close of his
mortal career, and feeling the shadow of the eternal world
coming over his spirit, as the flowers do when the sun is going
down beneath the western hills,—what did he say to this
attendant?—"You speak of empires and power. Well,
Alexander the Great, Julius Cæsar, Charlemagne and myself

founded empires, but on what did we found them? Force.
Christ founded His on love, and at this moment there are millions
ready to die for Him.   It was not one day nor one generation
that accomplished the triumph of religion in the world.   No.
It was a long war—a war for three centuries—a war begun by
the apostles and continued by successive generations.   In this
war all the kings and armies were on one side, but on the other
I see no army, no banner or battering ram, but yet a mysterious
power is there, working in the interests of christianity—men
secretly sustained here and there by a common faith in the
great Unseen.   I die before my time, and my body will be
given to the earth as food for worms.   Such is the fate of him
called Napoleon the Great.   But look to Christ, honoured and
loved in every land.   Look at His kingdom rising over all
other kingdoms.   His life was not the life of a man ; His death
not that of a man, but of God,"

Such was the utterance of Napoleon the Great in reference
to Christ shortly before his death, and if he could speak in such
terms then, more than fifty years ago, how much more now?
There were moments of bright spiritual vision, it would seem,
vouchsafed to him in which he could see more than most men,
and during which he felt something of the powers of the world
to come.   In some such moments he gave utterance to the
foregoing statements   He was not always blind to the "manifest
destiny" of the Lord Jesus—to the fact that all things are
hastening to one end—that all forces are gathering around their
Lord, and melting down under the reign of love.   He had
visions of God when he saw that after all it was not by the
sword or the battering ram or the great army mustered on the
field that universal empire was to be accomplished, but by the
Word of God that liveth and abideth forever.

Quite in accordance with these utterances has been the progress of christianity since Christ's day.   Look back over the
centuries and behold what God hath wrought !   In the first

century there were five hundred thousand christians; in the second, two million christians; in the third, five million christians; in the fourth, ten million christians; in the fifth, fifteen million christians; in the sixth, twenty million christians; in the seventh, twenty-four million christians; in the eight, thirty million christians; in the ninth, forty million christians; in the tenth, fifty million christians; in the eleventh, seventy million christians; in the twelfth, eighty million christians; in the thirteenth, seventy-five million Christians; in the fourteenth, eighty million christians; in the fifteenth, one hundred million christians; in the sixteenth, one hundred and twenty-five million christians; in the seventeenth, one hundred and fifty-five million christians; in the eighteenth, two hundred million christians; and in the nineteenth, before its close there will be, at a moderate calculation, three hundred million. At the beginning of the present century there were not over fifty thousand heathen converts; now there must be nearly two million in all heathendom; and, including native agents, fully twenty-five thousand labourers all over the Church, now waking up to its duty in regard to the heathen as it never did before. There are thousands of brave young spirits, both men and women, preparing to follow. The Lord is speaking to the Church as He has never done in the past, and calling upon His workers to go forth and possess the land; and this, not only for the sake of the heathen, but for her own sake. He had given the word, and even the women that publish the tidings are a great host. Kings of armies flee; they flee, and she that tarrieth at home (no less than those that go) divideth the spoil. Read this hymn in the light of the facts stated when gloomy doubts arise, and you will sing it with a grander strain and a "larger hope" than the little Doctor had any conception of in his day when taken to task by the grave deacons of his little church for his innovation. Peace to his memory! Among all the hymnists none has left a clearer tone. The calm, unsullied light of his fame is not dimmed by the lapse of years. His name is still fragrant, and his best thoughts, like ministering angels, traverse every land. His tomb in the unconsecrated dust of Bunfields still invites tourists, and his effigy in West. minster Abbey commands greater respect then the busts of kings. His request that nothing should be added to his name on the stone that marks his resting place but the words, *In uno Jesu omnia*, has been observed.

HYMN XIV.

HAIL TO THE LORD'S ANOINTED.

MONTGOMERY'S GREAT MISSIONARY HYMN.

TUNE—*Morning Light.* BY GEO. JAS. WEBB.

HAIL to the Lord's anointed !
   Great David's greater Son :
Hail, in the time appointed,
   His reign on earth begun.
He comes to break oppression,
   To set the captive free ;
To take away transgression,
   And rule in equity.

He shall come down like showers
   Upon the fruitful earth ;
And love, joy, hope, like flowers,
   Spring, in His path, to birth.
Before Him, on the mountains,
   Shall peace, the herald, go ;
And righteousness, in fountains,
   From hill to valley flow.

Arabia's desert-ranger
   To Him shall bow the knee ;
The Ethiopian stranger
   His glory come to see ;
With offerings of devotion,
   Ships from the isles shall meet
To pour the wealth of ocean
   In tribute at His feet.

Kings shall fall down before Him,
  And gold and incense bring ;
All nations shall adore Him,
  His praise all people sing ;
For He shall have dominion
  O'er river, sea, and shore,
Far as the eagle's pinion,
  Or dove's light wing, can soar.

For Him shall prayer unceasing
  And daily vows ascend ;
His kingdom still increasing,
  A kingdom without end.
The mountain dews shall nourish
  A seed in weakness sown,
Whose fruit shall spread and flourish,
  And shake like Lebanon.

O'er every foe victorious,
  He on His throne shall rest ;
From age to age more glorious,
  All blessing and all blest.
The tide of time shall never
  His covenant remove ;
His name shall stand for ever ;
  That name to us is Love.

We also in accordance with our custom would look at this
hymn through a mediæval dress, same measure :—

AVE, Dei Inuncto
  Permagni Davidi
Nato majori multo ;
  Et gloriæ regni !
Advenit ut frangat
  Oppressionis vim,
Advenit ut solvat
  Captivum miserum
          Regnans justitiâ,

Sicut in montes rores,
　Vel imbres vellera,
Vel via orti flores,
　Descendent munera.
Montibus tum præibit
　Heraldus albus, Pax ;
Collibus quoque fluet
　Æquitas tum sagax
　　　　Nobis per secula.

Ab Arabiâ quoque reges
　In Christo procident ;
Et Ethiopis duces
　Splendorem venient
Dotibus pretiosis ;
　Ab insulis naves
Opibus copiosis,
　Tributo ad pedes
　　　　Beati Domini.

Et civitates omnes
　Aurumque tus ferent ;
Et tyranni diademas,
　Eoque servient.
Ab orâ usque oram
　Regnabit, ab amni
Ad terminos terrarum,
　Quâ ala aquilai
　　　　Volare poterit.

Vota, thures orientur
　Secundum federa ;
Ejus regni tendentur
　Tum ultra sidera.
Eo educta proles
　Depascet vallibus,
Vitans torrentes soles
　Nunc parva, millibus
　　　　Sed semper amplians.

Undique victor throno
  Sedebit inclytus ;
Omni terrâ et homo
  Beans, Hoc beatus.
Ævi amnis non franget
  Statuta federa.
Amor ejus stringet ;
  Idem per secula,
          Nam manet Dominus.

JAMES MONTGOMERY, the author of this Hymn of surpassing excellence, was born 4th November, 1771, in the
little Scottish town, Irvine, on the Frith of Clyde, a
romantic spot and well fitted for the nurture of the fair-haired
child that was destined in the providence of God to be a sweet
singer in Israel. Designed by his father and mother for the
Moravian ministry, to which his parents belonged, he was sent
at the early age of six years to Fulneck—a Moravian settlement near Leeds, England,—and in the excellent Grammar
School connected with that institution he was taught the
necessary branches of learning, German, French, Greek, Latin,
natural science, etc. But James was slow to learn and his
teachers gave rather discouraging accounts of his progress from
time to time. But one fine summer day when he and a few
more of the boys were taken to the country under the escort of
one of those teachers he enjoyed a treat which made that day
memorable. In a shady spot in the fields this teacher read to
them,—with no idea that he was going to kindle a flame in the
heart of the young poet in the light of which many should
rejoice,—read Blair's " Grave." Young Montgomery was delighted. He mused much on the theme, and while he was
musing the fire burned, and nothing could restrain him from
versification. As his teacher despaired of ever making much
of him as a scholar, he was sent at the age of fifteen to serve in
a huckster's shop in the vicinity ; but even there, amid the

prosaic surroundings, he found time to write quite a number of
poems, and among others that much admired paraphrase of the
113th Psalm, "Servants of God in joyful lays," etc.　By and
by we find him in a newspaper office—1792—assisting the
editor of the Sheffield *Register*, and in full sympathy with his
chief's radical opinions.　Shortly afterward we find him editor-
in-chief, following in the same lines, advocating popular rights
and throwing the lustre of his genius over all his commu-
nications.　For his plain speaking and strong advocacy of
radical measures, under the shadow of the French Revolution,
the Government of the day threw him twice into the cells
of York Castle; but the poetic faculty was irrepressible even
here, and shortly after his liberation he published a small
volume of poems under the title of "Prison Amusements."
He published the "Wanderer of Switzerland" in 1806, which
in spite of the savage attack of the critic Jeffrey, in the *Edinburgh Review*, was received with great favour—12,000 copies
having been disposed of in twenty years, not speaking of the
American editions.

He had wandered about for many years; he had adopted
Socinian and other errors, but the remembrance of his saintly
father and mother, who died in the West Indies, and who had
given themselves to the missions of the Moravian brethren,
was fondly treasured by our author, and the little despised
settlement of the brethren at Fulneck was still a green spot in
his memory; and though more than thirty years had now passed
since he, a mere child, had taken up his residence there—
though none of its laurels had ever followed him—though none
of its calendars made honourable mention of his name, he loved
it, and at length determined openly and fully to identify himself
with the disciples of Christ; and so, at the close of 1814, he
was publicly received and recognized as a brother in the Lord
and a member of the Moravian Society.

It was on the forty-third anniversary of his birthday that he wrote the president of Fulneck, making his request for re-admission to the congregation, and it was at this time that he wrote these impressive lines :

> People of the living God,
>   I have sought the world around,
> Paths of sin and sorrow trod,
>   Peace and comfort nowhere found.
> Now to you my spirit turns—
>   Turns a fugitive unblest ;
> Brethren, where your altar burns,
>   Oh, receive me into rest.

Notwithstanding his success as a *litterateur*, he was poor ; but in 1835 he was relieved from all anxiety as to a livelihood by Sir Robert Peel placing his name on the pension list for £200 a year. Still he continued to be a voluminous writer to the last—29th April, 1854,—when a stroke of paralysis spared him the pains of death, and made a way of escape for the bright spirit that had learned to sun itself in the eternal light. Like Watts and Cowper and Ken and others, he never married, and like them, too, he found his sweetest enjoyment in sacred verse and in a hope full of immortality.

> " Heard ye the sobs of parting breath ?
>   Marked ye the eye's last ray ?
> No ! life so sweetly ceased to be
>   It lapsed in immortality."

"When seriously ill and far advanced in years," Mr. Duffield says, " he once offered some of his hymns to the attending physician, and that on his reading them to the sick man, he became very much affected, saying to the physician that every one embodied some distinct experience—adding he hoped they might be preferable to others."

The poet in his later years visited Edinburgh, and Hugh Miller, then editor of the *Witness*, gives the following description of him :

" His appearance speaks of antiquity, not of decay. His hair has assumed a snowy whiteness, and the lofty and full arched coronal regions exhibit what a brother poet has well termed the clear, bald polish of an honoured head ; but the expression of the countenance is that of middle life. It is a thin, clear, speaking countenance. The features are high, the complexion fresh, though not ruddy ; and age has failed to pucker either cheek or forehead. . . . The figure is quite as little touched of age as the face. It is well but not strongly made, and of the middle size ; yet there is a touch of antiquity about it, derived, however, rather from the dress than from any peculiarity of the person itself. To a plain suit of black, Mr. Montgomery adds the voluminous breast ruffles of the last age, exactly such things as, in Scotland at least, the fathers of the present generation wore on their wedding days."

A word now in regard to the genesis of this great hymn—the hymn on which his fame will chiefly rest. On the 14th April, 1822, there was a large and enthusiastic missionary meeting held in the Wesleyan Chapel, in the city of Liverpool, England. In those days the Church had little more than waked up as to its duty to the heathen world ; and when a missionary meeting was announced, speakers of great name felt honoured in being called to take part in the proceedings, at least to a greater extent than now ; and the Church as a whole took a warmer interest in this great question that had all but been neglected for ages.

Dr. Adam Clarke, the distinguished commentator, presided on this occasion, and among the speakers was the poet and *litterateur*, James Montgomery, now in the zenith of his popularity. He had made diligent preparation for this great meeting, and as a peroration to his speech gave the hymn under

K

consideration, which he recited with grand effect to the great assembly. Dr. Clarke was so delighted with it that he begged for a copy, and upon receiving it resolved to place it in his Commentary on Psalm 72, which he did. Now behold what God hath wrought ! In his " Original Hymns," published 1853, this is No. 267, and is entitled, " Christ's reign on earth."

The theme of the hymn, " Christ's reign on earth," has doubtless contributed largely to its popularity; for there is nothing so directly appeals to all that is best and greatest in our nature—nothing so much engages our best sympathies—than the prospect unfolded in the visions of ancient seers, who from time to time were carried away in the spirit to behold and describe the glory of the latter day. Such visions do not only address themselves to our faith and hope, but our imagination, and serve in no small measure to lift the Church into a higher life and stimulate her flagging energies. Amid all her successes and reverses, the conflicts and confusions of time, the onsets of infidelity and the storms of persecution, this has been the hope of the Church, and when a hymn like this is sung, or simply recited, as in this case—a hymn so fragrant with the atmosphere of Isaiah and coloured with the prophetic symbolism of holy men that spake as they were moved by the Holy Spirit—we need not wonder at its great popularity.

Blessed be God, the hope of the Church in this regard is a hope that maketh not ashamed; for the whole history of the Church points in the direction of this hymn; and as age after age passes on, each one paying in a larger contribution to the evidences of the faith, we can see more and more clearly how all this is to end. Every year we see a greater extension of the Redeemer's Kingdom—every year a brighter revelation of the great truth that Christ must reign till he put every enemy under his feet—till every evil be put down and every department of business be purged from its vices and every home consecrated to God—shining in the beauty of holiness—when, in the language of ancient prophecy—instead of the thorn shall come up the fir tree, and instead of the brier the myrtle tree and it shall be to the Lord for a name—for an everlasting sign that shall not be cut off.

We cannot dispose of this hymn without adding a word in regard to its special excellency. Some, notably, I. Bird, claim that it is the finest in the language, and certainly for wealth of imagery, for splendour of diction, for its exquisite polish, its smooth verse and delicious rhythm, and, above all, for the Christian sympathy beating in its every line, we do not see how it could be excelled. We are cautioned by some to bear in mind that it is only a paraphrase, that the materials were all furnished and prepared for his hand--that all that was wanted was a clever versifier to round them off into a glorious whole. True, but it is not given to every one to catch the spirit of inspiration, and to write as if sitting under the sound of David's lyre or the golden harp of the guiding angel that ministered to the Seer in Patmos. The spiritual insight, the far-reaching eye, the aroma that these forty-eight lines breathe, is the gift of the few, and speak to us of a soul that drank much of the crystal river that comes from the throne of God and the Lamb. Paraphrase or no paraphrase, this hymn is a wonderful work, and comes to ordinary mortals with something of the strange sweet surprise of a revelation. Any great work of art—a picture, a poem, a group of statuary,—appears to common people as nothing extraordinary. Many a one will walk through the Royal Academy, London, where the grandest works are on exhibition, and will see nothing calling for any great admiration. It takes genius to see genius and grace to see grace. No unction like that of the Holy One. No magnet so powerful in the experience of the painter as a rare work of art, however unworthy the frame, for the moment his eye lights upon it he at once recognizes the hand of a master, and delights in the contemplation. So with every true heart in sympathy with the

Master. Such was James Montgomery. The 72nd Psalm to him was a great revelation, for in him was great susceptibility, and to him was given not only the gift of spiritual insight, but the pen of description—a pen radiant with Pentecostal fire, and richly coloured with the symbolism and the aspirations of ancient seers who saw Christ's day afar off, and were glad. Because of this, God's special gift to James Montgomery, many will rise up and call him blessed, and his name shall be held in everlasting remembrance.

HYMN XV.

THERE IS A FOUNTAIN FILLED WITH BLOOD.

COWPER'S GREAT PENITENTIAL HYMN.

TUNE—*Southwold*, BY H. J. GAUNTLETT, MUS. DOC.,
or the old favorite *Fountain*.

THERE is a fountain filled with blood
    Drawn from Immanuel's veins ;
And sinners plunged beneath that flood,
    Lose all their guilty stains.

The dying thief rejoiced to see
    That fountain in his day ;
And there have I, as vile as he,
    Washed all my sins away.

Dear dying Lamb ! Thy precious blood
    Shall never lose its power,
Till all the ransomed Church of God
    Be saved, to sin no more.

E'er since by faith, I saw the stream
    Thy flowing wounds supply,
Redeeming love has been my theme,
    And shall be till I die.

Then, in a nobler, sweeter song,
    I'll sing Thy power to save,
When this poor lisping, stammering tongue
    Lies silent in the grave.

Lord, I believe Thou hast prepared,
  Unworthy though I be,
For me a blood-bought free reward,
  A golden harp for me ;

'Tis strung, and tuned for endless years,
  And formed by power divine,
To sound, in God the Father's ears,
  No other name but Thine.

Latin translation—same measure.

EST sanguinis repletus fons
  Ductus Immanuel ;
Submersus et lustratus sons
  Fit unus Israel.

Laetatus moriturus fur
  Jam tum fontem videns ;
Hic quoque vilus ablui
  Peccata penitens.

O Agnus Dei, iste fons
  Defecerit nunquam
Donec omnis redempta gens
  Allata gloriam.

Ab hinc vidique fluvium
  Fluentem Calvara,
Fuit mi sanctum gaudium,
  Erit per secula.

Tum dulcius, nobilius
  Laudabit carmen Te,
Quum balba vox non amplius
  Est mi, beato me,

Non dignus at existimo
Ut lyra aurea
Parata mi a Domino
In alta munera.

Existimo me ad thronum
Laturum carmina,
Laudantem Te et Te solum
Aeva intermina.

WILLIAM COWPER, the author of this exquisite hymn, was born 15th November, 1731, at Great Berkham-stead, of which parish his father was the much revered rector for many years. His mother Anne, daughter of Roger Dunne, of Ludham Hall, Norfolkshire, was a descendant, by four separate lines, of Henry III. Hence the memorable words :

My boast is not that I deduce my birth
From loins enthroned and rulers of the earth ;
But higher far my proud pretensions rise—
The son of parents passed into the skies.

He was only six years old when his mother died, but his memory of her was ever sacred, and, stimulated by a portrait of her that hung in the same parlor for at least twenty years, gave a color and character to many an exquisite line in his writings. Hear how one of his biographers speaks : " We see him yet at his nursery window listening with strange awe to the tolling bell, watching the heavily plumed hearse as it slowly bore the corpse away, gulping down his tears with childish resolve, but so pathetic in his silent grief that the servants, pitying him, assured him of the speedy return of her that should return no more. So beguiled, the days passed by in intense expectation till the orphan learned how sorely he was duped, and settled down into sad submission. But he was never to forget the sweet, short bliss of childhood. The "bauble coach" in which Robin the gardener drew him to school, arrayed in scarlet mantle and velvet cap ; the morning bounties of biscuit and candies; the nightly visits of his mother to the nursery ; the constant flow of love, even the tissue and pattern of her dress which she wore as she stroked his head and smiled on him, were living memories with the grief-worn man, when, half a century later on the receipt of her picture, he poured forth his love and grief in the most tender of elegiac stanzas, which have probably moved more men to tears than any poem in our language."

At the age of thirty-two he lost his reason and plunged into blank and absolute despair. How was the interval filled? Two years he spent at a dame's school in the neighborhood, where he had much to endure from the rough peasant children that attended—the dark memory of which followed him through life. Two years more he spent in London, living in the house of an oculist on account of the state of his eyes. Seven years more in the famous school of Westminster, where he distinguished himself for classic lore and no less for outdoor sports, excelling in cricket and football games. Here he had for his companions some that were to become ere long leaders in English society, such as Coleman, the *litterateur ;* Warren Hastings, the future Governor-General of India ; Thurlow, the Lord Chancellor of England ; and here his poetic taste awoke and revelled in Milton's "Paradise Lost," the "Odes of Horace," and the "Iliad of Homer." Happy days those were upon the whole that he spent in this famous school, although he had some periods of religious depression. Now he leaves school, exchanges a seat in the sixth form of Westminster for a seat in a lawyer's office, where he spends three years, having Thurlow for a fellow-clerk even as he had him as a companion in Westminster. In those three years he says he learned a

little law, but spent much time to little profit, much in
"giggling and making giggle."   And he was so fully aware of
this misuse of his time, that he said to Thurlow one day, who
in spite of his giggling and making giggle, was working his
way upward, "Thurlow, I am nobody, and shall always be
nobody, but you will yet be Lord Chancellor of England "—a
prophecy that in due time was fulfilled.

Now he leaves the lawyer's office, takes chambers in London,
and for four years practices on his own account ; but he does
not seem to have had much success.   Scarcely had he begun,
as he supposed, his life work, when a deep horror of darkness
as to his spiritual condition took possession of his soul.   He
was in great distress, "lying down in horror at night and
rising in the morning in despair," but the reading of holy Geo.
Herbert did much to soothe his troubled spirit.   He prayed
much and even wrote prayers and afterwards burned them,
believing that gaiety and society were his best friends.   Four
years more he spends in a strangely indefinite way—his life
purposeless, aimless, unsettled.   About this time, 1752, his
money is spent, but his father dies and his purse is again filled ;
but his life is not yet filled with any grand purpose or his mind
with any great object.   He meets with his old Westminster
boys in the coffee houses, spends happy evenings here and
there and occasionally writes an article for the periodicals of
the day.   He is described as being a great favorite amongst his
companions and friends at this time, as a young man of great
intelligence, elegant in his manners and prepossessing in his
appearance ; his face open and engaging and his figure erect and
well-proportioned.   But in spite of all such advantages, his
goodly personal appearance, highly scholastic attainments, pure
life and distinguished birth, he was the most diffident of men
and sensitive to a painful degree.   But he was social, gay and
comparatively happy among his friends.   This was his manner

of life for other two years, when we reach that dark period of insanity to which we have referred.

What was the immediate occasion? The answer is the two offices—the reading clerkship and the clerkship of the committee of the House of Lords—became vacant and were offered to him. He accepted them at once, but on reflection was so overwhelmed by extreme modesty as to surrender both in favor of the less lucrative clerkship of the journals. This acceptance involved an examination as to his qualifications—an examination before the House of Lords! This so worked upon his imagination as to totally unfit him for any preparations. And when the time came he cursed the day of his birth and reproached his Maker. With a disturbed brain and a soul pierced with a sense of guilt; with the feeling that he was doomed, and that there was nothing for him but endless despair, he fled from his friends and shut himself up in his chambers, revolving the idea of self-destruction. "In the darkness of a November night, with a bottle of laudanum in his side-pocket, he went forth into the fields, resolved to poison himself and die in a ditch. Back again to his chambers—forth in the darkness to the Tower wharf to drown himself—again to his chambers—putting the black phial of painless death twenty times to his mouth and as often withdrawing it—attempting to stab himself with a penknife—so the night passed. In the dismal dawn the poet whose works we now delight to peruse—the poet whom we love so well that even his spaniels, and his hares, Tiny, Puss and Bess, find a place in our hearts for his sake, the saintly man who afterwards sang, "Lord, I believe Thou hast prepared, etc.," hung strangled from the top of his door!

It was well that he was discovered in time. He was now delivered from the fear of an examination at the bar of the House of Lords, but not from the fear of appearing as a guilty man at the bar of God. His distress was very great. He could not bear the gaze of man, and he had a dreadful sense of

the scrutiny of God.   His nights were passed without sleep, or
in fearful dreams, and at one time he was tormented with the
recollection of one passage of Scripture, and at another with
another.   Having some notion of saving faith, he determined
on one occasion to prove whether he possessed it or no by
repeating the Creed.   While endeavoring to do this his thoughts
became confused, and he was unable to proceed.   "I considered
this," he says, "as a supernatural interposition to inform me
that having sinned against the Holy Ghost, I had no longer any
interest in Christ.   *   *   Being assured of this, I gave myself
up to despair.   I felt a sense of burning in my heart like real
fire, and concluded that it was an earnest of those real flames
that were soon to receive me.   I laid myself down howling
with horror, while my knees smote against each other."

Thus he suffered for about eight months, till reason abdicated
her throne, and the wild fancy raged without limit, driving him
into the fiercest paroxysms.   He was then placed under the
care of Dr. Cotton, a man of kind sympathy and much Christian excellence.   Under his skill the disease abated, and gradually
he recovered the serenity of former days, but not the serenity
of the Gospel which he so much desired.   How was this to be
obtained?   What did the Good Shepherd do for His weak
servant, at this time groping his way into liberty?   How was
the golden harp, so broken down and out of sorts, to be returned and prepared for the higher service?   The answer is, that
going one day into the garden he found a Bible and read the
story of the raising of Lazarus from the dead.   The narrative
greatly interested him; the Redeemer's character seemed so
lovely.   He wept to think that he had so far sinned against
one so beneficent, and longed to call Him his Saviour, too.   In
short, the effect upon his mind was soothing and sanctifying,
and he again sought consolation in the Scriptures.   One of the
first passages which he read was Roman iii. 25:   "Whom God
hath set forth to be a propitiation through faith in His blood,

to declare His righteousness for the remission of sins that are past, through the forbearance of God."   "Immediately," he says, " I received strength to believe, and the full beams of the Sun of Righteousness shone upon me.   I saw the sufficiency of the atonement that Christ had made, my pardon sealed in His blood, and all the fullness of justification."

It was this great event, we believe, that furnished the occasion of the hymn. "There is a Fountain Filled with Blood ;" not that it was immediately written, but that it was the first, or among the first, of the sixty-six hymns which he wrote as his contribution for the Olney collection.   It is, indeed, a great hymn, and in spite of the distasteful simile of the first line, is, perhaps, the most popular in the language.   True, many a cold critic has stumbled at this metaphor; so high an authority as James Montgomery objecting to it, offended at it, re-wrote the first verse thus :

> From Calvary's cross a fountain flows
>   Of water and of blood,
> More healing than Bethesda's pool
>   Or famed Siloam's flood.

But the Church has long ago decided against James Montgomery and adopted William Cowper still in spite of the critics. Such men forget that the poetry of intense feeling like the swelling stream, often overleaps the ordinary channels of speech and demands bold figures for its utterance—that the inner sense takes hold of such figures—interprets such figures and feeds upon them to an extent which it could never do upon hard fact or cold literal statement.   The metaphor of Cowper is truer to the spirit and sympathy of the worshipper in his better hours than the cold and faultless verse of Montgomery, and, therefore, it is not wonderful that the lines of the one should be forgotten and that these strong, red lines of the first verse should be so popular the world over. What a power it is to-day, and has been for the last hundred years! Beneath it is the beating heart of the poet that had just emerged from a great horror of darkness, and the warmth of that new-born joy which even now, amid the shadows of time and the ills of life is often a joy unspeakable and full of glory. "It is one of those elect songs which has gone forth into all the earth, speaking in all earth's tongues, uttering the language of all Christian hearts, linking them forever with Christ's universal Church. With its memories of the cross and its anticipations of the crown, it has been as often the first song of the redeemed as the last prayer of the pilgrim on whose ears the murmur of the river comes up through the falling shadows, mingled with the sound of harpers harping with their harps." We must not close these notes without giving one or two illustrations of its powers.

John Cross, a very benevolent man and a successful Sabbath School teacher, living in London, England, had for a neighbor a notorious infidel—a man that thoroughly detested the great Name, and could not conceal his hatred should a clergyman approach him. He was an invalid, and his good neighbor, Cross, knew that he was not long for this world. It was in vain that he had gone to see him several times, for he would see no minister, no Sunday school teacher—no one who would come to him on a Christian errand. The last time he had tried to gain an entrance the infidel's wife met him at the door with a stout denial. "You must let me in," said the good man, "for your husband is dying." "If you do," she said, "it will be over my prostrate body, for he has given me strict charges to let none of your kind in." There was nothing for Mr. Cross but to leave and come away home. He had not long sat down when he heard one of the Sunday school children who lived hard by, singing this glorious hymn, and, gifted with a sweet voice, she was making herself easily heard all around. "Mabel," cried the good man, " would you mind going up to the chamber of that window (pointing to it) and singing that hymn to a poor man that is dying there?" "No, sir," and immediately left her gambols and prepared herself for her errand.   Mr. Cross gave her a handful of flowers and suitable directions.   Off she went with a light step, little knowing the greatness of the mission on which she was sent.   She is freely admitted, and walks right into the room where the man was lying.   She laid the flowers down on the table beside the bed and commenced her song as directed, but before she had reached the line : " When this poor lisping," etc., the old man having turned round to the child, was greatly moved—moved to tears—and, raising himself on his elbow, said, with a trembling voice : " Where, Oh, child, did you learn your hymn?" " In the Sunday school, sir," was the reply.   " And who is the teacher?" he continued.   Then a pause.   " Would you tell Mr. Cross"—pause—" I would like to see him?" " Yes, sir," said Mabel, and the next moment was on her feet.   The result may easily be inferred—a brand plucked from the burning !

Another, which I take from Mr. Duffield's collection : During the last revival in Ireland, Belfast, had a large share in its blessing.   Soon after it began the curate of the parish visited one of the factories, in which two hundred girls were employed. On his entering the building with the manager a young woman near the door, seeing her minister, began to sing with a sweet voice, " There is a Fountain," etc., to its touching and well-known tune.   The girl next her took it up and so onward it ran down the mill, till all the girls joined in with much fervency.   Great as was the noise of the looms, the tender, subduing voice of praise rose above the din and clatter of the machinery.   They wanted no books to sing that hymn—it was known to nearly everyone there.   The manager, a Manchester man and an infidel and ever on the watch to make sport of religion, was so completely overcome by that outburst of psalmody that he ran ont of the mill !   Meeting the curate afterward, he said : " I was never so hard put to it as this morning; it nearly broke me down." How the author, Cowper, would have been cheered to hear that chorus ! The trouble with Cowper was his deep sense of guilt and along with that a sense of God's justice.

> Blood for blood and blow for blow,
> Thou shalt reap as thou didst sow.

When Æschylus uttered this sentiment he uttered the deepest feeling of the human heart—struck the central chord of man's life. The whole of Greek tragedy is resonant with the same sentiment and so with the theology of the whole heathen world to-day, with all its temples and smoking sacrifices and long pilgrimages to distant shrines. What is the burden of the world's cry to-day ? The same as that in the prophets' day. Wherewith shall I come before the Lord and bow myself before the most high God. Shall I come before him with burnt offerings, with calves of a year old ? Will the Lord be pleased with thousands of rams or with thousands of rivers of oil ? Shall I give my first born for my transgression, the fruit of my body for the sin of my soul ? The answer to that great question—the question of humanity—especially man in darkness smarting under a sense of guilt is Cowper's hymn : " There is a Fountain Filled with Blood," etc.

HYMN XVI.

ALL HAIL THE POWER OF JESUS' NAME.

PERRONET'S GREAT CORONATION HYMN.

TUNE.—*Coronation.* BY O. HOLDEN, 1793,
or *Miles Lane.* BY SHRUBSOLE.

ALL hail the power of Jesus' name !
    Let angels prostrate fall ;
Bring forth the royal diadem,
    To crown Him Lord of all.

Crown Him, ye martyrs of your God,
    Who from His altar call ;
Extol the stem of Jesse's rod,
    And crown Him Lord of all.

Ye seed of Israel's chosen race,
    Ye ransomed from the fall,
Hail Him who saves you by His grace,
    And crown Him Lord of all.

Ye Gentile sinners ! ne'er forget
    The wormwood and the gall,
Go, spread your trophies at His feet,
    And crown Him Lord of all.

Let every kindred, every tribe,
    On this terrestrial ball,
To Him all majesty ascribe,
    And crown Him Lord of all.

Oh, that with yonder sacred throng
We at His feet may fall !
Join in the everlasting song,
And crown Him Lord of all.

Latin Version.

O JESU ! prepotens Nomen,
   Procumbant seraphim ;
Efferte stephanon ; Regem
   Cor'nate omnium.

Pulsate auream lyram,
   Sereni cherubim,
Chorique albi ; et Regem
   Cor'nate omnium.

Clamantes, martyres sancti,
   Imis altarium ;
Laus Jesse Filio ; Regem
   Cor'nate omnium.

O Israel electa gens
   Allata gloriam,
Pulsate auream lyram
   Cor'nate omnium.

Memento fellis Golgathæ—
   Quoque absinthium ;
Tropœas ferte ad pedes ;
   Cor'nate omnium.

Jungamus nos illic turbæ,
   Semper lætantium
Salute hâc redemptûm !
   Nam Rex est omnium !

L

THIS great hymn first saw the light in 1780. The author is Edward Perronet. He published quite a number of others, and though they all bear the stamp of his genius, this is the one that has found the highest place and secured for him an undying name. It is regarded by many as the most inspiring hymn in the language.

The author was the son of the Rev. Vincent Perronet, vicar of Shoreham, England, for fifty years. Edward left the Established Church in early life and became a Methodist. He was a bosom friend of the Rev. Charles Wesley, with whom he often travelled and by whom he was familiarly called "Ned." He was one of the preachers appointed under the patronage of the Countess of Huntingdon, and, adding much zeal and industry to a warm and sympathetic nature, his labors were greatly blessed. But Perronet at heart was a Dissenter, and as such opposed to Church and State connection, and publishing an anonymous poem under the name Mitre—a satire on the State Church—he brought down upon himself the frown of that noble lady. Thereupon he severed his connection from the Church and became pastor of a small congregation of Dissenters—so small towards the close of his long life that he could gather them in his kitchen. Yet it was to this handful of godly people the hymn was first presented, and by them first sung ! So obscure was the origin—so humble the circumstances in which this plant of renown that has filled the land took its rise.

The author died at Canterbury, 1792. His was a grand life and a triumphant death, and as an evidence of that holy fire which warmed his heart and that all conquering faith which sustained him in dark days, we quote the following as among his last words :

> Glory to God in the height of His divinity,
> Glory to God in the depth of His humanity,
> Glory to God in His all-sufficiency,
> Into Thy hands I commend my spirit !

It is not easy accounting for the genesis of this hymn.   The author was a preacher as well as a poet, and it was not unusual for the poet-preacher in those days, as Watts and Wesley and Doddridge, to close his sermon with a fitting hymn as a peroration.   In this way not a few of our great hymns, it is believed, came into being, as "Jesus shall Reign," "O God of Bethel," etc., and it is not unlikely that it was in this way that the hymn under consideration had its rise—a very obscure rise —a very humble origin indeed ; but God gave this word, this regal hymn, and great has been the company that has published it.   How grand the strain !   How fragrant with the one Great Name !   Hear how one speaks : *

"Crown Him Lord of all, of all worlds, all sovereignties, all in the realm of redemption, in the realm of grace, in the realm of nature.   "For by Him were all things created that are in heaven and in earth, visible and invisible, whether they be thrones, or dominions, or principalities, or powers.   All things were created by Him and for Him, and He is before all things, and by Him all things consist.   And He is the Head of the body, the Church, who is the Beginning, the first born from the dead, that in all things He might have the pre-eminence ; for it pleased the Father that in Him all fullness should dwell ; and having made peace through the blood of His cross, by Him to reconcile all things to Himself; by Him, I say, whether they be things on earth or things in heaven."   Even in the light of humanity and measured by earthly standards how great are His claims on our devotion.   Others beside Napoleon the Great, the disappointed emperor, and Rousseau the fascin- ating writer on infidelity, have sung his praises without yielding their hearts.   But the day is coming when all hearts and all homes shall be filled with His devotion.   There have been many kings that have filled a great space in public eye, but He is the greatest.   Other crowns flash splendour from stones

* Henry Ward Beecher.

beyond price, but no stone ever yet was to be valued with those spikes of thorns for glorious beauty. What is a diamond, an emerald, an opal, but mere cold, physical beauty? But every thorn in that crown is a symbol of Divine love. Every thorn stood in a drop of blood, as every sorrow stood deep in the heart of the Saviour. And the great anguish, the shame, the indignation, the abandonment, the injustice, and that other unknown anguish which a God may feel but a man may not understand—all these were accepted in gentleness, in quietness, without repelling, without protest, without examination, without surprise, without anger, without even regret. He was to teach the world a new life. He was to teach the heart a new ideal of character. He was to teach a new power in the administration of justice. A Divine lesson was needed—the lesson that love is the essence of Divinity—that love suffering for another is the highest form of love—that love when administered carries with it everything that there is of purity and power and justice, and not only that love is the fulfilling of the law, but that God Himself is love, and this lesson He has taught us in the cross.

One great excellency of this hymn is its strongly objective character. It does not ask us to look in upon the working of our own hearts. It makes no demand on our experience, our patience, etc. Christ is an object—a person—not a doctrine. It deals with a great outward reality and not with the inward state—a living Church, His willing obedience even unto death, the grandeur of His triumphs, the glories of His reign, the homage of all ages and orders of intelligent beings in heaven above or on earth below, and calls upon them to join in the chorus; and this it does in terms so direct, simple, martial in their strain and withal so fitted to touch the imagination and quicken the soul that the coldest heart is ready to respond and the dullest intellect to take in the situation. Some of our hymns appeal to our love, our faith, our experience, to such a high experience in the Divine life that comparatively few can understand them or at least enter into their spirit; but this hymn is for all classes and all ages, the young and the old, the learned and the unlearned, the believer that is far advanced in the Divine life and the believer that has just taken christian ground and cast in his lot with the Lord Jesus.

We need not wonder then at the power of this hymn, and as an illustration let me cite the following: Mr. William Reynolds, of Peoria, Illinois, the well known Sunday school worker, tells the following, which he had from the lips of the missionary himself. This missionary, Rev. E. P. Scott, while labouring in India, saw on the street one of the strangest looking heathen his eyes had ever lit upon. On inquiry he found that he was a representative of one of the inland tribes that lived away in the mountain districts and that came down once a year to trade. Upon further investigation he found that the Gospel had never been preached to them and that it was dangerous to venture among them because of their murderous tendencies. He was stirred with much desire to break unto them the Bread of Life. He went to his lodging-place, fell upon his knees and pleaded for Divine direction. Arising he packed his valise, took his violin with which he was accustomed to sing and his pilgrim staff, and started in the direction of the Macedonian cry.

As he bade his fellow missionaries farewell, they said, "We shall never see you again. It is madness for you to go." For two days he travelled, scarcely meeting a human being, until at last he found himself in the mountains surrounded by a crowd of savages. Every spear was pointed at his heart. Not knowing of any other resource he tried the power of singing the name of Jesus to them. Drawing forth his violin he began with closed eyes :

All hail the power of Jesus' name ! etc.

Afraid to open his eyes he sang on till the third verse, and while singing this verse—

> Let every kindred, every tribe, etc.—

he opened his eyes to see what they were going to do, when, lo! the spears had dropped from their hands and the big tears were falling from their eyes. They afterwards invited him to their homes, an invitation which he gladly accepted. He spent two years and a half amongst them. His labours were greatly blessed, and he had so won upon their affections that when he was compelled to leave on account of impaired health for this country, they followed him for thirty miles. "O missionary," they said, "come back to us again." He has gone back and there he is labouring still.

We could fill many pages with illustrations of the power of this regal hymn—how in some instances it has roused whole congregations that had been at ease in Zion—lifted them to a higher life, breaking in upon the coldness and deadness and barrenness of souls, but this must suffice. Christ is King of glory, His name the mighty power that will expel every demon and fill every soul. How little was this apparent in the days of the flesh! We think of him going about continually doing good, making long journeys on foot, and sometimes sitting down weary by the way. We think of him dressed in the common serge of the people, content to eat the brown bread of the peasantry,—his face radiant with a holy enthusiasm, never darkened by improper emotion, always calm and self-possessed, never taken by surprise or thrown off his guard -- and so diligent that every hour was consecrated to some noble end. Often for him there was no rest. When others withdrew to their homes he often withdrew to his favorite solitudes, the mountain or the garden, where his head was wet with the dew and his locks with the drops of the night. "Oh could some prophet's prayer have touched the eyes of those that stood about Him, that for a moment they might have seen the sight behind and within the flesh, how strange would have been their gazing! How would the spiritual beauty and power have risen up before him! Stand by him now and look down through centuries to come." From this point of view interpret the passage, "Who for the joy that was set before Him endured the cross, despising the shame." Ages are to roll by; nations are to die, and nations are to rise and take their places; laws are to grow old and new germs from laws are to unfold; old civilizations are to crumble and new eras are to dawn with higher culture; but to the end of time it will be seen that this figure stands high above every other in the history of man! A Name which is above every name—like ointment poured forth, given to Him, not for the sake of fame, but for a far higher end—to win many sons and daughters to glory. The crown of thorns is the world's crown of redemption. The power of suffering love which has already worked such changes in the world is to work on with nobler disclosures and in wider spheres.

HYMN XVII.

JUST AS I AM, WITHOUT ONE PLEA.

THE GREAT HYMN FOR ANXIOUS INQUIRERS.

TUNE.—*Faith.* BY C. A. GARRATT.

JUST as I am, without one plea,
    But that Thy blood was shed for me,
And that Thou bidd'st me come to Thee,
    O Lamb of God, I come !

Just as I am, and waiting not
To rid my soul of one dark blot,
To Thee, whose blood can cleanse each spot,
    O Lamb of God, I come !

Just as I am, though tossed about
With many a conflict, many a doubt,
Fightings and fears within, without,
    O Lamb of God, I come !

Just as I am, poor, wretched, blind,
Sight, riches, healing of the mind,
Yea, all I need in Thee to find,
    O Lamb of God, I come !

Just as I am, Thou wilt receive,
Wilt welcome, pardon, cleanse, relieve !
Because Thy promise I believe,
    O Lamb of God, I come !

Just as I am (Thy love unknown
Has broken every barrier down),
Now to be Thine, yea, Thine alone,
  O Lamb of God, I come !

Latin translation—same measure.

T̲ALIS ut sum, cum sola spe.
    Tu immolatus sis pro me,
Et jubes ire me ad Te,
            O Jesus Te veni.

Talis ut sum ; nec demorans
Ut maculosus et purgans
Se frustra, flam innocens,
            O Jesus Te veni.

Talis ut sum, turbatus sim
Pavoribus, et fuerim
Tam opicus ; sed nunc vellim,
            O Jesus Te veni.

Talis ut sum, miserrimus,
Nudus, cæcus, obnoxius
Ubique, egens, omnibus,
            O Jesus Te veni.

Talis ut sum, recepies
Purgabis, libens ignosces,
Et quia credo, quam prodes !
            O Jesus Te veni.

Talis ut sum, tuus omnem
Defregit amor objicem
Et nunc me esse unicum,
            O Jesus Te veni.

THIS is one of the few hymns which immediately on its publication rose to the surface, and took rank as one of the great hymns of the church,—a position which it still holds, and which from its very nature it must continue to hold for ages to come. The authoress, Charlotte Elliot, was born one hundred years ago (18th August, 1788), at Brighton, England. She was granddaughter to the celebrated Henry Venn, minister of Huddersfield, the author of "The complete duty of man," and the friend and companion of John Wesley. Eling, a daughter of Mr. Venn, married Charles Elliot, Esq., of Brighton, and Charlotte, our authoress, was the third of their six children. Two of her brothers became clergymen and two of her sisters died early, and she lost her godly father in 1833. On the death of her mother, 1843, her home was broken up, and shortly afterwards she and her only surviving sister went to the continent. Finally they settled in Torquay, England, and for fourteen years it became their home. After this she returned to Brighton—her birthplace, which she never left except once and that only for a little season. There she died in 1871, at the great age of eighty-two. But though she reached this great age her health for long years had been very delicate and her sufferings often very great—sufferings all the harder to be borne from the fact that till the age of thirty-three she was a stranger to the consolations of the gospel, but not an indifferent stranger. On the contrary, she had many an hour of deep anxiety in regard to her salvation—many a doubt and fear—many an aspiration after the better life. Had she only been less sensitive—less cultured—less emotional she might have thrown aside her scruples, and dismissed those strange questionings that ever and anon arose in her soul. Walking in the shadow of an unsettled controversy from year to year; conscious of the truthfulness of religion on the one hand and her distance from God on the other, her felt isolation was distressing in the extreme. From her childhood she had grown up in an atmosphere of much refinement and piety, and like many a brilliant woman of a highly musical and æsthetic education, lapsed into a state of chronic ill-health.   Yet her fine sensibility and familiarity with suffering had much to do with her inward reach and grasp of thought—her poetic insight. We see the same thing in such cases as Anne Steele and Frances R. Havergal, and not less in such cases as Cowper and Francis Lyte.   Explain it as we may, there can be no doubt that suffering, both outward and inward, has much to do with this spiritual insight into truth—that it is the hand which "strikes the strings with fingers that ache and bleed which brings forth the sweetest music—that it is the soul that has been quickened by suffering, improved by culture and refined by grace that is able to rise on the highest wing and speak of the deep things of the Spirit.   Let no one attempt to write poetry whose experience in life has always been soft and easy—flowing on like a crystal tide—who lies down every night with soft content about his head, and rises every morning refreshed and rubicund from his unbroken slumber.   Who does not know that the ministry of suffering has not been wanting in the case of our greatest poets —that beneath the noblest of our hymns we may still hear the undertone of woe—the wrench, the buffetings of the world, the tramplings of the feet of the vintner in the wine press giving forth the blood red juice of the grape which we prosaic mortals so thoughtlessly enjoy ?   An appreciation of this fact should teach us to approach those great hymns of the church with reverence, and to handle them with piety—fitted as they are to bring us into fellowship with Him from whom cometh every good and perfect gift, and into closer communion with those bright spirits who labored, and into whose labors we have entered.

Now how about the *genesis* of this hymn —the circumstances under which it came into being ?   This question carries us back to 1822 when the Rev. C. Malan, D.D., of Geneva, made a visit to the family. From that date a new life was open to Charlotte. The blessed Spirit has spoken to her through the saintly teacher. Her weary soul was free, and in the thirty-third year of her age she was rejoicing in her newly found liberty. Dr. Malan did not attempt to unravel all her entangle-ments. "Dear Charlotte," he said, "cut the cable, it will take too long to loose it—cut it. The wind blows and the ocean is before you, and the Spirit of all power is waiting to be gracious." She cut the cable, "waiting not"—and how many since then have been enabled to follow her examples while singing these lines.

Just as I am, etc.

We have to add that Dr. Malan was a guest of her family at the time this took place —that the anniversary of his first visit to the family was ever observed as a festive day with its mem-bers and that for forty years—that is to the close of his life— he maintained a correspondence with Charlotte which proved to be a great blessing to her. Dr. Malan was a skilful physician of souls, and the remedy which he brought to bear on this desponding spirit was the simple remedy of entire trust in the words of God. Miss Elliot's tastes were literary, and up to this time she had given much attention to the poets and the best English authors ; but following Dr. Malan's advice she laid aside for a time desultory reading, and began the study of the Word, the glory of which every day dawned more clearly on her soul.

Charlotte Elliot had an invalid friend in Dublin, Ireland, Miss Kiernan. She was the successful editor of the *Christian Remembrancer*, an annual volume of texts, enriched and illus-trated by careful selections and original poems, all designed to minister to the higher life. This lady on her death-bed, expressed a desire that Miss Elliot should take up her work, and so carry on the *Yearly Remembrancer*. She did so, and in complying with Miss Kiernan's request, added a number of her own poems, and among these—*Just as I am, etc.* Thus quietly, even anonymously, this wonderful hymn began its career than which no one has been more honored and owned by the Master in the recent times of refreshing with which the church has been favored from on high. Many a heart has been touched by it. Many a one has rejoiced in its light. One English lady was so struck with it, while yet floating about anonymously, that she had it printed as a leaflet for the benefit of anxious inquirers with no idea of its authorship. It curiously happened while Miss Elliot was at Torquay, England, under the care of an eminent physician, that he one morning placed the leaflet in her hand, saying he was sure she would like it. Great was the surprise of both parties, she in recognizing her own hymn and he in seeing the author ! Perhaps there is no hymn in the language which reveals more clearly the way of salvation, and probably no one has led more souls to Christ, and has been more blessed in raising up those that were bowed down, and in carrying them forward into the glorious liberty of the children of God.

There is one fact that should be noted here before closing. Nothwithstanding her feeble health she went through a great amount of literary labor. Besides the *Christian Remembrancer* —the periodical referred to, which she edited for twenty-tive years, she contributed 115 hymns of her own—all anonymously. In 1836 she published " Hours of sorrow cheered and comforted," and about the same time a new edition of Miss Kiernan's " Invalid's Hymn Book," much enlarged by herself. Then all through she was a frequent contributor to the periodicals, and maintained in spite of her poor health a spirit of great activity and cheerfulness. Her religious experience is worth quoting : Speaking of her illness and consequent sufferings, she says :—" He knows and He alone, what it is, day by day, hour by hour, to fight against bodily feelings of almost overpowering weakness, languor and exhaustion, to resolve not to yield to slothfulness—depression and instability such as the body causes me to long to indulge, but to rise every morning determined to take for my motto, ' If any man will come after Me, let him deny himself, take up his cross and follow me.' "

The following lines are from a loving epistle to her sister written in the prospect of death :

> Sweet has been our earthly union,
> Sweet our fellowship of love :
> But more exquisite communion
> Waits us in our home above ;
> Nothing there can loose or sever
> 'Tis ordained to last forever.
>
> Place me in those arms as tender,
> But more powerful far than thine ;
> For a while thy charge surrender
> To his guardianship divine :
> Lay me on my Saviour's breast
> There to find eternal rest.

HYMN XVIII.

THE HOUR OF MY DEPARTURE'S COME.

TUNE—*Soldau.* BY H. DIBDIN. From an old German Chorale of 13th Century.

THE hour of my departure's come ;
I hear the voice that calls me home ;
At last, O Lord ! let trouble cease,
And let Thy servant die in peace.

The race appointed I have run ;
The combat's o'er, the prize is won ;
And now my witness is on high,
And now my record's in the sky.

Not in mine innocence I trust ;
I bow before Thee in the dust ;
And through my Saviour's blood alone,
I look for mercy at Thy throne.

I leave the world without a tear,
Save for the friends I hold so dear ;
To heal their sorrows, Lord, descend,
And to the friendless prove a friend.

I come, I come, at Thy command,
I give my spirit to Thy hand ;
Stretch forth Thine everlasting arms,
And shield me in the last alarms.

The hour of my departure's come,
I hear the voice that calls me home ;
Now, O my God ! let trouble cease ;
Now let Thy servant die in peace.

Latin translation.

MIGRANDI hora advenit,
   Audita vox hinc me vocat,
Nunc, O mi Deus, tristitia
   Cesset ; demumque gaudia,
Satûtus cursus et bellum
   Preteriti ; mi premium ;
     Nunc versatûrus angelis ;
     Nunc approbatus sublimis.

Ignoro innocentiam,
   Pronus ad te profiteam ;
Per sanguinem Jesu Christi
   Speravi veniam Dei.
Emigrans, est mi non dolor,
   Ni pro amatis versor ;
     Benignus eis, O Deus,
     Amicis orbis, et prodes.

Adsum ad tuum mandatum,
   Do in tuas manus animam,
Eternis protege alis,
   Defende me in extremis.
Migrandi hora advenit,
   Audita vox hinc me vocat ;
     Nunc, O mi Deus, tristitia
     Cesset, demumque gaudio.
          S. T. RAND.

THE author is Michael Bruce, fifth child of Alexander and Ann Bruce, whose eight children all died young— Michael outliving all the others. Their home was in the little hamlet of Kinneswood, on the banks of Lochleven, on the south-western declivity of the Lomond Hills, It is a place of surpassing beauty, and this must have been especially so in the poet's day, when as yet no whistle of steam train was heard, and no unsightly smoke stack was to be seen pouring forth its black volumes over the fair landscape. I can never forget my visit to that lovely spot some years ago, which, in spite of the unsightly spectacles referred to, and the huddling together of a mixed and foreign population, is a place where the tourist loves to linger. It is there, especially among the old ash trees that skirt the village, where you will hear the note of the cuckoo in the early spring, the song of birds in the gloamin', and the fall of distant waters, clear as crystal, making their way from the Loch to the Clyde—just the place for a poet to live in, like Hogg or Ferguson or Hugh Miller or Robert Burns, who all learned their first lessons from clouds and stars and stones and the ever-varying aspects of nature.

Here in this village, in a small thatched cottage, Michael Bruce was born, March 27, 1746. Here he herded cattle, making himself useful in many ways, learned his first and best lessons from his pious parents and fed upon the beauty of the landscape as a never-failing source of delight. He was a lovely child, "slenderly made," his biographer says, "with a long neck and a narrow chest; his skin white and shining; his cheeks tinged with red rather than rudy; his hair yollowish and inclined to curl." He was poor, for his father was a humble weaver; but, poor as he was, managed on the strength of a small legacy of two hundred marks—say sixty dollars—bequeathed to his father, and which his father had given to him for this end, to enter the University of Edinburgh. This took place in his fifteenth year; and at the age of nineteen we find him, during the summer vacation, teaching in a school, and at the same time preparing for college and writing poetry. One of his poems, composed at this time, is called "Lochleven," written in blank verse, possessing the simplicity, perspicuity—the truthfulness to nature—and all the liquid sweetness of a Grey, a Thompson or a Pollock. Another was his "Ode to the Cuckoo,"

M

said to be the finest of the kind in the English language, of
which we must give a few verses:

> Hail, beauteous stranger of the wood,
>   Attendant on the spring !
> Now heaven repairs thy rural seat
>   And woods thy welcome sing.
>
> Soon as the daisy decks the green,
>   Thy certain voice we hear ;
> Hast thou a star to guide thy path,
>   Or mark the rolling year?
>
> Delightful visitant, with thee
>   I hail the time of flowers,
> When heaven is filled with music sweet
>   Of birds among the bowers.

The poor young divinity student was happy in such engagements. His eye was bright with the fire of genius, and still
more with a hope full of immortality ; but the damp room in
which he taught (Forest-hill, near Alloway), the grinding
poverty of his humble lot, and the hard study which he had to
maintain from day to day, were too much for him. His slender
frame gave way. Consumption took hold upon his vitals, and
so he returned home to die—a home already made desolate by
the hand of death. On the 5th of July, 1767, the disease had
finished its work, and, feeling that the end was near, he wrote
these lines which have been so often repeated since his day :
"The hour of my departure's come," etc. Under his pillow
his Bible was found, marked at the words, Jer. xxii. 10 : "Weep
not for the dead, neither bemoan him ; but weep sore for him
that goeth away ; for he shall return no more, nor see his native
country."

But the saddest part of the story has to be told. At college

young Bruce had made the acquaintance of a classmate named
Logan, and to Logan he committed his writings with the view
of publication—a matter which gave sorrow to the old man,
the father, the humble weaver of Kinneswood; for Logan
proved recreant to his trust, and deceitful in every respect.
Often the old man would go to him, inquiring about his son's
papers. Many of the villagers knew of the poems and kept
speaking of them to him. Not a few could repeat his favourites
—especially the "Cuckoo." They, too, had been expecting to
see them in print, but year after year passed, and still no
appearance of anything of the kind. At length, in 1772, a
few of the poems were published; others in 1784; and still
more in 1787—that is, twenty years after the death of the
author.

Meanwhile Logan published poems of his own, or poems
which he claimed as his own, and, among these, the "Ode to the
Cuckoo." "But it happened," as Mr. Duffield says, "that the
Ode to the Cuckoo was a poem of such merit that inquiry was
set on foot, and Logan was detected and exposed. He had
boldly appropriated the writings of Bruce by confusing his own
with them – laying, in fact, his own cuckoo eggs in their
midst—and the controversy which grew out of this fraud was
destined to be among the most celebrated in English literature.
It is reviewed in the *British Quarterly* for 1875, pp. 500-513.
Principal Shairp also sums it up in *Good Words* for November,
1873. In every recent publication the case is decided against
Logan." And among the appropriations of Logan were eleven
paraphrases, which for long years bore the name of Logan,
but which should have borne the name of Bruce. These are:
8, 9, 10, 11, 18, 23, 31, 38, 53, besides the hymn under consideration. These eleven became part and parcel of the
psalmody of the Church of Scotland upon the recommendation
of a committee, and have now been in use for over a century.

The Rev. John Logan, whose name is now in such bad odour

became minister of Leith, and for a long time was looked up to as a man of mark, wearing the gay plumage of another, and well pleased to see so many burning incense to his drag.   For long years he played the part of a successful plagiarist, not only stealing hymns, but sermons.   But at length the judgments of heaven fell thick and heavy upon his devoted head.   Intoxicated with praise to which he had no claim, he became irregular in his life, dissipated in his habits, fantastic in his notions, and useless as a minister of Christ.   He took to the literature of the stage, and composed what he called the tragedy of " Runny-mede "—a matter which gave great offence to his parishioners. At length he passed away, " unwept, unhonoured and unsung," and now his name is hardly ever mentioned, but as furnishing an illustration of literary theft—the most villainous known in these last days.

But to return to Michael Bruce, the divinity student.   He died at the early age of twenty-one years and three months—penning this touching hymn as his last effort.   His biographer speaks of him in terms reminding us of Reginald Heber, con-cerning whom it was said that if all students were like him we might have reason to doubt the doctrine of original sin.

Like Heber, Bruce was a youth of beautiful character, pure in life—full of promise—but hear how he speaks :

> Not in my innocence I trust ;
> I bow before Thee in the dust ;
> And through my Saviour's blood alone,
> I look for mercy at Thy throne.

Innocence !   What does mortal man, born in sin, know about innocence in the sight of God !   What can the pale light of the oil lamp stuck in the miner's cap do in the light of the glorious sun ?   The saintliest life in eternal light is dark, and the most advanced Christian, in drawing near to the gates of death, can only say what young Michael Bruce said: "Not in mine innocence I trust," etc. It is strange how, in the presence of death, the purest life seems dark, and that the wisest and best feel their need, then above all times, of the great atonement. Bishop Butler, whose beautiful life was equal to his great attainments, and whose Analogy has proved such a bulwark against the foe, said to his chaplain on the eve of his departure, "There is one passage which gives me great comfort.—'Him that cometh unto Me, I shall in no wise cast out.'" (John vi. 37.) Similar is the experience of thousands of the wisest and best of our race, as to innocence.

The culprit that has brought disgrace on his name may, in other scenes—in other lands—rise above the repressing influences that follow in the track of a gigantic fraud, and rehabilitate himself with something like the prestige of former days; but in the higher relationship—in the case of the sinner uncleansed and unforgiven, there is no such possibility. In all places, in all ages, the eye of Omniscience will follow him, and the ban of an ostracism which no change of scene or lapse of time can lift. There is a possibility of wiping out everything that stands against him, and covering himself with an honour that will fill men with admiration; but in the higher relationship there is a strange indelibleness. Here the awful past, with all its hateful and repressing memories, must remain. Here conscience condemns, and if she condemns to-day she will condemn to-morrow—forever. In such a case the man is always on his trial; the judge is always on the bench; the culprit always at the bar; the blood stains are always crying from the ground. It is not only God that asks for an atonement, and the honor of His love to be maintained, but man himself that asks for it, and no easy good-natured act of forgiveness without such an atonement, will bring peace, even if that were possible. What the aroused conscience wants is not simply an act of amnesty, but an act of amnesty founded on

righteousness—on a law magnified and made honorable ; for
the conscience sympathizes with the law. So that the sinner
is condemned not only by an outward law, but by that inner
witness which also lifts its accusing voice and condemns him to
his face. There is a divinity within man as well as without
man that cannot take peace till it sees that it is a right thing .
for God to forgive sin—right for Christ's sake to restore men to
fellowship with the Father and the Son. The voice of condemna-
tion without and the echo within are one; so let no one look for
a deep and blessed peace without both the one and other being
satisfied. It is this great fact in our mental economy that
explains such an utterance in view of death as that of the poet,
" Not in mine innocence I trust," etc. For fair, beautiful, as
the life of young Bruce was, he felt that it was dark when held
up in the eternal light, and that his was a guilt which nothing
but the purest blood in the universe could obliterate.

I would not dismiss this hymn which, when read in the light
of its history, must always awaken a tender interest, without
giving at least one illustration of its quickening and refreshing
power; but here I must write under the restraints which
family connections impose, for the person now referred to was
one belonging to our home circle on the female side, one that
lived in the old land. Gifted alike by nature and grace, distinguished at once by the beauty of her person and the beauty
of her life, she had awakened a very considerable interest in
the country, at least in the circle in which she moved. Her
literary taste—her scholastic attainments, were far above the
average, and had her remains been published she would certainly have won for herself an honorable name. But this it
seems has never been contemplated, and it is not likely that it
will ever be done now. Like young Bruce, she became a victim
of consumption and, at an early age, a helpless invalid. She
knew that death was near, and, conscious of his sure, steady,
inexorable step, she often thought of this hymn, and when her

bright eye grew dim and lover and friends were removed into darkness, she repeated it as her own felt experience, and shortly after passed away, leaving the world without a tear save for the friends she held so dear. Much the same may be said of the Rev. A. Ogilvie Brown, minister of Campbellton, N.B., who died April, 1889, leaving the fairest record behind him and closing a young life full of promise. Almost his last utterance was that of the hymn :—" The hour of my departure's come."

HYMN XIX.

THE GREAT SCOTCH COMMUNION HYMN.

TUNE.—*Communion*, BY EDWARD MILLER, MUS. DOC.

'TWAS on that night, when doom'd to know
   The eager rage of ev'ry foe,
That night in which he was betray'd,
The Saviour of the world took bread :
And, after thanks and glory giv'n
To him that rules in earth and heav'n,
That symbol of his flesh he broke,
And thus to all his followers spoke :

My broken body thus I give
For you, for all ; take, eat, and live,
And oft the sacred rite renew,
That brings my wondrous love to view.
Then in his hands the cup he rais'd,
And God anew he thank'd and prais'd ;
While kindness in his bosom glow'd.
And from his lips salvation flow'd :

My blood I thus pour forth, he cries,
To cleanse the soul in sin that lies ;
In this the covenant is seal'd,
And Heav'n's eternal grace revealed.
With love to man this cup is fraught,
Let all partake the sacred draught ;
Through latest ages let it pour,
In mem'ry of my dying hour.

Latin Translation.

HAC nocte Jesus designatus
  Dare pœnas inquinatus,
Est proditus nocte eâdem
Salvator mundi cepit panem.

Tum Deo gratiis actis
Qui presit universis vitis,
Symbolum carnis Is fregit
Discipulisque sic dixit :—

" Meum corpus do fragendum
  Scelera ad expiandum ;
O edite ut revivatis
Et sæpe ritum renovatis."

Calicem quoque Is cepit,
Iratiis actis his dedit,
Dicens, omnes hanc bibatis
Ritum semper et colatis.

Sanguinem sic mi profundo
In februa vobis—pro mundo,
Hoc signatum testimentum
Dei gratiam ad monstrandum.

E proculoque hoc divino
Fideles bibant—repleno
Immutato mi amore,
In memoriam sacræ horæ.

This has been Scotland's communion hymn for generations ;
and though a goodly number of fair rivals have entered the
field since it first saw the light, it still holds its high place,
and bids fair to do so for generations to come. It has taken a deep
hold of Presbyterian worshippers, not only in Scotland but the

world over; and if anything will move the heart of a recreant backslider, who in former days and in other scenes vowed everlasting allegiance to his Lord, and in token of his allegiance sat down at his table in deep silence and solemnity, and took into his hands the sacred emblems of His broken body and shed blood, it is the singing of this hymn, while "the elders are preparing the table," to the old tune he loves so well.

And so, on the other hand, this hymn is no small means of grace to the faithful worshipper, to whom the dispensation of the Lord's Supper has ever been dear, and who in the wane of years and amid the lengthening shadows of his little day has his eye upon a far off land where the sun shall not go down any more, where the moon shall not withdraw herself, and the days of mourning shall be ended.

Any hymn that like this has maintained its place through the siftings of generations,—that has stood the crucible of the public taste and met the devotional feeling of the church in its deepest and purest hours for one hundred years and more, has asserted its right to live. There is not one in fifty of the new hymns that does so. What has been the doom of the great proportion of the Wesley's seven thousand hymns? Oblivion. Not more than sixty or seventy, at the most, can be found in all our modern hymnals, except in that of the Methodists themselves. And similar, though not to the same extent, has been the doom of the great proportion of the hymns of other writers. Even our paraphrases, culled with such care from many gifted pens, have suffered severely, so that no minister ever thinks of making use of more than one-half of them.

Now the consideration that this is one of the hymns that has stood the winnowing process of years—that it has not only a place in our psalter, but such a warm place in our hearts,— that it is in constant use in Scotland and the world over at communion seasons, proves that it must possess elements of a high order; and in looking over it once more, we should say these are purity, simplicity, spiritual insight, fidelity to the Scriptures and warm but not overstrained devotion.

The quality of age is an important quality in wine. A cask of Burgundy, twenty years old, is of more value than one only twenty days. And the quality of age, or rather the quality which is imparted to a hymn through age, is not to be lightly regarded. It is an adventitious quality, no doubt, but still a quality that carries power. A hymn that is entirely new— that has no tender associations connected with it—no hallowed memories stretching away back into past years, must from the nature of the case, occupy an inferior position, even though it should be equal in all other respects. It is a stranger, very pretty it may be, but it must be tried and tested, and found worthy of our affection before it is admitted to our friendship. The elements of age and association do not count for much with young worshippers, or with minds given to change, even when engaged in compiling hymnals, but nevertheless they are elements that contribute not a little to the power of a hymn; and for illustration of this fact we need not go farther than the one under consideration. Certainly, if any hymn can claim these qualities in a high degree, it is the thirty-fifth para-phrase—Scotland's communion hymn—the hymn which has been the vehicle of the purest devotion for over a century, when her children scattered far and wide, gather around the mercy seat of the everlasting Father.

The ordinary passage is one of the most solemn utterances of our Lord—an utterance that touches the imagination as well as the heart, and so far may be considered poetic, not in the sense of unreality, but in the sense of solemn beauty. The language our Lord uses, deals with a great mystery—one too high for us to understand, yet one in which we feel we have a stake—language which we cannot read without being struck with its simple majesty and its awe inspiring power. The translator has caught the spirit of the Master on that memorable night, in which the ordinance of the Holy Supper was instituted, and done justice to his words, for they have lost nothing of their power—their simple grandeur, or the spirit of deep reverence and awe which belong to the original. This spirit of reverence—this solemn beauty of which we speak, is common to all the great hymns, and especially the hymns of Scripture, like the Magnificat of Mary, or the song of Moses on the banks of the Red Sea on the morning of the nation's deliverance from the hosts of Pharaoh, and such furnish no warrant for the use of the fondling words and terms of endearment, that we often see in modern hymns, as "Dear Saviour," "Sweet Jesus," etc.

But how about the author of this hymn? That is a question which many a one has raised, for the name of the Rev. John Morrison, D.D., does not appear in any of the common manuals of English literature. How few of the many thousands of Israel that make use of his communion hymn on their solemn holy days, know anything about him? He seems to have been a man of a very retiring disposition, yet a splendid scholar, an able preacher, and one greatly beloved and honored in his day. From the few notices that can be gathered concerning him, it appears that he was born in the parish of Carnie, 1750, that he studied at King's College, Aberdeen, spent a few years as a teacher in the parish school of Thurso, and in the year 1780, at the age of 30, was ordained minister of the parish of Canisbay.

Gifted in a high degree with poetic insight, he must have felt the pleadings of the muse to linger around Parnassus, and give himself to such congenial engagements; yet his one aim seems to have been to instruct his flock in the great matters pertaining to the kingdom, holding forth the word of life, preaching Christ to the hardy fishermen of that northern shore, to the end that he might gather in a people that should be to the praise of His grace in the ages to come.

And would the reader like to know something of the scene of Dr. Morrison's ministry,—the parish where he labored,—the grave where his ashes lie? Then let him take his map of Scotland and look towards the north—away up towards the shores of the Pentland Firth—near the high cliffs of Duncansbay Head, and within a mile or so of Johnnie Groat's house; and he will find the parish of Canisbay, and the most northern church on the mainland of Great Britain. Here, amidst a rustic people, traders, sailors, farmers, fishermen, he labored for eighteen years—labored till he died, holding forth the word of life.

I have before me now a sketch of the church, kindly furnished me by the Rev. James McPherson, M.A., the present distinguished minister of the parish, to whom I am indebted for accurate information, and from this sketch I conclude that it must be visible to the vessels making their way along the neighboring shores of the Pentland. It is antique in its figure, unpretentious in style, while in its appearance, fitted to accommodate, say three or four hundred worshippers, and approached by a gently sloping path, leading upwards from the public road right to the church door. Then before the church on the green knoll on which the church is built, and over which this sloping path leads, is the grave yard of the parish where the ashes of some of our forefathers sleep, but where costly monuments and grand epitaphs are rare. Here is the resting place—marked in the sketch by the pencil of Mr. McPherson—of Dr. John Morrison. Here his ashes have reposed for about ninety years; and his last child, a daughter, dying about a year ago, left a five pound note, with the desire that an appropriate memorial-stone might be raised over her father's grave. To his credit be it said, Mr. McPherson has carefully seen to this matter, got the desired stone erected, and thereon a suitable inscription engraved, setting forth that he was minister of the parish for eighteen years, and that he was the author of the paraphrases

numbered in our collection :—19, 21, 27, 28, 29, 30, and 35—
this last the hymn under consideration.

We have only space to notice another question which may
be raised in connection with this great hymn,—and that is its
genesis.   How came it to find a place in the service of the
Church ?   The answer is, that in Dr. Morrison's early day, and
for long years before he became minister of Canisbay, there was
no such thing known in the Scottish church as hymns or paraphrases, though in the dissenting chapels in England, such
were beginning to make their way, and great was their popularity.   But the Scottish church had to content herself with
the often-rugged verse of the Psalter and the Psalter alone, and
celebrate the praises of God and the glories of redemption in
the terms of prophecy and in the symbolic language of the Old
Testament Scriptures.   This was all the more felt, seeing other
churches were now using hymns and paraphrases that did much
to quicken the spiritual life of congregations.   Then the poet
Burns, with his magic verse, was stirring the heart of Scotland,
and about the same time the mellifluous voices of Hogg and
Tannahill.   In these circumstances many a friend of the Church
was raising the question :—" Can nothing be done to improve
our congregational singing—might not the psalms of the Old
Testament Scriptures be supplemented by paraphrases of important passages from the New Testament Scriptures ?"   The
result was that a committee, of which the Rev. Dr. Hugh
Blair, the Rev. Dr. John Morrison, the Rev. John Logan, and
the Rev. William Cameron were members, was appointed (1775)
by the General Assembly to prepare such translations and
paraphrases as would likely supply the felt-want of the church
in this respect, and in six years later the paraphrases were
published in their present form, sixty-seven in number, with
five hymns appended.   The committee reported in that year
recommending the use of these paraphrases and hymns, but the
church to this day has taken no further action !   Their use is a

mere matter of tolerance, not of sanction. This is the answer
to the question, Whence the origin of Scotland's communion
hymn,

'Twas on that night when doomed to know, etc.

Dr. Morrison and the generation to whom he ministered
have long ago been gathered to their fathers, but through this
great hymn he is ministering to the church still—holding
communion with the church still—communion with all saints,
and will continue to do so till he, whose right it is to reign,
will come again without sin unto salvation, and gather in his
elect from the four winds of heaven an exceeding great army—
now stained with many imperfections, but then all shining in
the beauty of holiness, numerous as the drops of dew in the
womb of the morning! All around his once northern home
storms and tempests rage, and many a noble vessel is stranded
on the shore; but all is peace " over there,"—the holy calm of
the everlasting Sabbath—the rest that remaineth for the people
of God. Here, his communion with God must have been often
intercepted by the press of worldly care, and his vision of God
often dimmed by reason of human imperfection; but what is
there now to come between him and the eternal light, or break
in upon those pleasures which are forever at God's right hand?

HYMN XX.

SUN OF MY SOUL, THOU SAVIOUR DEAR.

KEBLE'S GREAT EVENING HYMN.

TUNE.—*Abends*, BY SIR HERBERT OAKELEY, M.A., MUS. DOC.,
also *Hursley*, a Huguenot melody and a great favorite in most congregations.

GRAY'S "Elegy" is a poem, which for finish, polish and the perfect smoothness of its versification, stands at the very summit of modern literature. The same remark may be made concerning the "Christian Year," the name of Keble's book of hymns; so called, from the circumstance that the hymns are arranged in the order of the festivals and fasts, or holy seasons, of the Church of England during the year. The book has had a wonderful success, ninety-six large editions having been disposed of in the author's lifetime; and in 1873, when the copyright expired, 305,500 copies had been sold; and, since that date, we know that the circulation has enormously increased both in England and America. A book that has commanded such a sale, and has taken such a hold of the hearts of thousands, stirring the very fountains of thought, and voicing the deepest aspirations of men, must be regarded as a great gift to the Church. Sir J. T. Coleridge, speaking of the hymns as a whole, says there is nothing equal to them in the language; and Prescott declares, "I know of no body of uninspired poetry where purity and power—the knowledge of the Holy Scriptures, the knowledge of the human heart, where the love of nature and the love of Christ, are so wonderfully combined."

The book was the work of years, the offspring of much

thought and revision. The author had intended that years of
labour still should be spent upon it, bringing the hymns up to
the loftier ideal in his mind; but such was the importunity
that was raised for their publication that he yielded. At the
same time, I venture the remark, that it is not so much for
their strength, as their calm beauty and wonderful finish, that
they have won their way to their high place. This is certainly
the case with the hymn under consideration.

English Hymn.

SUN of my soul, Thou Saviour dear !
  It is not night if Thou be near ;
O may no earth-born cloud arise
To hide Thee from Thy servant's eyes.

When the soft dews of kindly sleep
My wearied eyelids gently sleep,
Be my last thought, how sweet to rest
For ever on my Saviour's breast !

Abide with me from morn till eve ;
For, without Thee, I cannot live,
Abide with me when night is nigh ;
For, without Thee, I dare not die.

If some poor wandering child of Thine
Have spurned to-day the voice divine,
Now, Lord, the gracious work begin,
Let him no more lie down in sin.

Watch by the sick, enrich the poor
With blessings from Thy boundless store ;
Be every mourner's sleep to-night,
Like infant's slumbers, pure and light.

N

Come near and bless us when we wake,
Ere through the world our way we take,
Till, in the ocean of Thy love,
We lose ourselves in heaven above.

Latin Hymn.

O Jesu, tu Sol animæ,
  Quum propius non tenebræ,
Terrestria ne patere
Te oculis contegere.

Quum somni rores subdulcis,—
Quum cadunt pallebræ graves—
Sit cura ultima, Jesu,
Quiescam brachiis noctu.

Morator mane ad noctem,
Nam te absente non possum
Durare ; ac mortis umbrâ
Emittas, Christe, jubera.

Siquisque aberrans longe
Contempsit lucem hodie,
Cubare sine ne cæcum,
Illustra hac nocte eum.

O vigila juxta ægrum,
Ditaque donis inopem,
Nocteque sit mæsti somnus
Infantis similis dulcis.

Salvator ! adsis tu mane,
Periculis feram ante,
O semper in te quiescam
Ad seculorum seculum !

But who was this J. Keble who has proved such a blessing
to the Church, and wen for himself such a name? The answer
is, The son of the Rev. John Keble, vicar of Coln, St. Aldwins,
Gloucestershire, England. He became a classical scholar of
great distinction, taking many prizes, and graduating with a
double first (1810), though only eighteen years of age. Such
was his reputation that he was appointed professor of poetry in
the University of Oxford in 1831, and on the death of his
father (1835), he succeded to the vicarage, which he had held
for over fifty years ; but *that* he exchanged for Bisley, Hamp-
shire, the following year, and this he held for thirty years—
held till, under a stroke of paralysis, he sank into unconscious-
ness, and passed away into the great spirit land in his seventy-
fourth year, whither he was followed by his beloved wife,
Charlotte, youngest daughter of the Rev. George Clarke, of
Fairford, a few months afterward.

Will it be believed that this spirit, so devout—so ethereal—
this master of sacred song, whose life was so beautiful, and
whose heart was so responsive to the great truths of the Bible,
was the leader of the High Church party in England, and the
real author of the Tractarian movement (1833), which carried
so many gifted spirits into the bosom of the Roman Catholic
Church? Certainly this is the view of Cardinal Newman; but
in vain do we look for any tint or trace of Tractarian teaching
in these hymns. Great is their variety, great their scope and
compass ; many are the themes handled, and the voices raised,
but there is no dissonance in the notes, no false or uncertain
sound in the utterances—nothing to offend the most orthodox
ear. The hands may be the hands of Esau, but the voice is
the voice of Jacob—the inspiration that of the Father of Lights,
from whom cometh every good and perfect gift.

What is the genesis of this hymn? How came it to be
written? Was there any special providence in the life of the
author at the time that led to its composition? This is one

feature pertaining to the history of the great hymns of the Church which should be kept in view, seeing that a knowledge of the circumstances in which the hymn was written lends not a little to its charm and its power, but concerning this we find nothing authentic. All we know for sure is, that he had given himself to the task of preparing hymns adapted to all the holy seasons observed in the Church of England during the year, and that this is one of the course.

It may be that in his meditations on death, he had some presentiment of that fatal stroke of paralysis under which he sank—that his spirit, so ethereal, so bright with the beauty of holiness, pierced through the veil of coming years, realized in fancy that solemn hour when the wheel should be broken at the cistern, and the silver cord should be loosed, and in the way of anticipation sang

> Abide with me when night is nigh ;
> For, without Thee, I dare not die.

But all this is conjecture. This is a secret that eternity alone can reveal ; but there is no conjecture or doubt as to its power. Who that has ever heard it sung as it ought to be sung will ever forget it—and will not in his best moments thank God that He put it into the heart of John Keble to write this grand hymn ? It is one of those utterances that is fitted to touch every heart, saint or savage, young or old. It is only the other day I had a letter from a friend who is labouring among the Cree Indians, N. W. T., telling me that it has been translated into their vernacular and that there is nothing more popular than this sacred song among them. He often hears the children, he says, lulling themselves to sleep with the words upon their lips : Here is what he says :—

"I shall try to give you the hymn of which you speak in the Cree. We have but a poor translation and not much of it ;

still what we have is much appreciated by the Indians and even
our Indian children attending our schools, I frequently hear
them lull themselves to sleep by it.   You will notice that though
each line has the proper number of syllables there is no attempt
at rhyme.   Then the words are long and very little can be
expressed in one line.   I shall give you as a specimen one or
two verses, and the words as we sing them with the literal
translation, but though the hymn is a great comfort to the
Indians, the translation is poor—much inferior to that in the
English language.

Sun of my soul, etc.

Ne-ta-tchak O pe-se-mo-ma
No-pe-ma-tche-e-wam tche-sus
O a-ka-we-ya ka-sos-tow
Ke-ya ke-ta-tos ka-ya-kav

Literal translation.

O my soul, O Sun
    My Saviour Jesus
Do not hide
    From your servant

Es-pe a-te-ne-pa ya ne
Es-kwa-yach me-ka-kes-ke-sen
A-e-se-me-way-ye-tak-won
Tche-sas a-ka-ma-wa-ye-met

Translation.

When I go to sleep
    The last I remember
I shall be happy
    That Jesus keeps me

O we-tche-wen kapa-ke sehk
Ke-ta kan a wa-ye-me yav
O we tche wen ka pa te pisk
Ke ya ka-pe-ma tche e yak

Translation.

Be with me all the day
Keep me
Be with me all the night
Thou art my saviour

A deputation of the tribe or that portion of the tribe under the instruction of the Presbyterian Church in Canada, N. W. T. waited upon the synod of Manitoba, May, 1886, with the view of pressing their claims upon the church. They told their story very well and at the close sang this hymn and probably made a deeper impression on their hearers than they could have done by the most gifted oratory. This hymn is doing its work among the Crees and from this case we can see what a power there lies in sacred song. All through the history of the Church, notably in the sixteenth and seventeenth century it has been the great vehicle of instruction, often reaching hearts that could not otherwise be reached and doing a work for which the preacher as such was utterly incompetent. Who does not know that the living preacher,—the personal reproach, or the word of remonstrance, however kindly meant, often leads to a stormier opposition. But this is never the case with such sacred song as that we are now considering. They never provoke, their influence is silent as the dews of the night, and as effective too, casting down imaginations and every high thing which exalteth itself against the knowledge of God and bringing into captivity every thought to the obedience of Christ.

HYMN XXI.

ABIDE WITH ME !

TUNE.—*Eventide,* BY W. H. MONK.

ABIDE with me ! fast falls the even-tide ;
The darkness deepens ; Lord, with me abide !
When other helpers fail, and comforts flee,
Help of the helpless, O abide with me !

Swift to its close ebbs out life's little day ;
Earth's joys grow dim, its glories pass away ;
Change and decay in all around I see :
O Thou who changest not, abide with me !

Not a brief glance I beg, a passing word ;
But as Thou dwell'st with Thy disciples, Lord,
Familiar, condescending, patient, free,
Come, not to sojourn, but abide, with me.

Come not in terrors, as the King of kings,
But kind and good, with healing in Thy wings ;
Tears for all woes, a heart for every plea :
Come, Friend of sinners, thus abide with me.

Thou on my head in early youth didst smile ;
And, though rebellious and perverse meanwhile,
Thou hast not left me, oft as I left Thee :
On to the close, O Lord, abide with me !

Latin translation.

Maneto mecum ! Prepotens !
    Ad finem Vesper properans ;
Increscunt graves tenebræ,
Inopum Spes, maneto me.

Exilis ætas transiit.
Et orbis splendor defecit.
Fugacis gaudia vitæ,
O Semper Idem ! maneto me.

Non brevis mora, visio,
Sed globo ceu discipulo
Olim'; O clemens Domine !
Sic facilis maneto me.

Ne ceu Rex regum adveni.
Sed suavis ; ceu ros vesperi.
In pennis sanitas—lacte
Melæque fessis, maneto me.

Juventâ jam immemori
Perversâ subridisti mi ;
Et nunquam deserebas me
Toties deserentem Te,
        O maneto me.

THE name of the Rev. Henry P. Lyte, M.A., the author, has already been introduced in these notes, in connection with that no less admired hymn, " Jesus, I my cross have taken." Though of English parentage, he was born in Scotland, near Kelso, June 1, 1793. Admitted to Trinity College, Dublin, 1812, he rose to distinction as a student and three times won the prize for the best English poetry. In the same year he penned the celebrated ode to a spring flower,

"Hail, lovely messenger of Spring," reminding us of the yet more celebrated "Ode to the Cuckoo," by Mr. Bruce, said to be the finest in the language. He had intended the practice of medicine, but on his graduation we find him taking orders in the English Church, and soon after serving as curate in different places, one after the other, but all the while making good use of his time and writing not a few of his celebrated hymns. Those who have had the joy of gliding on the waters of the lovely river, the Dart, in Devonshire, will remember a point amid its green lawns and fenny slopes where the village of Detteshan lies in dreamy stillness and simple beauty. Here the wandering curate nestled in a cottage, going out now and then to officiate in Lower Brixham, which at length became his parish. Here for over twenty years he toiled away amid many a cloud of trouble—personal affliction, pastoral discouragement —amid a rough, sea-faring people that had been subjected to all the corrupting influences peculiar to a neighborhood where naval and military forces often had a footing during the French war. Here he carried on his blessed work, caring both for the bodies and the souls of men, preaching the Word, making hymns—hymns for the children, hymns for the hardy fisher-men, hymns for sufferers like himself. Bnt the hymn most admired of all, unless it be " Jesus, I my cross," is the one under consideration—the one that is sure to find a place in every collection. It was composed under very solemn circum-stances. His health, not being good at any time, had been rapidly declining, and he was advised to make a trip to the South to see whether a change of air and a warmer climate would not do something to arrest the progress of consumption. Some twenty years before this, when the symptoms first de-veloped, he had found relief by a sojourn on the Continent of Europe, and on his return tried the air of Bristol, then Lym-ington, where he wrote his charming tales on the Lord's Prayer. In the same way he found relief in 1842, 1844 and

1846. But now the disease was far gone, and there was little to hope from a change of climate. Still that was the prescription—leave the ocean and go to the south. Concerning this command he wrote a friend, saying :—" I hope not, for I know no divorce I should more deprecate than from the ocean. From childhood it has been my home, my playmate, and I never have been weary of gazing on its glorious face." However, there was nothing for it but to go. But before going, he, weak and scarcely able to crawl, resolved to meet once more with his people, administer to them the Lord's Supper, and say some parting words, and he did so. The scene was peculiarly solemn, and his words must have been memorable. There were the symbols of the Saviour's death—the broken bread and the poured forth wine—there the people to whom he had ministered so long, that had so often grieved him by their coarseness and carnality, but who were still dear to him—and there, too, was the weary minister, standing on the great border land, with the shadows of the long night gathering around him. Feeling that this was the case—anticipating the change that was coming on his mortal body—he spent the evening of that memorable day writing this hymn (originally eight verses), and thereupon handed the manuscript to a friend.

Shortly afterwards he started on his journey, but by the time he reached Nice, France, he was entirely prostrated. There he died, and pointing upward said, " Joy," " Peace." His age was 54. Now, in view of these facts, let us read over again this hymn, first in English, then in Latin (same measure as in English :)

Such was the genesis of this great hymn—the hymn that stands only second to " Rock of Ages," according to the vote of the readers of Sunday at Home. In their choice of the best one hundred they place " Rock of Ages," first, this second, the votes being respectively, 3,215 and 3,204.

The hymn was the offspring of sorrow—the last note of the

great minstrel, which swanlike, he had reserved for the last. It would seem as if our most precious things were born of suffering—that before the heart can utter anything that will be lasting and helpful to others, it must be rung with grief. The child's range on the gamut of life is limited, and the lover of ease, whose days pass on like a dream, cannot be expected to touch the lyre with a master hand. No heart can touch other hearts to any great extent which has not had a large experience and been made to drink of the bitter cup. Shakespeare, Byron, Burns, Coleridge, Cowper and the Wesleys must have had an inner history of which the great outside world knew nothing.

Let us deal gently in our judgments with the temper and the oddities we find in such writers,—those high priests of nature that, on coming down from the mount, gave way to a little feeling when handing us their messages :—

> " Be tender to the seers that lack
> The wild bird's song, the wild bird's wing to rise,
> And bathe their souls in light of summer skies.
> The poets who gather truth with bended back,
> And give forth its speech as on the rack—
> Speech urgent as the blood of grapes that dyes
> His garments who must tread it out with sighs.
> Think of the vintage which they bruise
> For you—the wine of life you daily use.
> Count it no marvel if they should pine
> Who feed on dregs of that poured forth as wine."

Be this as it may, the author of this celebrated hymn was a sufferer, a sufferer for many years. He early lost his father, Captain Thomas Lyte, an officer in the Royal army, and not long after his pious mother. He had to struggle hard to get through the university in consequence of straitened circumstances. He had to bear the stroke of wounded affection—slighted love—concerning which he wrote in 1815. " Yes! I am calm and humbled now !" Far more, he had to bear the hiding of God's countenance for a season and grope in darkness as one that had no light. In short, his was a long life of suffering—suffering from poor health and probably still more from poor success among his rough though warmhearted people. It was in such ways that our author poured forth his wine— the wine we daily use. So with F. R. Havergal, whose life was so beautiful and death so like a translation ; so with the gifted McCheyne, the saintly pastor, whose six years' work in Dundee did more for God and humanity than that of ordinary men prolonged over half a century ; so with Milton, whose blindness and domestic troubles seem to have quickened his spiritual sensibilities and enabled him to walk in the light that is inaccessible,

"The light that never fell on land or sea."

Count it no marvel, then, that H. F. Lyte should have been such a sufferer, that this polished shaft had to endure, for he could only be made perfect through suffering. Thank you, O gifted seer, for your work of faith and labor of love on earth, and especially for this precious hymn, breathed out on the evening of that holy Communion Sabbath when you spoke to your people for the last time. Thank you for its great lesson. It will help us in our life of faith—help us to realise the presence of the Master when all around is dark—help us in the evening of our little day, when the shadows of the long night are falling—help us by speaking of a Companion ever near, when lover and friend are removed into darkness and when the spirit, weary with the battle of life, is about to pass away into that sphere where the sun shall no more go down, where the moon shall not withdraw herself and the days of our mourning shall be ended.

HYMN XXII.

JESUS, I MY CROSS HAVE TAKEN.

Tune.—*Bethany.* By HENRY SMART.

JESUS, I my cross have taken,
　　All to leave and follow Thee ;
Destitute, despised, forsaken,
　　Thou from hence my all shalt be !

Go, then, earthly fame and treasure !
　　Come disaster, scorn and pain !
In Thy service, pain is pleasure ;
　　With Thy favour, loss is gain.

Man may trouble and distress me,
　　'Twill but drive me to Thy breast ;
Life with trials hard may press me,
　　Heaven will bring me sweeter rest.

O 'tis not in grief to harm me,
　　While Thy love is left to me !
O 'twere not in joy to charm me,
　　Were that joy unmixed with Thee !

Take, my soul, thy full salvation ;
　　Rise o'er sin, and fear, and care ;
Joy to find, in every station,
　　Something still to do or bear.

Think what Spirit dwells within Thee !
What a Father's smile is thine !
What a Saviour died to win thee !
   Child of heaven, shouldst thou repine

Haste, then, on from grace to glory,
   Armed by faith and winged by prayer ;
Heaven's eternal day 's before thee,
   God's own hand shall guide thee there.

Latin translation.

SUSTULI, Salvator, crucem
   Ut hinc sequar Te solum,
Inops, sperna, derelicta,
   Hinc Tu mihi omnia.

Vale, laus humana, nugæ
   Mundi ! mi deliciæ
Olim ; Christi munera, —
   Salutis pura gaudia

Quid quamvis homo fatiget !
   Propiorem me aget ;
Suavior quies erit cœlo,
   Labore tunc peracto.

Non est doloris nocere,
   Tuus amor perfulgens ;
Non est gaudii lætari,
   Tuus amor non fulgens.

Sume, anima, salutem,
   Cito, plenam, liberam ;
Curam omnem supersurge
   In Deo tam secura.

Puta dona Spiritûs—
   Christum qui sit mortuus
Pro te, et æternum domum
   Et magni Patris oculum

E gratiâ ad gloriam
   Propera, dans Deo laudem ;
Nunc, fide semper valida
   Seculorum secula.

THE origin of this hymn is interesting. According to
Henry Ward Beecher ("Plymouth Pulpit," page 410),
it took its rise from the case of a young woman born in
splendour, but disinherited by her father, because of a great
offence—her conversion to a faith which he despised, and her
quiet but resolute adherence to her profession.

There are parents, in a certain sense believers, and profess to
be believers. There are many that have just enough of faith
to shield their consciences, and save themselves from being
counted infidel. They believe in a kind of mutual protective
christianity which takes care of their anxieties and fears—a
christianity which allays all their troubles in this respect, but
nothing more. The idea of a perfect manhood, a cleansed
conscience, a purified heart, an imagination radiant with heavenly
truth—the idea of a great overwhelming affection that like the
sun pours its rays down upon all their faculties—the idea, in
short, of an entire consecration as the result of such down-
shedding, has never entered their mind. The world, the world,
the beautiful world, with its ambitions and its pleasures, is their
all. In these circumstances think of a daughter, young, beautiful,
opening up in all the graces of early womanhood—one who is
the coyest, sweetest thing in the whole neighborbood—one who
has studied in the best schools, and has taken on the most
graceful finish they can impart. She is an only child, and
many a suitor looks on in her direction. Many a one rises up

to call her blessed, for with an open hand she dispenses to the poor, and with an unconscious charm she makes her way to every heart, and, but for some noisy, ranting preacher, might have occupied a grand place in the world! It is vexatious to such parents to see such an one brought under his power, to see the child that is the joy of their hearts and the pride of their life carried away with religious excitement. Their hopes are crushed. The father is in a rage, and the mother is in grief; and they will not have it so. How does the child act during the storm? With simple modesty she is patient but tenacious, and bears the storm that is without by the blessed peace that is within. She is still loving and more obedient than ever, except on this one point. Having tasted the better portion, she will not give it up; and so great, some times, has been the rage of the father, that he has actually driven the child from his door and dispossessed her of every thing. I am here stating the case in a general way. I mean a case of fealty to Christ amid great temptations; and it was really such a case as I have drawn that gave birth to this touching hymn. Returning from a ball, the daughter of a wealthy man in England heard a Methodist service going on. She went in, and by the blessing of God was converted, and when she made known her faith and purpose to her father, and stuck to her purpose against all remonstrance, he cast her off in a rage and dispossessed her of every thing.

This is something like the representation given us by the great Congregational divine; but Dr. Hatfield who has earned the right to speak on such matters, gives us another version of the *genesis* of this hymn. He thinks it took its rise from the conversion of the author, the Rev. F. Lyte, then (1825) curate of Taghmon, Ireland. It seems that this distinguished clergyman, to whom we owe so much for his great hymns such as this hymn and

Abide with me, fast falls the eventide,

was called to see a brother minister who was at the point of
death, and found himself entirely unprepared for offering to him
the consolations of the Gospel. This led him to look into the
grounds of his own hope, and he was convinced that his heart
had never been savingly renewed. Together they sought and
found the Lord. His friend died in peace, and he himself lived
to serve the Lord as he had never done before. His was indeed
a real consecration. This took place at the time (1825) when
the hymn was written, and Dr. Hatfield thinks that probably
the poet's conversion was the occasion of its *genesis*. Still
there is nothing inconsistent with all this in the representation
which we have cited. Both of these may be perfectly true,
and the poet in drawing from his own experience would be in a
position to do ample justice to the case of the young woman
whose loyalty to the Great King in the circumstances must
have touched his poetic sensibility.

I would not here refer to the life of the author, delightful as
the theme is, reserving that for another occasion—my annotations on the hymn,

Abide with me,

certainly one of the great hymns of the Church, and having a
genesis than which there is nothing more touchingly beautiful
in the language. As to its power—the power of the hymn
under consideration—the power of awakening the godless to
serious thought—as well as the power of stimulating, refreshing,
encouraging those that have already taken Christian ground,
it has had a wonderful history. It is our one great consecration
hymn, and should be used on stated occasions, when consecration
is the theme of the preacher. The writer can never forget its
power in this respect on a particular occasion—how that on one
memorable Sabbath evening when specially addressing young
women, after pleading with them to take higher ground and
consecrate themselves afresh to the Lord, one remained to speak

o

with him and tell him how that under the divine blessing all
her scruples had been overcome by the appeal, backed as it was
with this, the closing hymn. She had lingered long, hesitated
much, but now she could resist no more, hold out no longer ;
and so she quietly, unostentatiously made herself over to God
in a covenant never to be forgotten.

This was the result of light admitted into the soul—of turning the eye of faith on the Lamb of God. And this if consecration is the universal result whether in Christian or Heathen
lands, and whether the sinner will or will not receive the grace
of God.

The very first convert in India won to Christ by Dr. Duff
furnishes us with an illustration of this kind. We refer to the
case of Mohesh Chunder Hose—a high caste Hindoo, and the
editor of the most influential newspaper in India. Dissatisfied
with the teachings of the priests he had secretly renounced the
faith of his childhood, but in the absence of something to rest
his soul upon, he was miserable. At length coming under the
power of the truth and the influence of such a saintly life as
that of Dr. Duff, the great Scotch Missionary, he could hold
out no longer, and in spite of himself became a convert, took
Christian ground and faced the storm of persecution which he
knew he would have to bear. This was the case with Dr. Duff's
first convert, and similar was the case of the second—Gopinah
Mundi – afterwards the distinguished missionary of Futtepore.
Giving up father, mother, houses, lands,—all their patrimony,—
for that is the penalty in India for apostatising from the heathen
religion and espousing Christ,—those two young men entered
into liberty and a richer inheritance. They soon found how
true the words of the Lord Jesus were : Verily I say unto
you no man shall lose father or mother or houses, etc. This
was their experience and so they could easily say,

"Jesus I my cross, have taken."

HYMN XXIII.

LEAD, KINDLY LIGHT.

A WONDERFUL HYMN.

TUNE.—*Lux Benigna.* BY REV. J. B. DYKES MUS. DOC.

JOHN HENRY NEWMAN, the author of this hymn of surpassing beauty and tenderness, has had a remarkable history.
We find him at the early age of fourteen (City of London,
England, where he was born in 1801) taking delight in such
authors as Hume and Tom Paine, in short, strongly infidel in
his tendencies if not in his convictions; but shortly after recalled to the faith of his fathers through the reading of Romaine
and other Calvinists, and immediately giving his heart to the
God of all grace, delighting himself greatly in the discovery
which he had made and making a vow of perpetual celibacy
that he might serve the Lord without let or hindrance.

He was a scholar of no mean rank, having been elected
fellow of Oriel in 1822, and chosen as Whateley's vice-president
at Alban Hall in 1825, where he began his famous university
sermons, published in 1841. I have never seen anything finer
of the kind than those sermons. They are not to be compared
with those of F. W. Robertson or John Caird for ponderous
strength and splendid utterance, but in spirituality of tone, in
solemn beauty, in touching tenderness—in his marvellous
insight into divine truth and his honest dealing with the
thoughts—yea the very fountain of thought which he stirs—
bringing all into view those special aspects of truth which he

would bring to bear on those thoughts—he is, in my humble judgment, unsurpassed.

As an evidence of the power of those sermons of Newman, I may mention that I tried their effect on one unusually sensitive in the matter of error, especially Roman Catholic error. I did so by reading a portion of them from time to time, carefully concealing the author's name. Again and again that person, delighted with thoughts set off in such felicitous style, would stop me and demand who the author was, who could so write and so move to tears through the dull, dead page of a book. Great was the astonishment and chagrin when at length the name was given—John Henry Newman, the supreme dignitary of the Roman Catholic Church in the British Islands. And as an instance—the only one for which we have room—of the power of this hymn, we give the case of Catharine Tait— the wife of Archibald C. Tait, Archbishop of Canterbury, whose memoir he wrote so wisely and lovingly, that to-day there is no more popular piece of biographical writing to be found. On drawing near the close of life, her daughters sang to her some favorite hymns; "Lo, He Comes with Clouds Descending" and "Lead, Kindly Light, Amid the Encircling Gloom." When they had finished, I (the Archbishop) repeated to her again the last lines, inscribed by her desire on the frame of Grispine's picture of the children we had lost at Carlisle:

> And with the morn those angel faces smile,
> Which I have loved long since and lost a while.

"Yes, yes," she repeated, and either then or a few minutes before she spoke of those of us, who had gone before stretching out their hands to welcome her. Soon she became unconscious. After I had offered the commendatory prayer, her breathing ceased with a gentle sigh. She was gone.

At page 35 of the book "*Apologia pro Vita Sua,*" we have a full account of the *genesis* of this hymn—the circumstances under which it was composed ; and I copy a few sentences culled by another hand setting forth these circumstances.   He had in 1832, thirteen years before his going over to the Roman Catholic Church, gone to visit Italy, and on his way home got becalmed on the Mediterranean—a whole week at the shoals of Bonifacio.   He had, moreover, been subject to great alternations of thought and feeling in the matter of religion and had by no means reached a state of rest for his soul, and so he was eminently in a mood for striking such a chord as that which runs through these lines.   "I was aching to get home, yet for want of a vessel I was kept at Palermo for three weeks.   At last I got off in an orange boat bound for Marseilles.   Then it was that I wrote the lines, 'Lead, kindly Light,' . . . I have for years had something of an habitual notion, though it was latent and had never led me to distrust my own convictions that my mind had not found its ultimate rest and that in some sense or other I was on a journey."

According to Mr. Rigand, of Magdalen College, Oxford, a great admirer of Newman, the thoughts of this hymn are expressed in one of his sermons, namely, the second of the second volume.

L EAD, kindly Light, amid the encircling gloom,
  Lead thou me on ;
The night is dark, and I am far from home,
  Lead thou me on ;
Keep thou my feet ; I do not ask to see
The distant scene ; one step enough for me.

I was not ever thus, nor prayed that Thou
  Shouldst lead me on ;
I loved to choose and see my path ; but now
  Lead thou me on !
I loved the garish day, and spite of fears,
Pride ruled my will : remember not past years.

So long thy power has blest me, sure it still
          Will lead me on,
O'er moor and fen, o'er crag and torrent, till
          The night is gone,
And with the morn those angel faces smile.
Which I have loved long since, and lost awhile.

We also furnish a Latin translation of surpassing excellence,
for which I am indebted to another hand.

DUC alma Lux, circumstat umbra mundi,
          Duc, alma Lux ;
Est atra nox, mei jam vagabundi
          Sis ergo dux ;
Serva pedes—non capio longinqua
Videre ; satis semita propinqua.

Non semper eram, ut nunc, doctus precari,
          Ductorem Te—
Magis me exploratorem gloriari ;
          Duc tamen me.
Præclara amabam, neque expers timorum
Regebam me ; sis immemor actorum.

Tam diu præsens adfui vocanti
          Divina vox.
Sic erit vel per ima dubitanti,
          Dum fugit nox ;
Et mane lucent nitidæ figuræ
Notæ per annos pallulum obscuræ.

John Henry Newman had scarcely settled down to his work
as a parish minister when he began to revolve certain great
questions of a theological character, which did much to unsettle,
not only his own mind, but the minds of thousands—questions
which at one time threatened to rend the great English Church

into two parties—the High, or Romanising party, and the Low, or Evangelical party. In June, 1833, he had written :

O, that thy creed were sound !
For thou dost soothe the heart thou Church of Rome.

He had been looking in this direction for years. He was Vicar of St. Mary's, Oxford, from 1828 to 1843, where his preaching produced a profound sensation. Here began the "Oxford movement," which has left such a deep mark on the Church of England, the results of which are still so widely seen and felt. "Its positions," says Rev. M. F. Bird, "were set forth in the famous *Tracts for the Times*," of which Newman wrote twenty-four, including No. 90, Feb., 1841. The outcry over this put an end to the series and cleared the author's way to his spiritual home.

We are curious to know something of the youth of one who has filled so large a space in the public eye for so many years— something of the opening grace of one whose ripe age is still so illustrious, and whose life, upon the whole so melancholy and phenomenal, has left such a deep mark upon the age ; but of this we have comparatively nothing from his own pen, but a writer in the *Catholic Times*, speaking of his early life, says : " On most Sunday afternoons during the last year of the first decade of the present century two boys, aged respectively 9 and 5 might have been seen playing in the gardens of Bloomsbury Square, London. The boys, both natives of the Square, offered the most complete contrast to each other in appearance. The younger, whose head was profuse with long, black, glossy ring- lets, was a child of rare Jewish type of beauty and full of life and activity. The other was grave in demeanor and wore his hair close cut, and walked and talked and moved in a way, which in young people is called " old-fashioned." He was of pure English race and Puritan family. The names of the children denoted these differences as much as their appearance. The one was Benjamin Disraeli, the other John Newman."

As to Newman's appearance in early life Mr. J. A. Froude, who was an undergraduate at the time Mr. Newman was made tutor in Oriel in 1826, describes him as "above the middle height, slight and spare. His head was large, his face remarkably like that of Julius Cæsar. . . . . His was a temper imperious and wilful—a disdain for conventionalities, but along with it a most attaching gentleness, sweetness, singleness of heart and purpose. He seemed always to be better informed on common subjects of common conversation than anyone present. He was never condescending with us undergraduates, never didactic or authoritative, but what he said carried conviction along with it. Perhaps his supreme merit as a talker was that he never tried to be witty or to say remarkable things. Ironical he could be, but not ill-natured. Not a malicious anecdote was ever heard from him, and for hundreds of young men '*Credo in Newmannum*' was the genuine symbol of faith, and is still unconsciously the faith of nine-tenths of the English converts to Rome."

The same authority, speaking of his sermons, says: "No one who heard them in those days can ever forget them. They were seldom directly theological. We had enough of that from the select preachers of the University. Newman, taking some Scripture character for a text, spoke to us about ourselves, our temptations, our experiences. His illustrations were inexhaustible. He seemed to be addressing the most secret consciousness of each of us, as the eyes of a portrait appear to look at every person in a room. He never exaggerated; he never was unreal. A sermon from him was a poem—welcome— how welcome—welcome from its sincerity, interesting from its originality, even to those who were careless of religion; and to others who wished to be religious, but had found it dry and wearisome; it was like the springing of a fountain out of the rock. On one occasion he described closely some of the incidents of our Lord's passion, then he paused. For a few moments there was a breathless silence. Then in a low, clear voice, of which the faintest vibration was audible in the farthest corner of St. Mary's, he said: 'Now I bid you recollect that He to whom these things were done was Almighty God. It was as if an electric shock had gone through the church, as if every person present understood for the first time the meaning of what all his life he had been saying. I suppose it was an epoch in the mental history of more than one of my Oxford contemporaries."

From the book referred to, " *Apologia pro Vita Sua*," we can trace the path which led him to the Church of Rome and the successive steps he took in that direction. Strange that the reading of Butler's " Analogy " should have been one of these ! From Sumner's book on " Apostolical preaching," he accepted baptismal regeneration ; from " Dr. Hawkins, on The Authority of Tradition," he accepted Apostolical succession ; from Rev. W. James and Butler's " Analogy " the doctrine of a visible Church in the Roman Catholic sense. Nay, he went a step further, and contended that every abstract truth should be presented to the people in a visible emblem, as under the ancient dispensation. Then his friendship with Froude, Keble, Pusey and others of that class developed in him an admiration for the Church of Rome in spite of all its errors, and a strong dislike for the Reformation with, as he thought, its blind iconoclasm and its ruthless spoliation. Accepting these and kindred views with all the power of a warm and sympathetic nature, it is not strange that he should at length throw up his living (vicar of St. Mary's and chaplain of Littlemore) and go over to the Church of Rome, which he did in 1845.

Dr. Newman is an extensive author. His writings run up into some thirty volumes, including his poems—or, as he calls

them,—verses on various occasions ; of which we give a specimen
in closing.   It is the piece on " Warnings."

When heaven sends sorrow,
  Warnings go first,
  Lest it should burst,
  With stunning might,
  On souls too bright
To fear the morrow.

Can science bear us
  To the hid springs
  Of human things ?
  Why may not dream
  Or thought's day gleam
Startle, yet cheer us ?

Are such thoughts fetters ?
  While faith disowns,
  Dread of earth's tones,
  Recks but Heaven's call,
  And on the wall
Reads but Heaven's letters.

It was in 1879 that Father Newman was called to Rome to
receive the highest honor at the disposal of the Pope—the
honor of Cardinal.   The ceremonials lasted four days, conducted
with great pomp and before large assemblies and high dignitaries
of that Church.   At the close he sank under the fatigue and
excitement.   He was prostrated by fever, and for some days it
was feared that he would not long survive the occasion ; but
when his strength rallied the Pope permitted him to choose his
future home, and he gladly returned to the quiet retreat of
Edgburton cloisters, where he was received even with tears of
joy.   There he lives in the ripeness of a rare old age spending
his days in quiet study.   There the aged pilgrim now tranquilly

awaits his summons to the better country where all the great
names of earth and the great leaders of men, such as Calvin,
and Arius, and Knox, and Pusey, and Wesley, and Whitfield,
and Newman are forgotten and merged into that great Name
which is above every name in heaven and in earth, where the
great distinction is not sprinkling or dipping or genuflexion,
but righteousness and peace and joy in the Holy Ghost.

HYMN XXIV.

MY FAITH LOOKS UP TO THEE.

Tune.—*Olivet,* By Dr. Lowell Mason

MY faith looks up to Thee,
   Thou Lamb of Calvary,
      Saviour divine ;
Now hear me while I pray ;
Take all my guilt away ;
O let me from this day
      Be wholly Thine !

May Thy rich grace impart
Strength to my fainting heart,
      My zeal inspire ;
As Thou hast died for me,
O may my love to Thee
Pure, warm and changeless be,
      A living fire.

While life's dark maze I tread,
And griefs around me spread,
      Be Thou my Guide ;
Bid darkness turn to day,
Wipe sorrow's tears away,
Nor let me ever stray
      From Thee aside.

When ends life's transient dream,
When death's cold sullen stream
      Shall o'er me roll,
Blest Saviour, then in love,
Fear and distrust remove ;
O bear me safe above,
      A ransomed soul.

Latin translation.

FIDES vertit ad Te,
    O Agne Calvaræ,
  O Lux mundi,
Audito dum orem,
Auferto mi labem
Ut pro Te unicum
    Me fieri.

O sint opes tuæ
Labente me fusæ
    Agentes me !
Es quia mortuus,
Mi amor perpetuus,
Divinus, mutuus
    Delectans Te.

Dum ambulans cæcas
Vias, obnoxius,
    Me regito
Affer Lux tenebras,
Absterge lacrymas,
Et semper venias
    Auxilio !

Quum finis omnium—
Quum vitæ somnium
    Evanuit ;
Amore in tuo,
Salvator, abferto
Mi metus ituro
    In gloriam.

DR. RAY PALMER, son of Hon. T. Palmer, Compton,
    Vermont, besides being a noted preacher for forty years,
    and a popular writer for about half that time, is a poet
of no mean order. His is the gift, in a remarkable degree, of
infusing a spirit of tenderness into his lines and clothing even

his common places with a solemn beauty which is itself poetic. We quote the following as characteristic :

> My angel mother ! Long, long years have gone
> Since thou, yet young and fair, passed from my sight
> .   .   .   .   .
> E'er since I see thy gentle face each day,
> And in the silent night, and still there play,
> In those soft eyes, the self-same smiles that made
> Thy presence a deep joy in days of yore.

But though Dr. Palmer has written much, both as a divine and a poet, we believe that this one hymn, struck out in a glorious hour of spiritual exaltation, will do more to preserve his name from sinking into oblivion than all his other writings put together—that when those will be laid upon the shelf as having served their day, this, like a crystal stream revealing itself by a green belt of vegetation amid the desert sands, will live and minister to the devotions of thousands yet unborn.

The same may be said of Charles Wesley's " Jesus Lover of My Soul," or Perronet's " All Hail the Power of Jesus' Name," or Toplady's " Rock of Ages." It is plain that Toplady regarded this, his great hymn, a mere trifle in comparison with his great controversial volumes on Calvinism ; but where are all those controversial writings now ? They have shrunk into small space and to a great extent are forgotten, whereas his peerless hymn is heard in almost every church, on the lonely sea, in the crowded mart, from many a cottage home and fisherman's boat, from the lips of childhood and the faltering accents of old age.

The same may be said, though not to the same extent, of the hymn under consideration. Dr. Palmer will hereafter be known—not by his books—" What is Truth?" "Remember Me, or the Holy Communion," " Closet Hours," " Doctrinal

Text-Book," etc., but as the author of "My Faith Looks Up to Thee." God gave a great gift to the Church on the day (12th November, 1808, Rhode Island), when Ray Palmer was born ; for if he had done no more than write this hymn, he has ministered to thousands that will rise up and call him blessed. He is still with us,* and though the snows of seventy-seven winters are on his head, his eye is not dim and his tongue has lost nothing of the fluency and ease of former days.

Ray Palmer was a student of Andover, where he spent three years, and then entered New Haven (1826), and graduated in 1830—that is when about the age of twenty-two. From a sketch of his life lying before me, I gather that, having graduated, he took to teaching in a famous school in New York, where he taught for three hours a day. There the young man had plenty of time on his hands, and many temptations to face ; but by this time he had taken Christian ground and cast in his lot with the Lord Jesus ; and so much of his spare time was given to Christian service and heavenly meditation. At this time he was in the habit of carrying about with him a little book, in which he jotted down short poems and single verses as expressive of his deepest emotions; and one day, alone in his chamber, with a deep feeling of his great need and a solemn sense of the great realities of the eternal world, he wrote this precious hymn—wrote it as the spontaneous ex-pression of his experience, with no design of publication, with no design to say fine things or win the *popularis aura;* and when he had written the lines down he was so moved by the subject that he covered his face with his hands, and his heart,

---

* Since writing the above, we have heard of Dr. Palmer's death. He died 29th November, 1887, Newark, N.J., United States. He had had two strokes of paralysis under the effects of which he gradually sank till the close—his last audible words were :

> Jesus, these eyes have never seen
> Thy glorious form divine,
> The vail of flesh hangs dark between
> Thy blessed face and mine.

filled with emotion, found relief in many tears. These four
verses are still to be seen in the old morocco-covered memo-
randum book as they were written more than sixty years ago.
There in that little book they lay hidden for years. No eye
saw them till they were shown to Dr. Mason, who had been
inquiring for a contribution from him in a Boston street car.
That was a memorable time in the city. A wave of deep
religious feeling was sweeping over the country, and a new
demand had risen for hymns. Dr. Mason, who was preparing
a collection, took a copy of the verses and prepared a tune—
Olivet—to suit the words—the tune to which it is still sung in
every clime by tens of thousands.

When Dr. Ray Palmer was asked for the origin of this
hymn—his first and best—he replied :—" It was written because it was born in my heart and demanded expression. I
simply gave form to what I felt by writing with little effort
those verses, I wrote them with tender feeling and ended the
last lines with tears." " You may live many years, Mr. Palmer," said Dr. Mason, on meeting the author a few days afterwards, " and do many good things, but I think you will be
best known to posterity as the author of this hymn." That
prediction is verified. In 1840, the hymn was introduced into
England, and since that time it has been received with great
favor, and translated into over twenty languages, among which
are the Arabic, Marathi, and the Syriac. Mrs. Layyath,
Baraket, a native Syrian woman, educated in the mission
schools of Beirût, and sent out as a teacher to Egypt, made
large use of this hymn in her work. She and her husband,
driven out in 1882 by the insurrection of Arabi Pasha, came to
the United States and soon found friends. While in this
country, Mr. Duffield states that she addressed some large
audiences to whom her earnestness and broken piquant English
proved unusually attractive. Among other incidents, she told
how she had seen her whole family—Maronites of Mount

Lebanon—among whom was her mother, aged seventy-two,
converted. In this case it was the child that was the teacher,
and this hymn was the chief lesson. She told how the two
would often sit together on the roof of the house, after the
manner of the orientals, to repeat it to one another in the
Arabic; and when the news came back to Syria that this
woman was safe in the United States, the aged mother could
send her no better proof of her abiding faith than that contained
in the words of this hymn.

Many interesting incidents in which this hymn has figured
have been related. One of the most affecting is an incident of
the late war in the United States. In one of the tents eight
Christian young men were gathered. They knew well that the
coming dawn would be the signal for a sanguinary conflict,
from which they could not all hope to escape. In that hour
they came together for prayer. Before they parted they spoke
freely of the improbability of their surviving the morrow, and
one of the number suggested that they should draw up a paper
expressing the feelings with which they went to stand face to
face with death, and all sign it; and that the same should be
left as a testimony to the friends of such of them as might fall.
The suggestion was unanimously adopted, and after consultation
it was decided that a copy of " My faith looks up to Thee," etc.,
should be written out and subscribed by all present, so that
father, mother and friends should know in what spirit they had
laid down their lives. They did not all meet again, but one of
the survivors saw the arrangement carried out.

A multitude of instances are also on record of souls seeking
the light, who have found it in the same hymn, and of Christians in circumstances of trial and heart-breaking sorrow who
have gained strength by its perusal.

Dr. Palmer has had the happiness of seeing his hymn owned
and honored of God to a wonderful extent—an extent of which
he had no thought on that day when sitting in his chamber he

P

penned the lines with many tears. It is not given to every earnest worker to see the seed that he sows ripen so fast. Many a one at the close of a long life can see nothing but leaves. It is not for us to know the times and the seasons which God has put in his own power. Still every true worker will have a reaping time—a glorious reward. And it is good for us to look away from ourselves and to cease from man, hearing only the words of the Master, " Therefore, my beloved brethren, be ye steadfast, unmovable, always abounding in the work of the Lord, forasmuch as ye know that your labor is not in vain in the Lord."

HYMN XXV.

I HEARD THE VOICE OF JESUS SAY.

DR. HORATIUS BONAR'S GREATEST HYMN.

TUNE.—*Vox Dilecti.* BY REV. J. B. DYKES, MUS. DOC.

I HEARD the voice of Jesus say,
  "Come unto me and rest ;
Lay down, thou weary one, lay down
  Thy head upon My breast."
I came to Jesus as I was,
  Weary, and worn, and sad :
I found in Him a resting-place,
  And He has made me glad.

I heard the voice of Jesus say,
  "Behold, I freely give
The living water ; thirsty one,
  Stoop down, and drink, and live."
I came to Jesus, and I drank
  Of that life-giving stream ;
My thirst was quenched, my soul revived,
  And now I live in Him.

I heard the voice of Jesus say,
  "I am this dark world's Light ;
Look unto Me, thy morn shall rise,
  And all thy day be bright."
I looked to Jesus, and I found
  In Him my Star, my Sun ;
And in that light of life I'll walk,
  'Till travelling days are done.

Latin translation.

AUDIVI vocem Jesus :—
    " O fesse adveni,
Nunc tandem requiescas,
Mi tutus pectori."
Tum talis erat veni,
Tristisque debilis ;
Asylum Hoc inveni
Nunc sum lætabilis.

Audivi vocem Jesus :—
" En aquam infero,
O sitiens, ut vivas,
Inclina, bibito."
Adveni Jesum, et bibens
Vivende fluvio
Restincta sitis, et vivens
Lætabilis nunc Illo !

Audivi vocem Jesus :—
" Sum cæci Lux mundi
Adverte, tibi ortus
Indies lucidi."
Adversans Hoc inveni
Et solem et stellam ;
Hâc luce peregrinus
Adibo terminam.

IN these days when a grateful appreciation of sterling worth and consecrated genius is moving many to do honor to Dr. Horatius Bonar and celebrate his ministerial jubilee—twenty-one years in Kelso and nineteen in Edinburgh —it may not be out of place to introduce this, his greatest hymn, and the one by which he will be best remembered when he is gone.*

---

*Written after he died.

If it be asked what was the *genesis* of this great hymn, "I Heard the Voice," etc., the answer, I think, must be that deep and dark religious experience through which he had to pass before entering into liberty. His little book, "A Night of Weeping," is understood to set forth that experience—a book which has been like a lamp burning in the chamber of many a suffering saint since the day it was published. No voice more tenderly and truly gives the sentiments of the seeking and sanctified heart or touches its deeper chords with the unction of the Holy One. From no other author in these last days are more copious selections made, both from prose and verse, and no one was better fitted to write on such a theme as that of this hymn. He had had a long night of bondage, as is generally supposed, and when he emerged into the fuller light and purer joy he was the better able to handle such a theme as the glorious liberty of the children of God. Out of the eater God brings forth meat and out of the strong he brings forth sweetness.

This hymn has had a wonderful history. God has honored it with many a seal of His approval. To mention only one case. The last time that Henry Ward Beecher was in his pulpit—6th March, 1887—he remained for some time at the close of the evening service listening to the choir practising, and was evidently moved by their rendering of this hymn. While sitting and listening he noticed two street arabs coming into church to enjoy the music also. He came down, and speaking to them tenderly he drew them to his heart and kissed them. Whether this touch of humanity was due to the hymn or simply the response of his deeply emotional nature in seeing two unfortunates before him, with all their undeveloped possibilities, we cannot say, but of this we are sure, that the last grand utterance that he heard in his church was this hymn: "I Heard the Voice," etc., for, a few hours afterwards the shadows of the long night fell upon his ethereal spirit; the silver cord that bound him with the outer world was loosed, and though the soul still lingered over the mortal frame which she had filled with an abundant life for seventy-four years, as if loath to depart, the eyes, the senses were all but sealed, and the lips on which listening thousands had hung for half a century were silent. It was fitting that he who took such an active part in the emancipation of the slave should close his life under the inspiration of this tender hymn, and take those two street arabs to his heart as representing the humanity he loved so well !

But, strange enough, this hymn, that has had such a blessed history, has a very obscure origin. The author has no recollection of the immediate circumstances in which it was written. As to the fact of its being the fruit of his own religious experience there is no doubt. Still, he has no recollection of the *immediate* circumstances. "I have nothing on record but a little scrap of paper without a date and the hymn written in pencil." That is all the author has got to say on the subject. Yet this same hymn, which first saw the light some forty years ago in the manse at Kelso, is now recognized as one of the grandest hymns of the church through all its denominations. Only a few months ago it was rendered in high class manner in Christ's Church cathedral, Montreal, notice of which was published in the newspapers, and looked forward to as the chief attraction in the services of the day. The notice ran : " 10th September, 1887. There will be services in Christ's church to-morrow (Sunday) at eight a.m. Holy Communion . . . quarter past four p.m. Choral Litany, Saviour of Sinners, by Cherubini. Seven, evening service, T. Stainer's in A ; anthem, "I Heard the Voice of Jesus Say," etc., by G. Couture. Preacher, Rev. Cannon Norman.

We have seen many strange things in these days, but none stranger than this—that a congregation, distinguished for its High Churchism, should lay its dainty hand on a Dissenter's

hymn, and on one of its high days make it the vehicle of the
devotions of the people when they would enter the holiest of
all.   Away down at the bottom of the scale, in the region of
controversy and fierce debate, churches are broken up into many
parts, each contending, as is supposed, earnestly for the faith
once delivered to the saints ; but away at the top, on the sunlit
mountains of devotion, they meet and mingle as the children
of one common Father, and they will continue to do so in spite
of themselves, for there is a higher power at work than themselves, till every passion is laid, till every disturbing element
is cast out—till, in short, with clean hands and pure hearts they
enter on the higher ministry.

The Calvinist and Arminian both engage in singing " Rock
of Ages," though the author and John Wesley were angry
disputants in their day ; and the Episcopalian and the Wesleyan
both sing, in their holiest hours : "Hark, the Herald Angels
Sing," though the author was ostracised and the church doors
of the Establishment were closed against him.   Then the
Baptist, the Presbyterian and the Episcopalian, High Church
and Low, are now all ready to acknowledge the author of
" Jesus Shall Reign," etc., as the greatest name in hymnody
and to accept his sacred songs, although some of us can remember the time when they severally dealt heavy blows at one
another, and how each and all united in hurling anathemas at
the little doctor.   More remarkable still is the fact that hymns
purely Roman Catholic in their origin, and hitherto regarded as
the exclusive property of that Church, such as " Veni Creator
Spiritus," " Jerusalem the Golden," and " Lead, Kindly Light,"
etc., are no longer confined to the Roman Catholic Church, but
are to be found in all the hymnals ; so that in spite of ourselves
we unite with the Roman Catholic and the Roman Catholic
unites with us in those moments rich in blessing when we make
our nearest approaches to God !   But the most remarkable thing
of all is that the Romanising party in the English Church should

make use of our Presbyterian hymns, as in the case cited, and publicly advertise in the *Star* as the chief attraction of the day : " I Heard the Voice," etc., T. Stainer's in A, anthem by G. Couture. Has it come to this, that creeds so divergent, voices so discordant—that churches that have so long stood apart in frowning attitude are becoming more tolerant in regard to error or more charitable in regard to duty ? Yes, more charitable in regard to duty—more open to the fact that the Church of God is wider than the fold—than all the folds—that the Divine Spirit is richer in his grace and wider in his sphere of operation than we in our ignorance or bigotry have any conception of, that He in His saving and sanctifying power is preparing hearts in ways and places undreamed of by theologians that will be to the praise of His grace in the ages to come.

One remarkable circumstance, as we have seen, connected with this great hymn is the obscurity of its origin—that it dropped, as it would seem, almost unconsciously from the pencil of the author—that he has no record of it but a scrap of dateless paper and no remembrance whatever of the immediate circumstances in which it was produced, of so little value did it seem in his eyes. But the same thing may be said of many of Charles Wesley's hymns—of the Rev. G. H. Gilmour's hymn, " He Leadeth Me "—of Mr. J. Luke's hymn, " I Think When I Read That Sweet Story of Old "—of Phœbe Cary's hymn, " One Sweetly Solemn Thought," etc. We are accustomed to look for great things only as the result of great labor for grand success only as the reward of human wisdom and high-born genius ; but God has chosen the foolish things of this world to confound the wise, and the weak, etc. Great things in human estimation are often great failures, but anything done for Christ has the stamp of immortality, and however feeble or foolish in itself it may seem, will be owned by God, taken up amid the great redeeming agencies of the Cross and carried through all the ages. Dorcas is still making garments for the poor ; and the penitent at the feet of Jesus has not yet poured forth all her precious ointment. Toplady has not yet done with "Rock of Ages" or Dr. Bonar with "I Heard the Voice of Jesus Say," which he began almost unconsciously on some quiet evening in the manse of Kelso, more than forty years ago.

The hymn under consideration is a specimen of what may be called the *subjective* class—a class now more in request than in former years — that is, hymns dealing with the inner life, the religious experience of the worshipper. Those hymns that celebrate the perfections of God, the glories of Redemption, etc., are properly *objective* in their character, and for long centuries were, with few exceptions, the only hymns known to the Church. But in these last days hymns of a *subjective* kind—hymns dealing with the human heart—its hopes and fears, its joys and sorrows, its failures and its faith, often taking the form of confession and prayer, are now common, and in the hands of Wesley, Cowper, Newton, Newman, Bonar, have become a great success and given a new color to our devotion, a new form in presenting the aspirations and longings of our souls before God. Dr. Bonar's is one of the best of its class. The danger here is *unreality*, making the worshippers sing in terms far beyond their experience, and use language which is not only foreign to their feelings, but positively unsuited for common people and the rough and tumble of life's terrible conflicts.

> "And now triumphantly come down
> And take our souls to heaven."

are lines from Charles Wesley, but how few of the many thousands of Israel really feel like *that* when they stand up to sing !

These notes would be incomplete without some more extended notice of the author. He was born in Edinburgh in 1808, won distinction as a student in the University of that city, pub-

lished his first edition of "Hymns on Faith and Hope," in
1856, and was raised to the Moderator's chair of the Free
Church in 1883. "I met him," says a friend of mine, "a few
years ago and was delighted with my interviews. He was then
a fine genial old man, with a full, round head, a quiet, thought-
ful expression—in short, a charming man. And another,
writing of Dr. Bonar in his youthful prime, gives me the following reminiscences: "His name calls up a scene enacted many
years ago, when I was a divinity student, and he was a minister of ten years in Kelso. The occasion was an evangelistic
service in a school room on a week-day evening. There was
something about the service, and about the man that made you
feel that you were standing on holy ground, and that the
service was far above that which usually goes by that name.
To give you an idea of the earnest preacher and his great subject, imagine before you a youth of slender build, somewhat
below the common height, with dark complexion, finely rounded
head surmounted with an abundance of auburn locks, large,
lustrous eyes full of intelligence and strong emotion and a
countenance well defined, every feature indicating a sensitive
kindly nature,

> "Sicklied o'er with the pale cast of thought,"

and you have a glimpse of the Rev. Horatius Bonar, D.D., in
his youthful prime, and when you have read the outline of his
beautiful discourse you will see how true it is that the youth is
the father of the man. His text was Ezek. xxxiv., 29: "I
will raise up for them a plant of renown." He saw Christ in
the text as the plant of renown—the plant of Jehovah's right
hand planting: and he showed that it was renowned for (1)
being a shelter from the wrath to come, (2) for its precious
fruit, (3) for its beauty and grand proportions, and (4) for its
durability, its amaranthine character. These were the strong
lines of his discourse, and he held them up to us in all their

grandeur, and pressed home the lessons which they convey upon the hearts and consciences of his hearers in a style which I at least can never forget."

Here then, on the one hand, we have a picture of Dr. Bonar in his youth, and on the other hand, one in old age, full of years and honors. Look on this picture and on that, and who would not say : "Surely all flesh is grass, and all the glory of man as," etc. But look again and you will see that while the outward man is perishing the inward man is renewed day by day because fed from an everlasting fountain—that beneath the fading exterior there is the outshining of the power of an endless life, the immortal love strong in death, the beauty of a rarer grace than nature can bestow, the faith that deals with the unseen, in virtue of which the saint puts on the robes of immortality and walks with a steadier step as he nears the eternal world.

O, Horatius Bonar,[*] man greatly beloved, author of the sweet hymn, "I Heard the Voice of Jesus Say," we shall soon miss thee in thy accustomed place and fail to hear thy voice once so rich and resonant, but we shall still sing the songs we learned from thee and take up thy name with reverence; and, encouraged by thy example as well as warmed by thy ministry, we shall also press on in the same narrow path you have trod —often dark, but ending in light, ending at God's right hand where there are pleasures for evermore.

The following beautiful and affecting lines were found among Dr. Bonar's papers, after his death. It is believed they were the last he ever wrote :

> Long days and nights upon this restless bed,
>   Of daily, nightly weariness and pain !
> Yet Thou art here, my ever-gracious Lord,
>   Thy well-known voice speaks not to me in vain ;—
>   "In Me ye shall have peace

*Died since this was written.

The darkness seemeth long, and even the light
  No respite brings with it ; no soothing rest
For this worn frame ; yet in the midst of all
  Thy love revives.   Father, Thy will is best.
      "In Me ye shall have peace !"

Sleep cometh not, when most I seem to need
  Its kindly balm.   O Father, be to me
Better than sleep ; and let these sleepless hours
  Be hours of blessed fellowship with Thee.
      "In Me ye shall have peace !"

Not always seen the wisdom and the love ;
  And sometimes hard to be believed, when pain
Wrestles with faith, and almost overcomes.
  Yet even in conflict Thy sure words sustain ;—
      "In Me ye shall have peace !"

Father, the flesh is weak ; fain would I rise
  Above its weakness into things unseen.
Lift Thou me up ; give me the open ear,
  To hear the voice that speaketh from within :—
      "In Me ye shall have peace !"

Father, the hour is come ; the hour when I
  Shall with these fading eyes behold Thy face ;
And drink in all the fulness of Thy love ;—
  Till then, oh speak to me thy words of grace ;—
      "In Me ye shall have peace !"

HYMN XXVI.

"HOLY, HOLY, HOLY."

THE GREATEST HYMN ON THE TRINITY IN THE LANGUAGE.

TUNE—*Nicæa* BY REV. J. B. DYKES, MUS., DOC.

HOLY, holy, holy, Lord God Almighty !
  Early in the morning our song shall rise to Thee ;
Holy, holy, holy, merciful and mighty,
  God in Three Persons, blessed Trinity !

Holy, holy, holy ! all the saints adore Thee,
  Casting down their golden crowns around the glassy sea ;
Cherubim and seraphim falling down before Thee,
  Which wert, and art, and evermore shalt be.

Holy, holy, holy ! though the darkness hide Thee,
  Though the eye of sinful man Thy glory may not see,
Only Thou art holy, there is none beside Thee,
  Perfect in power, in love and purity.

Holy, holy, holy, Lord God Almighty !
  All Thy works shall praise Thy name in earth, and sky, and sea ;
Holy, holy, holy, merciful and mighty !
  God in Three Persons, blessed Trinity !

Latin translation—same measure.

SANCTE, sancte, sancte ! O Deus prepotens !
   Primo mane laudetur tum tua lenitas
Sancte, sancte, sancte ! clemens et prepotens !
   Deus tribus personis, beate Trinitas !

Sancte, sancte, sancte ! pii Te celebrant ;
   Jaciunt coronas ad mare vitreum ;
Angeli, archangeli—omnes Tibi procidunt !
   Qui eras, et es, qui eris perpetuum.

Sancte, sancte, sancte ! quamvis abditus
   Ægris mortalibus ob delicta eorum
Sanctus tamen : ac semper validus,
   Clemens, misericors, plenus amorum.

Sancte, sancte, sancte ' O Deus prepotens !
   Cuncta Te cantant per terras lucidas,
In mari, in silvis, cœlo lætificans
   Deus tribus personis, beate Trinitas !

THIS is certainly the grandest hymn in the language on the subject of the Trinity. We have twenty-four on the same subject by Charles Wesley, but there is not one of them comes near this. It holds not only the first place in regard to this great mystery, but it does so at a great distance, and the compilers of our Presbyterian hymn book now in use have shown their good taste in giving it the first place in their collection. It is the first hymn, and is likely to be the first hymn for many years, while our theology remains what it is ; while the fourth, fifth and fifteenth chapters of Revelations remain, and the Song of Moses and the Lamb is appropriate, this hymn will hold a warm place in the Church as a suitable expression of her feelings—especially in those grand elate moments when the breath of the Divine Spirit stirs the inner chords of her devotions, and all that is truest and best is ready to rise from the harp of a thousand strings which is slumbering in every soul.

The state of the heathen world had for years engaged the best thoughts of Reginald Heber, and when called upon by the Dean of St. Asaph to write a hymn for a missionary meeting the words dropped easily from his pen:

From Greenland's icy mountains.

Then when Dr. Middleton, the first Bishop of Calcutta, died (1823), it is not strange that he, so full of missionary zeal, should hail the appointment of being his successor and tear himself away from his parish—Hodnet—and, as soon as his consecration was over, hasten to the coral strand. In India he had to contend with the same difficulty that Dr. Wilson, Dr. Duff—perhaps every missionary, more or less—have had to contend with, namely, opposition on the part of the Hindoos and Moslems to the doctrine of the Blessed Trinity, their cavils and conceits, their slowness of heart to believe in a threefold dispensation of love—in short the gospel of redemption.

We are not sure about the *genesis* of this great hymn, " Holy, Holy, Holy, Lord God Almighty," whether it took its rise in the quiet study of Hodnet, or amid the contendings and debates which the author had probably with the best intellects of India ; but we are sure that the heathen conception of God, whether Moslem or Hindoo—the monotheism of the East prevailing in so many forms and meeting him in so many ways, must have intensified his conceptions of the truth as it is in Jesus, on which his own soul rested so securely.

His career in India was brilliant, but short—only three years. He had, in his missionary travels, made his way to Travancore —April 1, 1826—and on the day after his arrival he conducted

two services at the fort, one of which was in the Tamil tongue;
afterwards he retired to the bath, where he was drowned.   It
would seem that the shock had been too great for him, for on
his servant, who had waited longer than usual, entering he was
found lifeless in the water.   Thus, at the early age of forty-
three, the second Bishop of Calcutta came to the close of his
earthly career.   Thus the bright light under which so many had
rejoiced for a season was quenched, but eternity alone can reveal
the value of his labors.

It is interesting to note the prominence that this great doctrine of the Trinity has had in the whole history of the Christian Church from the days of the Apostles down, and the part
which these hymns on the Trinity have played in preserving the
truth.   Great as the mystery is, the fact was accepted and most
surely believed, along with the other great mysteries of the
faith, and not only so, but felt to be spirit and life to souls of
men.   The dying martyr Blandina, A.D. 177, (Lyons) cried
out in her torments, "I believe in the Father, and the Son, and
the Holy Ghost, one God, blessed, forever, Amen!" The Venerable Bede passed away with the "Gloria Patri" on his lips;
and when Grotius lay dying he requested that Heber's hymn on
the Trinity should be repeated to him.   We have the same
truth presented to us in that old Latin hymn, the "Veni,
Creator Spiritus," said by some to belong to the fifth century.
The hymn closes:

> Gloria Patri Domino
> Natoque, qui a mortuis
> Surrexit, ac Paracleto
> In seculorum seculum, Amen!

Then among the few fragments of the Saxon Church, established by Augustine and his forty monks in the sixth century,
there is one hymn addressed to the Trinity which is much ad-

mired. The translation is from the "Codex Exoniensis," beginning, "Holy, holy art thou, Lord of archangels," etc. So, again in that great hymn to the Trinity, which has made its way to us from the early Bohemian Church—fourteenth century—which we would like to insert had we room. Moreover, it is not a little remarkable that one of the earliest battles of the Church with the State was waged on this great article of the faith, and won by means of hymns—hymns giving honor unto the Son as unto the Father and Holy Ghost—though the battle turned chiefly on the supreme divinity of the Lord Jesus Christ.

The Milan Cathedral, over which the good Bishop Ambrose presided in a part of the fourth century, has witnessed many a storm, but none that touched the hearts of the people more than that referred to—the storming of the Cathedral by the imperial troops because its bishop and the bulk of the inhabitants refused to accept the heresy of Arius. The queen, Mother Justina, was an Arian, and demanded one of the churches of Milan for her sect. Ambrose refused, and at length when the bishop was conducting divine worship, a military guard was placed around the cathedral. None were suffered to leave. All night the people were shut up in the sanctuary. The city itself was beseiged, and many weary days and nights the citizens had to endure. But the singing of the simple hymns then in use on the Trinity did much to sustain their faith. The soldiers were powerless to produce apostacy within the Basilica, while the walls resounded with such strains as:

> Thus suppliant with the Father's own,
> Together with the King, Thy Son,
> And Holy Ghost, one Trinity,
> With lowly hearts beseeching Thee.

"Truly," said the good Bishop Ambrose, "those hymns have in them a high strain, above all other influence. Can anything

Q

have more influence than the confession of the Holy Trinity proclaimed day and night by the whole people? Each is eager to rival his fellows in confessing, as he well knows how in sacred verse his faith is promoted in Father, Son and Holy Ghost." The result was that Ambrose and the orthodox party were successful in maintaining this great article of the faith.

Thus, all along the line we can see traces of the truth set forth in this glorious hymn, and the holy fire, like lightning amid the dark banks of clouds leaping forth and hear voices breaking forth in adoration to the Father, the Son and the Holy Ghost, one God, blessed forever. Many a volume has been written in defence of this great mystery, and among other writers Hilary, Bishop of Poitiers, wrote twelve, but we venture to say that any one of those hymns to which we have referred has done more to preserve the truth than all of the books put together. What cared the people for those ponderous volumes, or even those solemn decrees of councils coming from Nice or Nicomedia with such authority! One grand hymn like that of the Bohemian brethren referred to, was better than all—scattered to the winds the subtleties of the learned—the darkness of their own minds, and lifted them into a region of blessed peace—holy light in which they could see all things clearly. And it was not only from the calm retreat of the cloister those hymns came, but rather from the stormy heights of duty—from the fierce heat of controversy, from spiritual conflicts and great battles for the truth. They are the legacy of the days when theological terms were bandied about among soldiers and mobs, and when the old pagan rites were still a part of State ceremonial. Those hymns to the Trinity held their place in the hearts of the people, stimulating and strengthening them for brave duty and ministering to their faith when all was dry as summer's dust around them. Then when the great wave of spiritual life broke over the British Islands in the seventeenth century the same high theme is resumed, and from many a pure and lofty spirit arose songs of praise to the Father, Son and Holy Ghost, fresh as the mountain spring. Charles Wesley pours forth from his consecrated heart (twenty-four, published in 1746 under the title "Gloria Patri," and one hundred and eighty-two, in 1767, "Hymns on the Trinity," a great number. And what shall we say of the contributions of hundreds more that have followed, all fragrant with the same truth and bearing the seal and signature of the divine approval? Still we know no hymn, either ancient or modern, on the Trinity to surpass, or even equal, that of Reginald Heber, and therefore we are well pleased to see it put down as the very first in the collection used by the Presbyterian Church in Canada.

HYMN XXVII.

FROM GREENLAND'S ICY MOUNTAINS

BISHOP HEBER'S GREAT MISSIONARY HYMN.

TUNE.—*Missionary Hymn.*   BY DR. LOWELL MASON.

FROM Grenland's icy mountains,
    From India's coral strand,
Where Afric's sunny fountains
    Roll down their golden sand,
From many an ancient river,
    From many a palmy plain,
They call us to deliver
    Their land from error's chain.

What though the spicy breezes
    Blow soft o'er Ceylon's isle ;
Though every prospect pleases,
    And only man is vile ;
In vain with lavish kindness
    The gifts of God are strown ;
The heathen in his blindness
    Bows down to wood and stone.

Can we, whose souls are lighted
    With wisdom from on high,
Can we to men benighted
    The lamp of life deny ?
Salvation, O Salvation !
    The joyful sound proclaim,
Till each remotest nation
    Has learnt Messiah's name.

Waft, waft, ye winds, His story,
  And you, ye waters, roll,
Till, like a sea of glory,
  It spreads from pole to pole ;
Till o'er our ransomed nature
  The Lamb for sinners slain
Redeemer, King, Creator,
  In bliss returns to reign.

Latin Translation—same measure.

GREENLANDO glaciali,
  Orisque Boreæ,
In India coralli
  Quŏ aquæ auriferæ ;
Antiquis rivis multis
  Campis palmiferis,
Adfertur nobis luctus
  Captivis miseris.

Quid refert ut Zephyrus
  Ceylonis insula
Inflet aromaticus
  Amœna omnia ?
Et quid refert largītus
  Ut Deus, quoniam,
Quisque est captivus
  Idolis ejus coram.

Num tu tam luminosus,
  Moraris lampadem
Iis tam tenebrosis
  In longum seculum ?
O animarum salus !
  Jesu forte nomen !
Te læti indicamus
  Terrarum per orbem.

O venti rem fertote,
  Extremis incolis ;
O undæ, omnes estote
  Vos pro apostolis !
Redemptor, Rex, Creator
  Fulgens hoc lumine,
Per omnes terras ametor—
  Effuso sanguine.

THE author of this very popular hymn is Reginald Heber, D.D., second bishop of Calcutta, one of the youngest men that ever wore the Episcopal mitre, having scarcely reached his fortieth year when he was called to the honor. He was born on April 21st, 1783, at Malpas, county of Chester, England, the rectorship of which his father held for many years. He was a distinguished graduate of Oxford, carrying off many prizes, not the least of which was by his poem on " Palestine."

It was a great day for young Heber when called to read this poem in the Convocation Hall of the College, and great was the favor with which it was received by his friends and fellow-students ; but the praises which greeted him though encouraging were far from spoiling him. At the close he hastened to the vicarage, withdrew to his own room, bent down before God, and offered up thanks for the honors which had been conferred upon him and the joy which those honors had yielded his parents. His was indeed a beautiful character, so much so that one of his biographers says *that if all our students were like Reginald Heber it would be hard to make out the doctrine of original sin.*

One so gifted both by nature and grace could not but prove a living power wherever he should go, and so when he became rector of Hodnet—1807—then only twenty-four years of age, it was felt by the flock that a man after God's heart had been given them for their spiritual guide. For sixteen happy years he labored in this place, drawing much of his inspiration from on high.   Under the ministration of a spirit so gifted we may well suppose that on many a dark mind fell a light "such as never fell on land or sea."   His church was the birthplace of souls, and *when the Lord shall count—when he writeth up his people it shall be seen that this man and that was born there.*

But how about the hymn: "From Greenland's icy mountains," etc.   What is the *genesis*?   What were the circumstances that led to its birth?   The answer is that the author had gone to hear his father-in-law—the Dean of St. Asaph—preach the annual sermon for the "Society for the Propagation of the Gospel," and it seems that the clerk whose business it was to select the hymns for the choir could not find one sufficiently appropriate.   In his perplexity he came to the dean telling him his trouble.   Whereupon the good man turning to young Heber, said: "You are a bit of a poet, could not you help us?"   Heber retired to his room, and within two hours returned with the manuscript in his hand to see whether his lines would suit!   Strange enough this same manuscript was found not long ago with the author's name appended in the old vicarage where the scene took place which we have just described!

Young Heber had grown up under the influence of the great missionary movement that took its rise about the beginning of the present century; that is, shortly after he was born.   The great movement had then all the charm and romance of a glorious enterprise.   It had met with comparatively few disasters and delays, but such as came from the ignorant or the indifferent within the bosom of the church herself.   It was as if the command of the Master, after the lapse of ages, was heard anew, like a bugle blast,—*Go ye into all nations, etc.* The most apathetic were moved and were opening their eyes with wonder, and many a bright young spirit was saying: "Lord, here am I, send me."   The generation has not entirely

gone that saw the Careys, the Martyns, the Marshes, and the
Duffs go forth with their lives in their hand, but strong in God
and in the power of his might. And then when the charm of
novelty had passed away, and the glory of the enterprise begun
to fade some of those brethren returned with the fire in their
bones to tell of God's doings among the heathen, so that both
they that had gone to the foreign field, and those that tarried
at home, rejoiced together and divided the spoil.

The visits of those princes in Israel, those hardy pioneers that
went forth to land upon unknown shores, counting all things
but loss, etc., can never be forgotten—their influence never
arrested. Think of Dr. Duff in the General Assembly of 1867,
Edinburgh! He had been out in India twenty-five years. He
had returned to visit his brethren and awaken a deeper interest
in behalf of missions; but how different from the sprightly
youth that had left them a quarter of a century before, so
wasted and worn, but with the light of immortality in his eye
and the fire of Pentecost in his heart! The General Assembly
had money, but they could not get men, and it was the getting
of men that was his theme. He spoke an hour and a half and
then fainted. He was removed, and on being revived, said :—
"Where was I? Yes; I was making my plea for India for
men. Let me go back that I may finish my speech." No, no!
You are too weak, was the reply. "I *must* go back. They
don't meet for a year, and then I'll be dead." So he was taken
back ; and never was such a sight seen as that which he presented in the General Assembly. Everybody rose on his enter
ing in, and the old man stood before them with his hand on the
rail, and spoke another hour like a messenger from the eternal
world, closing his speech in such terms as these :—"Is it true,
fathers and brethren of Scotland, that you have no more sons
to go to India? If the Queen calls to recruit her army there are
many to respond, but when the Lord Jesus calls, how few? Is
it true, moderator, that Scotland has no sons for India? Well,

then, let it be announced that there is one poor old man ready ; and though his health is shattered and his power not what it once was, that he will spend it, such as it is, and close his pilgrimage in India."

How different all this to the spirit of the General Assembly that met in Edinburgh, 1796, when a motion for commencing missions to the heathen world was negatived on a division, the yeas and nays being respectively 44—58 ! What changes have taken place in the matter of missions ! Think of the sons of the savage chief that took part in the clubbing of missionary Williams on the blood-stained shores of Erromango now engaged in Sabbath school work, clothed and in their right mind ; and in the year of grace, 1888, 1400 delegates assembling for conference in London to tell of God's dealings among the heathen, and to take counsel of one another as to the best plans for the world's evangelization ! God hath done great things for us whereof we are glad. How true that word, " They that sow in tears shall reap in joy, and he that goeth forth weeping, bearing precious seed, shall doubtless come again bringing his sheaves with him.

Young Heber early heard the call of the Master, and gladly renounced the fairest worldly prospects in obedience to that call. It was not that he was insensible to the ambitions of earth and the glory of a grand name among men, for in the field of scholarship he had wrestled hard and successfully too in this regard. The glory of worldly success is a magnet that every soul more or less feels ; but there is a glory that excelleth, and this filled his whole soul and dwarfed into insignificance all the kingdoms of the world ; and the glory of them ; and so when the way was opened he turned his back upon all that was dear, and hastened away to the coral strand. But in three years from that time—a brilliant ministry—his labors were brought suddenly to a close by accidental death. His sun went down while it was yet day.

HYMN XXVIII.

HARK! THE HERALD-ANGELS SING.

THE GREAT CHRISTMAS HYMN.

TUNE.—*Bethlehem.* BY MENDELSSOHN.

HARK! the herald-angels sing
 Glory to the new-born King,
Peace on earth, and mercy mild,
God and sinners reconciled !
Joyful all ye nations rise,
Join the triumph of the skies ;
With the angelic host proclaim
Christ is born in Bethlehem.
 Hark ! the herald-angels sing
 Glory to the new-born King.

Christ, by highest heaven adored,
Christ, the everlasting Lord,
Late in time behold Him come,
Offspring of a virgin's womb,
Veiled in flesh the Godhead see !
Hail, the Incarnate Deity !
Pleased as Man with man to dwell
Jesus, our Emmanuel.
 Hark ! the herald-angels sing
 Glory to the hew-born King.

Hail, the heaven-born Prince of Peace !
Hail, the Sun of Righteousness !
Light and life to all He brings,
Risen with healing in His wings.

Mild He lays His glory by,
Born that man no more may die,
Born to raise the sons of earth,
Born to give them second birth.
　　Hark ! the herald-angels sing
　　Glory to the new-born King.

Latin translation — same measure.

EN heraldi hi in cœlo
　　Dantes gloriam sic Deo
Celebrantes Infantem
Natum nocte Bethlehem !
Sit laus Deo altissimo,
Pax in terra, benignas viro ;
Hinc terrarum per orbem
Christum nasci Bethlehem.
　　En heraldi hi in cœlo
　　Dantes gloriam sic Deo !

Rex adoratus in cœlo,
Rex supremus in mundo,
Serus venit, parvulus
Purus proles virginis !
Salve ! Tu Immanuel
Placitus in Israel
Habitare ; Ecce Deus
Incarnatus, humilis.
　　En heraldi hi in cœlo
　　Dantes gloriam sic Deo !

Salve ! O Tu Princeps pacis,
Salve ! O Sol æquitatus
Lucem, vitam afferas ;
Tuis alis sanitas ;

Mitis, decus seponit,
Formam hominisque tollit !
Sic fit homo Eum mori
Natus est nos renasci.
　En heraldi hi in cœlo
　Dantes gloriam sic Deo.

THIS is one of the earlier hymns of Charles Wesley—one of the eighteen he wrote on the Nativity of our Lord, and from its great popularity must have rendered signal service in teaching and keeping this doctrine before the public mind, especially in an age when sermons were often obtruse and books comparatively rare. In this we have a specimen of the great didactic power of song. The sermon, indeed, is the great vehicle of instruction and preaching God's great ordinance, but there are periods in a nation's history—transition periods and special states of society when the truth as presented in song must be the chief dependence of the people. Clearly this was the case with ancient Israel. It was not on the readings of the law in the synagogue or even the occasional burdens of the prophets, but rather on the songs of Asaph and Heman and Jeduthren who prophesied with harps before the Lord that the people depended for instruction. Any one may see from such psalms as the 78th or the 136th that while praise and honor and adoration rose to God from the many thousands of Israel— all led on by a choir of hundreds of trained minstrels, the instruction of the people was steadily kept in view. All through the centuries the song rather than the sermon has been the great popular instructor. Bardesanus, an agnostic of the second century, composed some one hundred and fifty hymns with the view of propagating his errors—errors that had a long and mischievous career. On the other hand, Ephrem Syrus wrote hymns, it is said, to the number of twelve thousand in the interest of orthodoxy, and so did much not only to stem the tide of evil but to indoctrinate the people in the great facts of the Gospel story.

This work of hymn writing for the purpose of propagating truth began about the close of the second century, and to such an extent did the hymn prevail that in the fourth century Chrysostom found the articles of Arius popular melodies in the streets of Constantinople and set himself to the work of composing orthodox hymns as an antidote. St. Jerome, the earliest Greek hymn writer, declares that by the close of this century hymns had so permeated the nominal church world that one could not go into the fields without finding " the plower at his hallelujah " and the " mower at his songs." Then if we come down to Reformation times we find the same thing—the use of hymns for propagating the truth—sometimes a single song winning whole towns to the new faith as if by one blow ! Scarcely was it composed till it was sung before every door. Crowds gathered round to listen, and though they heard it for the first time they were ready to join with joyful voice in the last strophe. Luther himself was a great contributor to this volume of song that arose in Germany; and to make his hymns spread the more rapidly he set them to familiar melodies—chants which had been sung on pilgrimages or airs of popular songs, and the new words made their way wherever the old ballad was sung. He wrote for the people ; he wrote for the children, and the chief of all Christmas hymns in Germany is one which he wrote for his little boy, Hans, then only five years old. In this respect the hymns of Martin Luther were greatly blessed, and more than one hundred years after this the hymns of Decuis, Eber, Gerhardt, etc., were found to be more potent instructors of the people than all the pulpits and presses of Germany. One day the people of New Bradenburg heard a baker's boy sing a new hymn, and they listened while he sang and learned the song. Other towns caught it up from them till in every household was known that most touching of all

German hymns : "Leave God to order all thy ways," etc.　The author, Decius, a monk into whose heart the light had found its way, leaving the cloister—coming under the spell of the glorious liberty but feeling the storm of a relentless persecution rising on every hand, gave utterance to his feelings in those immortal lines.　It was the utterance of his own bursting heart, and it fled with incredible speed from the one end of the country to the other.　No need in such cases for ingenious puffing or friendly notices from paid journalists.　It was what every bursting heart in the land yearned after.　It was the utterance of that joy unspeakable that had seized emancipated spirits—spirits that had seen the darkness—the crushing weight of centuries of superstition rolled away.

The hymn has ever been potent as an instructor of the people. Explain it as we may there is a nameless charm in rhyme as in the boom of the wave on the sea-shore or in the measured tramp of men on their way to the battlefield, that gratefully affects the popular ear and makes a way for itself to the popular heart.　It is not the scholar alone that feels the force of the *ictus*—the cadence of the rhythm, but man, saint and savage the world over.　Hence, I say, the hymn has always been a popular vehicle of sentiment whether true or false, and when presented as a ballad—the narrative style—like many of the psalms, it is all the more instructive.　Much of the power of such songs as: "There were ninety and nine," "Jesus of Nazarth," "Hark the herald-angels sing," "I heard the voice of Jesus say," etc., comes from this that they are narratives of facts, God's great mercy to sinful men, Christ's nativity, death, and as such will always be fresh and fragrant in the estimation of the church.

The Reformation hymns are chiefly of the ballad order, carrying us away back to Calvary, the Cross, the Creation, the Fall, the Exodus, etc.　They are in many cases abrupt, rough, unfinished things—poor in language and halting in measure, but, still they served their purpose and had a marvelous popularity. They were linked with many tender associations in the families where such names as Huss and Jerome were household words. They held a sacred place in the children's hearts in after years with memories of their home and of martyr tales heard by the fireside on the long winter nights. Those hymns we say, served a great end, rough and unfinished as many of them were. They nourished the faith of the rising church. They guarded the essential doctrines of grace as the vestal virgins guarded the holy fires in the sacred shrine when all around was dark—like them those hymns preserved the truth as it is in Jesus; and they have done much to preserve it till this day amid all the subtleties of rationalism and the ridicule of scorners sitting in high places. In this way the holy fire has been continually burning, warming otherwise cold devotions, rebuking lifeless orthodoxy, testifying against Arian error and bringing light and cheer to many a pilgrim. And when the roseate flush of the Reformation was over—when the enthusiasm consequent on the discovery of the great truth—*the just shall live by faith*, had subsided, it gave way not to lethargy but to a calmer, a more settled faith in things unseen, and clearer conceptions of the plain practical duties of the new life. Then as one sacred poet after another arose, Decius, Speratus, Eber, Hermann, Gerhardt (in whom the German hymn culminated) new aspects of truth were dealt with, and the personal experiences and aspirations of such hymn writers and hymn singers were found to be a great contribution of strength to souls that had but recently come into light and had shaken off the superstitions of ages. John Wesley, the more gifted of the two brothers rendered a great service to the church as a hymn writer but we venture to say, far more as a hymn translator. Of the nineteen German hymns that we have in our collections, all rich, strong utterances and beautiful as well as strong, we owe to John Wesley the translation of seven of the best. With such hymns in com-

mon circulation among the people it was impossible for them to
rest contented in the Roman Catholic Church—to rest contented
with anything short of the glorious liberty of the children of
God. We can easily understand that such hymns would be
offensive not only to the priesthood but the rationalist, the
Arian and the unenlightened, and that if they had had the powers
as they had the will, every one of them should have been suppressed. As Paul, the Arian, bishop of Samosata, banished the
Gloria Patri, Gloria in Excelsis, The Magnificat and other hymns
from the pulpits in his diocese because Christ was addressed as
God : as Frederick the Great found the *Geesangbuck* bar the por-
gress of rationalistic tenets in his day, and sought to tone down
its red evangelism to the neutral tint of a negative theology ;—
and as the Semiarians of the eighteenth century demanded that
nothing should be sung in public worship but the Psalms of
David, so there are many in these days whose hearts are not
right with God, not *en rapport* with the Divine Spirit, to whom
the supernatural element of the Gospel is an offence, and the
great mysteries of redemption are folly, that would gladly see
all this supernatural evangelism set forth in hymns swept away
like fuel for the burning. But in spite of the sneer of the
sceptic and the distaste of thousands of *litterateurs* at what
they call " bloody hymns," they are growing in number and
growing in favor with God and man, and no one has found
greater favor than the beautiful hymn under consideration.
Every Christmas season as it comes finds a greater number to
join in its holy strains, and rejoice that *unto us a child is born,
a Son is given, the wonderful, the counsellor, the mighty God.*
Every Church, the Presbyterian, the Methodist, the Baptist,
and, not the least, the English Church, have given it a foremost
place in their collection of Christmas hymns. Strange that the
Church out of which the Wesleys came—not as dissidents, but
as the apostles of a purer faith—that this church which closed
its doors against them, 2nd April, 1739, when they took to

field preaching — should now give a place in its hymnals
and prayer-books to their writings—that the living preacher
should be ostracised, but being dead should be made welcome as
a minstrel—that all the people, rich and poor, in the highest
and lowliest temples the world over, should unite together in
their devotion on this high day—Christmas—and be led by the
strains of men that it followed with the anathema, the scorn
and contumely of an unrelenting persecution for forty years !

How did this hymn, "Hark, the herald angels sing," etc.—
find its way into the English prayer-book ? By what authority
has it won for itself such a commanding position ? Much in the
same way as the five hymns at the end of the Scotch paraphrases
found their way to that place. The story is that about the year
1818, shortly after the new version of the Psalms was introduced by the order of William III., an anonymous printer, connected with the University of Cambridge, where the Bible, the
prayer-books and psalm books were then exclusively published.
Finding that he had a blank page at the end, filled it up with
six hymns, of which "Hark the herald angels sing" is one—a
matter which was not noticed at the time, and has never been
cancelled since.

The curious fact is that being in, there is no getting of it out
without legislation. Ritualists have fought against it and
rationalists have denounced it, but still it holds its place in the
hymnals of the Church and the hearts of the people; and in all
the services of the round year none is more hearty—devotional
—than that which is borne on the wings of this noble hymn to
the golden altar where the angel offers up the prayers of all saints.
Then his Easter hymn: "Christ the Lord is risen to-day,"
appropriately opens the morning service on that occasion; and
his ascension hymn: "Hail the day that sees him rise"—the
finest in the language of this kind—leads the praises of the
worshippers on Ascension day; and it is not enough that the
Church from which he was driven, should hear his voice, but

R

that all churches, orthodox and heterodox, should accord him an honored place in their hymnals—that on whatever shore Britain drops her anchor—wherever she hoists her flag,—whether on lands savage or civilized—wherever, in short, the English tongue is spoken the songs of Charles Wesley are heard and the God of Charles Wesley is adored. Surely they that sow in tears shall reap in joy, and he that goeth forth weeping, bearing precious seed, shall doubtless come again with rejoicing, bringing his sheaves with him !